THE FIX

THE FIX

Dorian Fliegel

Houghton Mifflin Company
1978   Boston

Library of Congress Cataloging in Publication Data

Fliegel, Dorian.
The fix.   I. Title.
PZ4.F619Fi [PS3556.L528]   813'.5'4   78–9475
ISBN 0–395–25700–X

Printed in the United States of America

S 10 9 8 7 6 5 4 3 2 1

This book is for Kat

That we may discover anew where dreams end and where illusions begin . . . Then we may know where we are, and each of us may decide for himself where he wants to go.

—DANIEL J. BOORSTIN
The Image

PART ONE

ONE

I first met him late in the season, at a bar up on the West Side. It was a cold wet Sunday night and New York had just beaten Boston to take the division title. The place was packed and roaring in celebration. All that joy and goodwill was starting to get to me, and I was about to leave when he squeezed onto the stool beside me and ordered a drink.

"That guy plays with that thing too much," he said to me. Halfway down the bar the ex-horseplayer who ran the place was up on a crate giving the TV set its postgame rubdown. The rest of the place wasn't much to look at, but the owner treated his big color TV like a thoroughbred. Apparently my friend hadn't caught the act before. "What's that they say," he said, "about goosing the cock that laid the golden egg?"

He didn't seem to be putting me on. "I don't think it goes like that," I said.

"Something like that," he said, wrapping his hands around his glass. He was a big man with a rugged face and an awkward, chest-out, stiff-shouldered way of holding himself, as though his body were something he wore, as though it were a suit of armor and he was afraid if he moved too abruptly he'd come crashing down off the stool. He had "Art" embroidered in gold thread on the sleeve of his jacket, which I thought was a nice touch considering the size of him and his overall appearance. His nose was a real work of art, all right. Whoever or whatever had taken it apart had been a lot more thorough than whoever put it back together.

"Pouring like a bastard," he said. "Hell of a night." I nodded. He said he hated nights like this, that every time he came out on a night like this he got lost and caught a chill. Normally, on a night like this, you couldn't pay him to come out. He only came out to see Boston, because of Burke. Burke was a hell of a coach, didn't I think? They would never have beaten him without all those early calls. He said he thought it must have been a terrible heartbreak for Burke, making it sound as if the man was a personal friend.

Well I didn't want to get into any of that with him then. He seemed like one of those gullible, bumbling, true-believing fans, a twenty-buck bettor who would talk your head off if you gave him half a chance, and all I wanted in the world right then was just to forget about it, just to let the whole thing drift quietly off into the mist. That was one thing you could always count on, watching the games. Whoever was the hero, or whoever got the blame, whatever anyone did or didn't do, once the picture faded you were only sitting in a darkened room.

"Two things you want to watch out for in this town," he was saying. "Getting lost and catching a chill. I been here seven years and I get lost still. Of course you can get lost pretty good, too, where I come from, down around Boston. That's a beautiful town for getting lost in."

"You don't say?"

"Oh yeah. Lot of out-of-towners get lost down there. How about yourself? You from around here?"

"No," I told him. "Xanadu."

"No shit. Well in that case, Prince," he said, leaning towards me with a little confidential smile, "let me give you a word of advice, if I may, seeing as how you're from out of town and all. You want to be very careful about what New Yorkers tell you. People here'll tell you anything. Just between you and me, Prince, I think some of them are full of it."

He had clear blue eyes and an easy smile. I couldn't help smiling back at him.

"How about another of those," he said. "You feel like another?"

"No thanks."

He took a swig of his drink and wiped the back of his hand across his lips. We sat there, two islands in a beery sea of celebration. "Barrooms," he said, looking around. "Smoke. A lot of hot air. What do they know, you know?"

"They knew something today."

"We should've had it," he said. "C'mon, how about another? Help me try'n shake this chill before I catch it."

"No thanks."

"Sure?"

"Thanks."

"Fix you up."

"I'm fine."

"Is that right, Prince?" he said, smiling at me with his eyes. It was a smile that could have gone either way, crazy or wise. I shrugged and tried to concentrate on what was left of my drink. He started drumming on the bar with his fingers. He had some set of fingers all right. They went beautifully with the nose.

"Looks a little to me as though maybe you got killed," he said, and for the first time I heard the Boston in him good and strong.

"Does it?"

"Just a bit," he said, fingering a matchbook, turning it over and over again with the sharp, crisp snap of a dealer laying out a hand. "They were a bargain opening at three, so what does that make them at a price like six or better?" He snorted out a laugh. "Who in the world would have ever figured them to lose by more than six?"

I suggested he could start by asking around the bar.

"So what if the public likes New York? These New Yorkers have been without a winner so long they've lost all sense of values. So what if they make a solid team six-and-a-half-point dogs. Beautiful. You wait all season for one like that. They give you an opportunity like that and you go all the way, you know?"

"I know," I said.

He stared at me for a long moment. "No," he said finally, "no you don't. You probably don't know a goddamn thing about it."

Well as a matter of fact that was one thing I did know about right then, that and the folly of trying to make up for an entire season all at once. I thought I knew a little something about values, too.

He was still staring at me. "How much?"

"Five grand."

He didn't bat an eye. "Can you cover?"

"I don't know."

"For five dimes plus the juice you'd better know. And fast."

"I'll get it."

He shook his head, smiling.

"You think it's funny, do you?"

"Misery," he said, "likes a little company from time to time. I lost just about everything I had. Twenty altogether."

"Jesus."

"How about a drink, Prince?" he said. "I'd really appreciate it if you'd have that drink now."

The crowd had thinned out, but the celebration was going stronger than ever. The rain was still coming down outside and the little red Christmas lights over the bar were blinking merrily away. We moved over to one of the wooden booths. I wasn't feeling too bad now. The heavy, heartsick feeling was gone and it seemed I could float wherever I wanted — look down on the heads of the men at the bar, see the rain and the pinpoint lights of cars in the canyons of the city. I felt enormously calm. I felt as though I had attained the perfect state.

"Sixteen points," he said staring down into his drink. "No way they were sixteen points better than us. All those calls," he groaned.

It was worth groaning about, all right, straight from the opening kickoff when the refs gave a fumble back to New York on a quick whistle. The replay clearly showed the ball popping loose with the hit, and that was the last replay of a key call we were shown all afternoon. Mostly it was the holding. They say you can call holding on almost any play in the pros, but they sure picked the worst possible times to do it. It was like a bad dream. On one long touchdown run, a ref stumbled and fell, but he still managed to get up in time to throw a late flag that took away the score. And when Burke rushed out onto the field they hit him with an additional fifteen-yarder. The men in the booth had plenty to say about the coach's action, about the kind of bad example it set for youngsters, but they didn't have much to say about what was going on out on the field. They weren't supposed to undermine confidence in the League or the officials. Not with forty million witnesses looking in, and so much riding on the outcome. After a while it didn't seem to matter much anymore anyhow, and all the images began to blur.

Except for one. There was a close-up of Burke on the sidelines, off by himself towards the very end of the game. He was standing in profile, staring straight ahead at the field, the skin around his eyes a leather web of wrinkles. The hand-held camera was jiggling slightly, the shifting glare of the stadium lights coating the lens like a film. In that unnatural light Burke's face seemed to blaze with a clenched-jaw, hair-trigger intensity. And just when it seemed for sure they would cut away — had to cut away for the sake of decency — the camera closed in even tighter. Burke turned then to face it squarely, his features, like a man answering the door, suddenly filling the screen. This image stuck in my mind: Burke looking straight out through the screen as though it were a window, not in the cold fury I had expected but instead stricken, desolate, lost in a question for which he asked no answer.

"You want to know what really happened?" my friend said, his face looking more than just a little glassy now. "I'll tell you. They stole it from us. They did. They took it from us in broad daylight. They don't care what they do. They walk right over you."

Well there it was, I thought, the good old red-blooded All-American loser's cry: we wuz robbed. No doubt it was being repeated in bars and cars and living rooms the length and breadth of this great land. The refs had stolen it from us. In theory, of course, nobody was supposed to feel anything like that anymore. The League's recent reorganization of the referees was supposed to have removed any doubts about their competence and trustworthiness — which only proved that the occasional impulse to strangle a ref was too deep-rooted to be eliminated by a commissioner's public relations gesture. What was the difference anyhow? If you won you called it the breaks. And if you lost . . . what was the point? What was over was over.

But Art wouldn't let it rest. There was just something about it all, he was saying, something about the way it happened. "Look," he said, "let me tell you something about the average bettor. Most of them haven't set foot on a football field in their lives. They don't even go to the games. They're TV fans, see. They like teams that look good on the tube — wide open, flashy teams. They don't care about what's going on in the line where it's won or lost. The camera isn't showing it, anyhow, can't show it really. Even when they do show it, nobody understands it. They can see it — but they can't feel it. They think they know the game and they think they know values — but they don't."

"And you do?" I said.

He said he was in a position to know a little about what the fast guys were up to. He said he'd done some work for a "friend." He said it wasn't just what he'd seen on the screen today: it was the whole thing, the pattern, the way the money had been moving all week long. I asked him pointblank what he meant, but it was just what I expected: he couldn't say. He just sat there nodding as though he had all kinds of inside information.

I didn't want to start with that. Every place you went there was some kind of might-have-been hanging around, ready to pass off his opinion as solid edge. They all had been stars once upon a time at some school or other, and they all would have made it big if they hadn't told somebody-or-other where to go. They all had inside information. There was no percentage in listening to them. The ones who knew the game best made the worst handicappers.

I got up and put on my coat. He just sat there with those fingers wrapped around the glass, his body bolt upright in that silly stiff-shouldered way.

"I mean it," he said. "You don't know me. But if I thought for sure one of those fast guys had touched that game I'd go after him with everything I had. I really would."

"Sure you would," I said. "Well so long now. Take it easy."

Outside the rain had turned to snow — the first of the year. I stopped for a second to breathe in the air and watch the big flakes come tumbling down through the streetlights and vanish into the wet pavement. Then my friend came rushing out after me. I noticed he had a limp.

"Look," he said, "back in there just now, I don't know what I was saying. First I felt like I had to talk to somebody; then, I don't know, you know?" He said maybe I was right, the thing to do was just try and forget it. He held out his hand and told me his name was Cooper. It sounded like some kind of Indian dialect the way he pronounced it with his Boston accent — "Aht Coopah." I shook his hand and told him my name and asked where around Boston he was from and he said Somerville and I told him I had spent some time around there once and he guessed it was at Harvard. So we talked about all that for a minute or so and then stood around a while longer with the snow falling and our breaths showing on the air and the traffic swishing by on Broadway. For what his opinion was worth he said he didn't think the bookmakers would be in too charitable a mood this Christmas, not with all they'd been holding on New York, not with the crazy kind of year it'd been. He wanted to make sure I understood this was no time for playing around. I should do whatever I had to do to come up with the money fast.

"What do you do for a living anyhow?" he said.

"At the moment, I'm a ghost."

He shot me a skeptical look. "The kind that goes 'boo,' right?"

"The kind who writes things for other people."

"No shit. I like to read. Ever write any books for famous detectives?"

"No."

"You got a family? You got somebody?"

I shook my head.

"Well all I can say is it's a crying shame."

"We did have a little something to do with it."

"Sure. Sure, nobody should bet what they can't afford to lose, but Jesus, a game like this, how could you afford not to, you know? I sailed my shirt down the river. And don't tell me it doesn't go like that."

"It doesn't."

"Well however the hell it goes it's not coming back — yours neither."

"I don't care."

He stood there staring down at me, and for the first time it struck me how big he really was.

"You don't care," he said. "You're a real case, you know that, Prince? You're not supposed to not care. It doesn't mean anything at all if you go into it like that." He said he felt like getting a bite to eat. Hell, we still had to eat, didn't we? We'd take a cab, it'd all be on him. I just shrugged and stood there looking at the way the snow was dusting his shoulders — like I was looking across a valley to a distant mountain ridge. I didn't mean anything by it. None of it was real to me — not really. That was the worst time in my life and that was the way I looked at everything then, myself included.

"All right," Art Cooper said, "suit yourself, forget it, so long," and with a have-a-nice-evening he was headed up to the corner to look for a cab, and I stood there watching him go, a big, dark hulk of a man carrying himself in that strange awkward way. From the distance it hit me just how bad the limp was.

All at once something cleared inside me, the way your head clears suddenly when the train starts up from the bottom of the tunnel. I shouted his name and he glanced up just as a cab came clanging over a manhole cover to a swerving stop.

"Cooper, hey, Cooper, listen," I said rushing up to him. "Didn't you once play ball? Back in the early fifties?"

He stood there with one hand on the cab door, staring at me as if I were babbling in a foreign tongue.

"Sure, Christ," I blurted out, a damn fool kid grin spreading like a stain across my face. "For Pittsburgh. The center, Art Cooper. There was something you did, something special. You were some kind of hero once, weren't you?"

He had his eyes tight on me, as if he recognized me now for a madman. I couldn't blame him, but I couldn't help myself, I couldn't wipe the damn grin off my face. But he didn't understand. He took it all wrong. He thought I was putting him on again. He said he had been nothing, a nobody who played part of one season. Nobody remembered him, why should they? He wanted to know how come I had remembered him, but I couldn't say.

The cabbie rapped sharply on the window. Cooper told him to hold his horses, then turned back to me with a smile. "You know what I'm thinking is going to be real nice? We're going to wake up and all this is only a dream and Boston really won it. Won't that be nice, though, Prince? We'll wake up in the tropic of Xanabull or whatever, with your crown and all our dough. How's that sound to you?"

"Right now," I said, "I'd be willing to settle for that bite to eat."

The easy smile faded. I heard the windshield wipers squeaking, I felt the damp cold through the soles of my shoes.

"I'm sorry." Stretching out his bad leg he lowered himself down into the cab, and the cab pulled away.

TWO

Litwin had said something about inviting a few people up for drinks, but when I stepped off the elevator I could tell from the laughter spilling out into the hall that he was staging one of his full-scale productions. The maid who let me in was a new acquisition. I edged into the crowd and began to work my way towards the bar. Litwin had the place all done up for New Year's Eve, with crepe paper streamers, silver balloons and big glittering letters that spelled out HAPPY NEW YEAR. But it wasn't New Year's Eve yet. The new year was still more than a week away.

I got a Scotch and took it over to the picture window with the famous view. After a while Litwin spotted me and gave me a big wave. I watched him making his way through the crowd, nodding and smiling at his guests. He was wearing a black velvet suit and looking very debonair.

"Jack, how the Christ are you?" he shouted above the party. "Jesus it's great to see you here. Isn't this a terrible crowd? One starts with a simple desire to have a few close friends up for a quiet drink and look what happens. X is in town and you can't have him without both Ys and she's so awful you might as well have the Zs. Before you know it you're talking squares, not pairs," he said, rocking happily back and forth on his heels, his eyes grazing the room with satisfaction.

It was an impressive crowd all right: you had to give him that. I recognized a lot of the faces right away.

Litwin helped himself to a glass of champagne from a passing tray. "That Montgomery girl's here. She really has a most astonishing mind."

Even if you tried you couldn't have missed the big blonde on the far side of the room surrounded by an appreciative male audience. She was the society girl who had done the book on underdeveloped nations and gone on to stardom on the talk show circuit. Given the depth of her neckline you didn't need an advanced degree to see that the quality of her mind wasn't her only astonishing attribute.

"She's invited me down to play at her place in the Islands," Litwin said.

"With her mind?"

"No. Tennis."

"What about what's his name, the Englishman? I thought they were the perfect couple."

"Oh but they are. He's off doing some hunting in Africa, and she's doing hers right here." Litwin laughed out loud. He was in top form. "But how are you?" he said. "You came alone, I hope? There are quite a few other interesting numbers here. The ways things are going tonight I can fix anyone up, even you."

I looked past him. Beyond the big picture window the city blazed against the night like an ocean liner. "I can't stay, Eliot."

"But you must. Haven't you even noticed? I'm celebrating New Year's Eve tonight. A real New York New Year's: the mob in Times Square, Guy Lombardo, the whole bit. I had one of the guys at the office rig it up on video. I decided I owed it to myself — every year now I seem to be down in the Islands. Come on, Jack, it's going to be just like the real thing. I've even got old bowl games on in the other room, for the real men like you to be sneaking off to watch. I'll skip the introductions and all that if you want. Christ — I'm just glad to have you here." He started rocking back and forth again. The light gleamed off his face. Eliot was very handsome, with sleek fair hair and a high broad forehead, the skin smooth and clear and the cool blue green veins showing just underneath. Not even he with his fabled Midas touch could have cast anyone better to play himself. To say that Eliot was one of the most successful independent television producers in the country didn't begin to encompass the range of his interlocking political and commercial activities. On a strictly private basis I did odd writing jobs for him — whatever he wanted even his closest professional associates to believe had sprung full-blown from his own head. We'd been friends long enough now to know how perfectly we complemented each other: where he was all ego and ambition, I needed the work.

"Eliot," I said, "I need some money."

He went right on rocking. "I was under the impression," he said, scanning the room, "that everything was all right. You did say everything was all right, didn't you? Or is this one of your jokes?"

"I just need the money."

"A loan?"

"An advance. The one you said I could have whenever I wanted."

"That's hardly the point."

"What is?"

"Frankly I had assumed we were beyond this stage by now." He turned to me with his eyes. His eyes were extraordinary, like stones, as green as emeralds and flecked with gold. Looking into them now I wondered for the hundredth time if it was only an accident of coloring that gave the impression he never really saw you.

"How much?" he said.

"Five thousand."

He pursed his lips. He wasn't looking at me now, but he wasn't rocking either. "Five thousand," he said, tilting his head back and reflecting, as if some contractor had just quoted him a price on a few alterations. He sighed heavily. Poor long-suffering Eliot, to whom life had only handed every break in the book. The least I could do, he said, was to tell him how I was doing, how I was really doing; but before I could say anything he started off on how he had been rethinking his whole position, how there were things he wanted to do politically, things of his own, things that counted. It was a new year and he was full of new plans. We really had to sit down and talk.

"And the money?"

He flashed a smile as broad as a blank check. But it wasn't for me, it was for the blonde, "Mikey" Montgomery.

"Eliot darling," she said taking his arm, "where do you ever get all your brilliant ideas from — it's like every New Year's party I've ever been to in the States: the women are ravishing and the men utterly incapable of discussing anything but football. Please don't go off and leave me again like that, darling. I'm liable to be bored to death by another Viking or Ram."

"Well you're safe with me," Litwin said laughing. "I couldn't talk about football if my life depended on it. All I know is the ratings are finally up again, so the right teams must be winning."

She threw back her head and laughed throatily, tossing her long blond hair and showing a big horsey mouthful of gleaming white teeth. It was as though somebody off-stage had yelled "cheese!" and inside her a whole battery of gears and levers had swung into action, pulling apart her lips, spreading them wide, holding them in place. On television she came across with a certain voluptuous energy. Up close her flesh had a heavy, pulpy quality, and her eyes were crusted with make-up, though that didn't prevent them from taking in every wrinkle in my suit.

Eliot skipped the introductions. Placing a hand on her bare back, he steered her away. "Jack," he said over his shoulder, "I'll look forward to getting together as soon as I get back from the Islands."

Good old Eliot. The thing was not to let him throw you, to remember just how much he needed you. The thing was not to leave until you had the money.

Somebody gave me a back-thumping greeting and proceeded to talk my head off about Someone, Something Incorporated until he realized that I wasn't who he thought I was. Then I bumped into a stunning redhead in a sheer silk gown, a slinky fashion-model type with dreamy eyelids and a pair of nipples that froze me in my tracks. She put a cool hand on my wrist and asked me if it were true that they were going to show blue movies. A man in Phoenix had once offered her ten thousand dollars to star in one that he swore would be in good taste. I was just starting to wonder whether or not I should let her in on the ground floor of a few blue projects of my own, when a guy chomping on a cigar said, "Rita, c'mere, here's somebody to meet." "Excuse me," she said, polite as a schoolgirl. "I have to go talk now to a man."

I set out across the room, picking my way through the clusters of executives and clients, the lawyers and the agents, the celebrities and the glamorous women. A high-powered bunch, no question. An elite who liked to think of themselves as servants of the public. And somewhere out there, down below in the network of dark streets and the liquid republic beyond, lived the creature they served. He was an elusive, mysterious little critter, but fortunately they didn't have to worry about any one individual specimen. They served the public, and serving the public, as many have long known, is a very good business. For the public has no voice and no mind; all it has are servants who claim to be its voice and mind. And all they ever need to know about the poor sap down there is that he lives in partial darkness, full of a hunger to be touched by something larger than himself.

The people in that room could touch him all right. They were all of us and none of us, just as we were all of them and none of them.

So I picked my way through them, on past the tables heaped with shrimp and cheeses and little sandwiches with silver spears stuck through them; past the pantry and the kitchen where I startled one of the waiters taking a nip, his fingers like claws around the bottle; down the long carpeted corridor, whole columns of me tramping through the infinite gold-bordered fields of the opposing mirrors, descending past the bedrooms, all the way down to the cool, dark, walnut-paneled study with the sweet smell of pipe tobacco, the leather chairs, and the heavy, solid oak door, which I shut.

I poured myself a drink from the special stock in the cabinet beneath the trophies and the shelf full of Eliot's speeches and his articles. I drank the Scotch off with a shudder. Then I poured another. When I was ready I settled back into the deep leather chair with the high back and faced it.

Because it was all there, all neatly matted, framed and hung on the dark-paneled walls: the snowmen in Harvard Yard; the long spring shadows of the sycamores on the bank of the Charles; the house on the Cape; the time with backpacks in Spain, under the gnarled little tree that shed leaves with each rustling of the breeze, and me grinning over my shoulder, half suspecting, even then, that it was only for Eliot's wall.

It was all there, arranged chronologically in rows so that you only had to look as far as you wanted. You didn't have to look at what came later if you didn't want to — at the cocky young men with their feet up on their desks, or at the women, the ones with their gay, sad good looks, and the one whose eyes, I knew now without looking, hid nothing.

It was only paper and glass and you didn't have to look at any of it if you didn't want to.

I took the bottle over to the couch and turned on the TV. The Knicks and Rangers had both won, the Jets were training hard for their upcoming playoff game, and as a footnote to the 29–13 trouncing he had suffered at the hands of New York, Boston head coach Wilson Burke had been slapped with an unprecedented five-thousand-dollar fine by the League office, for his criticism of the officials in that game.

Well Burke should have known that when it came to the purity of its image the League brooked no cheek. He had restrained himself to the point of not specifically mentioning the officials, saying only that "they" had cost him the game, that "they" knew who they were and what they had done. But neither the reporters nor apparently the commissioner had had any trouble figuring out exactly whom he meant. Burke must have been crazy to sound off like that, and although I had never cared much for his stone-cold image I drank a toast anyway to the old man's audacity.

Then I greeted my friendly weatherman with another toast, but he didn't say anything back except to predict fog by morning, which wasn't very friendly of him or precisely accurate either, since where I lived it was already plenty foggy, with small buzz warnings in effect off my extremities, and a nice warm front burning its way up the coast of my gut.

It must have been very late when Litwin finally came in. He was sitting there in his shirt sleeves when I woke up with a pounding head and a mouth dry as sand. I didn't attempt to sit up.

"Sounded like a big success," I said.

"It was."

"Your little friend still around?"

He shrugged. He said you could reach the point of diminishing returns very quickly with someone like that. He said he'd looked all over for me. He thought I'd left. He said he should have known, if I bothered to show up at all, where I'd end up. Then his eyes found their way to the wall, and he looked at it for a long time as if I weren't even there. Then he said it: "There was no one else like her, was there?"

"She had her points."

"And in this picture especially. I don't know what it is."

"It's the eyes. They follow you."

"Is that it?"

"Wherever you go. I'm sure there must be some technical explanation for it."

He turned slowly back to me. "She could have had it all," he said. "She could have had anything she wanted." What he meant, of course, was that he was the one who could have given it to her.

"I don't think she ever wanted to be anything but herself, Eliot."

"Maybe," he said. "Perhaps." Then after another moment: "At least we had her for a while."

Well that had to sound a little strange to me coming from him, considering that Lauren was the one thing I'd had that he wanted for himself and was unable to have. Even though, near the end, when she was confused and uncertain enough, he had, in his way, had her too.

Litwin was peering at me, his head tilted back, his hands folded under his chin as if he were sighting over the notches of his knuckles. "One year," he said. "You don't think that's long enough?"

"For what?"

"To go on the way you do."

"Sometimes I do all right."

"Meaning?"

"That there are stretches."

"But you still blame yourself. Even though it was an accident. Even though she didn't know what she was doing."

His words came at me like blows. There was nothing I could say, even then. If only I had been able to take my life more seriously; or maybe, as she used to think, if I had managed to find work that mattered to me at any of the schools or in any of the jobs. Maybe then I would have been able to accept her love. Maybe then her own troubles might not have seemed so overwhelming. At least then it would never have been necessary to wonder whether she really meant to take the pills.

"All right," he said at last. "Have it your way. Except now you've gone through all the money. Just pissed and gambled it away."

"From a certain point of view you might say that."

"From the point of view of the person who's expected to bail you out?"

"I'll work it off."

"Will you?" he said, swiveling into profile. The light struck him differently now, so that I could see the great vein that rose alongside the bridge of his nose to split his forehead. "Good old Jack. Still chasing after rainbows, aren't you?"

"Let's just say the bets help fill the time."

"Not very productively I'd say."

"I produce for you when I have to."

"Don't you think I deserve more than that?" he said, and he started in on his favorite speech about the obligations and responsibilities of the productive individual in a corporate society. Eliot loved to make speeches, but he could've saved his breath on me. I already knew the words by heart. I should have. I'd written almost every one of them for him.

"Eliot, why don't we just skip the lecture this time, all right?"

He stopped. "I don't give a damn about the money, Jack. You know it isn't that. I'm speaking to you now as your friend."

So while he spoke to me as my friend I lay there on his couch and breathed a lot easier. I should have known as long as Eliot's ego and ambition were safely intact I needn't worry. Dealing with him was a simple transaction: you either added to his world or subtracted from it. He always thought in categories — and I wasn't just someone who worked for him, or a business or social friend, I was his personal friend. He always said I was his best friend, and every time he said it I flinched. He assumed, of course, that I was jealous of his success. What he could never see was my indifference. Lauren once said he lacked the imagination to enter any world but his own. That made him, to her, poor beyond words. And it was this disability, rather than his obvious assets, that had moved her in the end. She had only wanted to be kind to him, she said. But maybe in saying that she was only being kind to me.

So I listened to him trying to fill me with the importance of himself while all along I was making those unspoken but exact calculations by which we trade away so much time and self for something else, wondering why it should be in the end that the thing we gain always feels like less.

"Eliot. It's late."

He stopped as if noticing me there for the first time. "Why don't you stay the night?"

"I can't."

"Some other time then. You'll come back soon and we'll have a nice long talk."

"All right. Now what about getting me the money?"

"The money? Oh yes." But he didn't move. He said it was about time we stopped kidding each other. As my friend he had an obligation to do what he thought best for me. As my friend he had to help me stop thinking I could go on in this condition forever, that I could come running to him whenever I wanted a handout. He thought it best not to give me any more advances.

I sat up so suddenly the room rocked. "As my *friend?*" I shouted. "As someone who wants to *help* me? Who the hell're you kidding? You don't give a fuck about me — if you did you wouldn't be going back on your word."

Eliot sat there with his eyes on me as cold as stones. "Whatever made you think," he said quietly, getting to his feet, "that in your present condition you could possibly be of any real use to me?"

I stared blankly at him, not understanding.

"I've waited more than long enough for you to shape up. There isn't going to be any more work for you, Jack."

Then he tossed me the envelope.

In the envelope was a check for $5000. He'd had it ready for me all along.

Well I knew I couldn't stay in that room any longer, not with her eyes on me like that. Out in the big room the crepe paper streamers were trailing on the floor and there was party debris everywhere. I stood for a while staring out the picture window at the fog-shrouded city, struggling against the shame and the helplessness.

But when you feel dead inside you tell yourself it doesn't matter. Things are the way they are and it doesn't matter. Nothing changes. Nothing happens. Nothing can make it any different now.

THREE

I could hear the phone ringing, but I was having one of my dreams, one of the good ones, and all I wanted was to hold on to it. Which I was never going to do as long as that damned phone kept on ringing.

I reached for the receiver, knocking over the clock. *"Jack Rose?"* The words pounded inside my head and I realized it was two days straight now I'd been drunk.

"*The* Jack Rose from the joint on Ninety-fifth?"

"Look — who is this?"

"Just another Boston nut, Prince."

"Christ — Cooper?"

"In person. You have any idea how many Roses there are in this town, Rose? My fucking finger's about to fall off. You could have told me your number."

"You could have asked."

"Rose, listen — about taking off on you like that — I don't know what came over me."

"Probably just the shock of being chased by one of your fans."

"Fans. You don't know the half of it. All them broads lurking down in the lobby, lusting up the hallways. You wouldn't by any chance have a broad up there now yourself, would you Rose? It's no use holding out on me. I've got a detective's nose for these things."

"Well then you'd better take it in for a tune-up. I was sleeping."

"Sure. One o'fucking o'clock on a lovely Friday afternoon, what else is a young guy like you going to be doing?" He paused. "You make out all right?"

I told him I'd gotten the money. Otherwise, aside from being broke and out of work, I didn't think I wanted to know how I felt yet for a while. I told him I'd call him back later some time when I knew. But he said that wouldn't do. He had to talk to me now.

"That was really something, though, wasn't it, Prince? You remembered it all for chrissake. I swear if I hadn't bolted you would even have had my number."

"What was your number?"

"Fifty-two."

"I wouldn't have had it."

"The hell you wouldn't have. And you were just a kid that year. Listen, Rose, you're not one of them trivial nostalgic freaks, are you?"

"Look Cooper, you had a good game. You got injured. It happened to stick in my head, all right?"

"Lots of people have good games. Lots of them get hurt. I was a nobody. Why should you remember me?"

"Who knows? I was a kid. You know how kids are. Maybe I felt sorry for you. Maybe I made a hero of you for a while. I tried to look it up; what difference does it make?"

"Look it up how? Where?"

"At the library," I said, realizing the instant I said it it was a mistake.

"Tell it to me," he said.

"Why?"

"I've just got to see." He sounded all excited, like a kid. So I told it to him:

How at Forbes Field, Pittsburgh, on a crackling cold December 3, 1950, the Steelers hosted the New York Giants; and how the Giants, needing a victory against this disappoint-

*ing Steeler team to stay alive in the race for the Conference
title, moved out easily to an early lead.*

And it felt a little strange. There I was lying in bed with
one hell of a hangover in what seemed like the middle of the
night, what might just as well have been the middle of the
night for all I cared, with everything stopped like a ship dead
in the water — there I lay in bed repeating into the telephone
to someone I hardly knew the words of an old newspaper account I'd read on microfilm in the basement of the public
library of a game I'd heard over the radio as a kid. At the
other end there was only silence, and I said the words but it
wasn't as if I believed there was anything real behind them
— anything living, anything whole. The words came, but
they were only words to me. It wasn't as if they had anything
to do with me, as if anything real could come of them. It was
just a story:

*How it started snowing before the half, and how the snow
kept swirling down and how the Steelers, in a game that meant
nothing to them, behind the quarterbacking of Wilson Burke
and the blocking of a rookie center, came back. How, still
trailing by four and with time expiring and the field completely white with snow, they mounted their final drive. How
with no more time-outs Burke ran out-of-bounds inside the
five to stop the clock, leaving time for just one play, two at
most. How the stands were half deserted; and you could
barely see the two teams through the blizzard, how the snow
had completely erased the goal line. And how the first play
inside came up short, the clock moving now, the Steelers trying desperately to line up for one last play — except for the
one that was down on the snow, clutching his leg.*

"Christ yes," cried Cooper, breaking in so suddenly the
words seemed to come from inside my own head, "that was
when I looked up, Jack. I looked up and saw him standing
there above me," he said, and he went on, the words just
pouring out of him. The crowd was cheering like crazy and

usually when they were like that you felt as if they were a wave right on top of you. But this time, there was none of that. Just those big flakes floating down in that perfect padded silence, and Burke leaning over him; just the two of them in that silence as if the rest of the world had vanished. It was fixed forever in his mind. He could see it now clear as day — see Billy, the way he looked then, leaning over him panting hard, his chin strap dangling, his nostrils flaring in and out, his face blackened, bruised, running with sweat, and his mouth half twisted into this funny smile, as if he was just a little pissed off, as if he would really appreciate it if Cooper would stop jerking off and get the hell up off his ass.

He saw all that and he saw something else — that power of Bill's, that private knowledge he seemed to have. Cooper came to his senses. He saw the ref, he remembered the moving clock. He couldn't feel the leg; hell, it was too cold to feel anything.

Burke had called two plays in the huddle; the second, in case it was needed, a sweep left. But as Burke helped Cooper to his feet he told him he was taking it in over his back. That was a great Giant line and Bill must have figured they wouldn't expect him to go a rookie's way again.

"And you?" I said. "What about your leg?"

"When I tried to get up the knee was gone. What does that matter now? I just had to see. I just had to be sure . . ." All of a sudden his voice went funny and he stopped.

"What is it, Art?" I asked.

"Bill's dead," he said. "Last night, down in Boston. His car crashed. Jack, I've got to talk to you right away. It's very important. Can you come down to the park? Can you make sure to come alone? Please."

I went up the long promenade, through a corridor of bare trees and empty benches. The sun was out, but the air was bitter cold. Cooper was waiting for me at the fountain. He looked up with that little smile of his, and just then several foreign-looking men with cameras came over the hill. "Come on," Cooper said, grabbing my arm.

We cut down the hillside, Cooper limping furiously along. We took the path under the highway, coming out alongside the river.

"My eyes aren't so good," he said, glancing quickly over his shoulder. "Are they still there?"

"Who?"

"The ones with the cameras. The ones who were watching us."

There was no one. We started walking up river. The air was wet and tarry. "Art, what's this all about?"

"What else?" he said, his face tense with urgency. "That goddamn game." He'd been working on it ever since he'd left me. He'd never seen the bookmaking people so uptight before. All right, it had been a crazy season all along — scoring galore, upsets, close games, tight races, New York, L.A. and the other big-city teams winning big. A good year for the public, a great year for the League, and just in the nick of time, too, with the networks' contract up for renegotiation — it looked as if they'd finally turned things around. But it had been a disaster of a year for the books. With this last game they had their backs to the wall and they weren't looking for any smart answers. He'd already been warned more than once to lay off the questions.

But he was more sure of it than ever: that game wasn't on the level. He wasn't just talking now about how much money had been handled or the way the line went up. It wasn't just the jump; it was the action. It was who was moving what, and which side was hot, which side the fast guys were laying off of. It was all the same to the fast guys. They'd bet one side up to a certain price, then switch. They didn't give a damn about the game down on the field. Their game was playing with the spread, setting off movements of money in which they guaranteed themselves the inside track.

Well if Cooper had known what the score was, why in hell had he gone against it?

Because this stuff was going on all the time, he said; because sometimes it meant something, sometimes it didn't. What bothered him more was a story he'd heard about a "beard," or a guy who places bets for somebody who wants his identity concealed. This particular beard made a very late play on New York — $200,000 worth. Naturally with so much so late he had a hard time getting down. The opening line was three, the closing six, six and a half. To make a long story short, he got down by giving eight. Why he waited so late with the price moving up was one question. What it was all about was another. Because it seems his client's identity was not all that well kept a secret. It seems this client's name was Morris Kauffman, an old-time Miami high roller with Vegas connections and enough of a reputation to worry the big boys. Usually one guy means nothing in the scheme of things, but in this situation where they were already holding so much on New York, this one guy was enough to trip the alarm. The rumor was they nearly took the game off the board.

"Art, Christ," I said, suddenly remembering that close-up of Burke's face. "Are you saying it really was fixed? That Burke knew it?"

Cooper turned up his collar against the wind and shook his head. He said he didn't know for sure what in hell he was saying, but as far as Bill's death went, it wasn't related, at least not in the way I meant. If Bill had known anything about a fix, anything at all, he would have spoken out and let the chips fall wherever the hell they wanted to. He wasn't the kind of man to ever hold back anything like that, any more than he was the kind to do away with himself the way some of them were already saying. Burke may never have been an All-Pro, but he was as good a player as Cooper wanted to know and he had been Art's friend. For a man who had been out of football as long as him, he had accomplished wonders with Boston in three short years, but they had sacked him yesterday because he hadn't made the play-offs, because of that one lousy game. Why the hell that goddamn upstart general manager Greenley had to pick the middle of the night to fire him, Cooper didn't know, but it must have broken Bill's heart to have to go out like that. It seemed he'd stopped for a few drinks afterwards: he was going over a hundred when he hit the bridge abutment.

"No," Cooper concluded, "Bill may have been upset, he may have sensed something was wrong — but he couldn't have known for sure what it was."

But Cooper thought he knew. "Those refs," he said, turning to me as we walked. "Those goddamn refs."

"Refs are refs," I said.

"Obviously, Rose. I'm not talking now about the fact that they're dumb homers who've been blowing calls since the beginning of time. This is different. It wasn't the number or even the kind of calls. It was the timing. Those early calls broke Boston's back."

"Your feelings aren't proof."

"I know, I know," he said, flinging himself down on a park bench. "That's why I need your help."

"To do what?"

"To fix the bastards."

"You've got to be kidding."

"We could do it, Rose. I'm telling you, together we could do it."

"Cooper, for chrissake, c'mon, will you? Even if you actually had any evidence what the hell could we possibly begin to do about it?"

"I've had some experience. I read a lot and I watch TV. Everybody knows a little about how you go about something like that."

"Oh Christ," I said turning away from him. We were way the hell uptown now. I could see the George Washington

Bridge and the bare rocks of the bluffs on the Jersey shore.

"Jack, I mean it." His voice trembled with intensity, as if sheer conviction could make him right. "I'm serious. You've got to try to understand what all this has meant to me. I worked for them, yes. If people want to throw their money away gambling that's their business. It wasn't like I was pushing narcotics or something. I wasn't really one of them; it was just something I did. I didn't remember what I was until you came running after me."

"What are you?" I said. "The guy who breaks the legs?"

He laughed. It wasn't like that at all. Sports betting had become respectable now that football was so big on TV. Football, TV and gambling all went together like ABC. It was just a business. You tried to avoid bad credit risks and collect your debts when you could. Cooper was just a cog, a runner, nothing more than a glorified errand boy. But he needed the easy hours and the easy money. Every year he tried to put something away, but the knee wasn't getting any better and these New York winters were killing him. At the rate he was going rigor mortis'd be setting in before he could make his move. He figured if he could scrape together everything he had and double his money in one fell swoop . . .

Well it was all gone now. That game had taken care of his money and his lousy job, too. The bookies had trusted him all these years because he wasn't a bettor; then he made one big bet, asked a couple of questions and all of a sudden they didn't want a drunk tending bar.

All those years. He had gotten so far away from himself he hadn't even known it anymore. I had to try to understand. Football meant everything to him and when he lost it so young he thought he'd lost it all. "I don't know how to explain it, Jack," he said, looking up from the bench. "If it's wrong to make more of a thing than it is, isn't it just as wrong to make it less? God help me, I know it was only a game and that there was an awful lot of shit to take, but I didn't exactly have much in the way of a background to boast of, and that game gave me a clean, honest shot, and for me it was a pure thing. It was real Jack, the realest thing ever. It gave me a special thrill, don't get me wrong, a clean new feeling each time I took the field knowing again in my heart that every moment counted, that anything could happen as long as I believed it could."

He was looking at me then, holding himself in that stiff-shouldered way, his cheeks red and his eyes shining in the cold. I knew he expected me to say something, but all I could think was that he had it all wrong about the person you thought you would be and the stranger you wanted no part of; they were one and the same, and there was hell to pay somewhere along the line for the illusion of thinking it was any different. There was no going back, no fresh start, no new season, no magic eraser to wipe clean the slate.

"What's the point, Art? You haven't got a shred of proof."

"But if I had," he said excitedly, "that might be different, right? If I had, you might be willing?"

"I might," I said, as much to end it as anything.

He broke slowly into a big, broad grin. "Then listen to this, Prince. You remember that crazy clipping call?"

"Art, for chrissake . . ."

"I know, I know — why go beating off in the bushes with a dead horse. Just answer the question."

"In the first period," I said. "On the late flag."

"That's it. Where the zebra falls. There's even a quick shot of the turkey hobbling around. The bastard was blind to begin with, now he's lame to boot. But they leave him in for the express purpose of tormenting us — that guy, the umpire, John Murdock, was the one who killed us with those holding calls. The other night I'm in the sack, and my mind's working away the way it does and it says to me, jeez, they're getting one hundred thousand bucks per commercial minute and the League can't afford a ref with two good legs. A big game like that, you figure there's just got to be at least one spare bastard standing around just dying for an opportunity to get into the act coast to coast. So I called this acquaintance of mine who used to do some officiating.

" 'That was a good play,' he says. 'Murdock had to haul ass to stay with the ball,' and he's off on the importance of keeping the ball boxed at all times. I said I don't care if they've got a herd of zebras holding hands around the ball, I don't like my calls being made by some guy who couldn't outrun a parked truck. He says you don't throw just anybody into a pressure game like that. These guys are pros. He says that was in part the point of the reform, of making them full-time employees, of assigning them to fixed crews. He says the crew develops a working rhythm, just like a team does. I said I thought their rhythm stunk. He says, yes, if you want to talk some other plays, some of the holding calls for instance looked a little hesitant.

"So I ask him to make a call for me. It seems Murdock got to the stadium just before kickoff; he pulled a muscle because he didn't have time to warm up properly. Officials have to warm up same as anybody else, he says to me, like I'm some kind of donkey. But I can't help thinking what in hell Murdock's doing showing up minutes before the biggest game of the season. Under the new procedures they're only given a couple of days' notice of their game assignments, ostensibly to minimize the possibility of any outside influence, but they're still supposed to be in town twenty-four hours before the game, and at the stadium a couple of hours before the kickoff. The weather, probably, my friend says, these things happen this time of year. But I take the weather with my sports and unless that turkey was flying in from the Yukon the weather wasn't all that bad and these things aren't supposed to happen. A guy like Murdock can get away with it, he says: he's one of the inner circle of holier-than-thou types who benefited most from the reorganization, the kind of guy who lives and breathes the League. Style-wise he was a bit of a showboat, but other than that my friend didn't see what I was so worked up about. But I had him make one more call for me.

"And Rose, guess what? It turns out that our Murdock was a last-minute substitution. He flew in from Gladiola, on the west coast of Florida, where he winters at a motel owned by a company called M. K. Realty. Want to know what company he worked for in the off-season back in Ohio until he suddenly, prematurely, retired last year? M. K. Realty. Now, Rose, hold on to your helmet. Guess who the boss of M. K. Realty just happens to be? Morris Kauffman — some old-time Miami high roller with big Vegas connections who just happened to place a last-minute two-hundred-thousand-dollar bet on New York."

"Jesus Christ. Are you sure?"

"Absolutely Rose, now listen. I've only got a little dough left but it's enough to get us down to Florida to see face to face what Kauffman and Murdock have to say for themselves."

"Cooper, there's no way we can . . ."

"The hell we can't. Why can't we?"

"Because we just can't. Because two guys just don't up and do something like that."

"Well what the hell are we supposed to do then? Sit back on our laurels for the rest of our lives? Or are you just afraid?"

I shook my head. "That's not it."

"Well you should be. These people play for keeps, Rose."

"Cooper, what difference does it make? I wouldn't be any use to you. I'm just a fan, a spectator. I don't know anything about something like this."

"Don't worry, I know enough for the both of us. Just come down to Florida with me, just go that far with me, Jack, and we'll see. It's not like we've got to nail 'em all by ourselves. We just get the goods on them and let the cops do the nailing.

We just can't let the bastards get away with it, can we? Call it a job, Rose, call it a vacation, crazy, whatever you want. What the hell better have you got to do anyhow?"

Him and his little smiles. I stood there looking at him in that way you do when you can't seem to fix in your head the way someone really is. He was just a big overgrown kid looking out from inside a man's body. But then, too, he had been there. Otto Graham, Marion Motley, Sammy Baugh — names from books; he had been on fields with them all.

"What do you say, Prince? Are you willing? Are you in?"

"All right," I said. "What the hell. I'm in."

PART TWO

FOUR

Three days later we flew to Miami. Cooper had it all worked out. Miami would be our base of operations; an old book-making friend of his down there was taking care of all the arrangements. What we had to do, Cooper said, was find out as much about Kauffman as we could as quickly as possible, then confront Murdock. Once we had the stuff to knock them out of the water we could surface and blow the whistle on both of them. But the timing, as Cooper kept reminding me during the flight, was going to be the key. We were going up against the big boys now. If we pushed too fast, if they found out we were onto them before we had the hard goods — they'd clean our clocks for sure. But as long as we played it smart, Art didn't think we'd have too much trouble. All we had to do was flush them out into the open and bluff them into showing their hand. He figured we should be able to wrap it up in a week or less, which was just about all the time we had money for anyhow. Of course once we had handed it all over to the proper authorities, Cooper didn't see why I shouldn't be able to sell the story to someone and recoup some of our losses. Who knew — maybe there'd even be a reward.

Well I had to admit I was pretty impressed. It had seemed to me a very hard thing — an almost impossible thing — for two ordinary guys just to pick up and begin something like

this. But for Cooper, beginning posed no problem at all:
you just began.

Art's friend wasn't on hand to meet us at the gate in Miami.
We waited a couple of minutes, then hiked to the main con-
course feeling a little dazed. Miami International could have
been history's own Hollywood warehouse, with all the stars
and extras from all the epics, romances and fairy tales of the
New World milling around between productions: cowboys in
ten-gallon hats, rednecks with loony grins, old black porters,
beehived southern honeys, fiery Latin women with strutting
walks, whores and pimps, nuns and priests, South American
planters, dark-bearded revolutionaries, sailors, marines, am-
putees. And everywhere female flesh, more sudden naked
tanned female flesh than a guy straight off the plane from a
New York winter knew what to do with.

From out of nowhere a white-haired, gold-toothed little
wisp of a Cuban rushed up to us, talking a mile a minute.
I thought we were in for some kind of tourist hustle, but it
was only Cooper's friend, Confianca Martinez.

"Big Art," he cried in his high-pitched Cuban voice. "I
know I almos' miss you, bu' jus' you gib me one more minute.
Man, have I ever got the surprise for you."

Grabbing our bags he led the way to the main exit, and
we stepped out into the blast furnace of the tropics. The
surprise — illegally parked and freshly ticketed — was right
out front: a two-tone green and white 1950 vintage Chevy
coupe with whitewalls and mudguards, portholes on the fen-
ders, rockets on the hood, and on the rear window the words
"Vaya con Dios." Docked there alongside the curb the car
looked like an outlandish underwater vessel — something on
the order of a bathysphere. For Cooper it was love at first
sight.

"Jesus," he said, running his hand along its flank, "I had
no idea you could rent something like this."

"Hee hee," laughed Confianca. "A car like this is no' for

rent, Big Art." He explained that as it happened this car belonged to his nephew, Luis, who for a small consideration would be honored to part with it for the duration of Big Art's visit. The terms weren't important at all. They could all be worked out later, said Confianca with a smile that showed off all the gold in his mouth.

Cooper, his eyes riveted to the Chevy, wasn't listening. "What year did you say it was again?"

"It's a fi'ty, Big Art."

"How about that, Jack?" Cooper said full of wonder. "My year."

It was hard to say exactly what was wrong with that car. I didn't know much about cars, but I assumed that if the muffler made a terrible racket and clouds of black smoke trailed out behind you, you might have a problem somewhere. Cooper, however, siding with Confianca, seemed to take all that sound and fury as a sign of excess power. He kept braking and clutching in fits and starts as if afraid to give the car free rein. But over the roar of the engine he managed to question Confianca. Kauffman, Confianca reported, was temporarily out of town. Cooper was right about him, though, he had some reputation all right. He was a hard guy to get to and right now he was making a point of keeping himself scarce. People were being very careful about what they said. Confianca said we were waiting to hear momentarily from a friend of a friend. Once we did, though, we'd have all of Miami at our fingertips.

Cooper was pleased. "Well we're on our way now, Jack," he said, patting the dashboard. "Hell — we're in Miami, aren't we?"

There was no denying that — even through a pair of eyes stinging from the acrid smell of burning rubber and hot exhaust. Directly in front of us, just beyond the causeway and the brilliant turquoise bay, rose the shimmering wedding-cake towers of Miami Beach. Then we were skimming in low over the dazzling water, with a cool, fresh, salt breeze blowing and the sweet smell of seaweed. Right beside us a fishing boat was churning home and overhead gulls were crying and wheeling against an armada of towering, flat-bottomed clouds asail in that vast summer sky; and pouring down over it all, flooding everything, the warm afternoon sun.

Base of operations turned out to be the El Paradiso. Confianca had worked out some kind of deal through his nephew, Luis, who was a bellhop there. Art and I were given a deluxe double on the tenth floor with a balcony overlooking the Atlantic and the pool below. It struck me as a little extravagant, but Cooper was more struck with what he considered the astounding fact that I hadn't thought to bring a bathing suit along. He insisted on buying me one immediately and sending me out to the pool for the rest of the afternoon. It was a good idea, he thought, for at least one of us to be out there appearing to enjoy himself; and that had to be me because he was sensitive to the sun. Besides he had to monitor the phone for that important call. He also wanted to get started on a letter to the D.A. that would serve as a hedge against our being captured by Kauffman's men. I should act perfectly natural, just like I was on vacation. I should charge anything I wanted to his account. He'd let me know as soon as anything big broke.

I spent the afternoon as instructed. I had a drink, read the local papers, and even swam the series of laps in the pool that Cooper had prescribed as a means of getting me into some kind of shape. Afterwards I sprawled beside the pool and talked with a beautifully tanned brunette. She was from Kansas City where she said the weather now was "muckymuck." She guessed New York was pretty "yucky," too. I bought her a drink and began working my way around to telling her what a perfect candidate I was starting to consider her for a bangy-wangy, when she told me she was checking out of the hotel for K.C. in less than an hour.

Upstairs Cooper was propped up in bed, the floor around him littered with the crumpled rejects of his letter to the D.A. He had just heard from the friend of a friend, the bookmaking contact who was going to put all of Miami at our fingertips.

"Well?" I said.

"Aaaah," Cooper said, looking away. "He's just a scared stiff like all the rest of them."

"What did he say, Art?"

"He says I'm suffering from TV on the brain. The hell with him." It was probably all for the best, anyhow, Cooper said. The more we relied on outside people the more we only ran the risk of being sold out. It didn't matter. Kauffman was out of town; we still had plenty of time.

"So I guess that means we'll probably be going to Gladiola," I said.

"For what?"

"To try to talk to Murdock. What else?"

Cooper gave me a sidelong look. "Boy, you really don't know a thing about how it's done, do you?"

"Well then how's it done?" I said, beginning to get annoyed with him.

"Not by running all over the goddamn state like a cock with your head unstrapped. With a little class, Rose, a little savoir flair. What's the first thing your big-time special investigator does? He sets up a phone number. You think he does that because he likes to get calls?"

"Flair," I said.

"That's right. And he drives a distinguished automobile and he has himself a nice base of operations." Cooper slapped the bed. He pointed out that every great investigative detective down through history from Eliot Ness to Nero Wolfe had had his own distinctive personal style. There was nothing for me to worry about, everything was perfectly under control. At that very moment Confianca and Luis were hard at work putting out feelers for us. All we had to do was sit back and wait for the information to start rolling in. Until then I could just stop aggravating him with unnecessary questions and do my job, and right then my job was to get the hell out, and for chrissake to drop the long face and attempt to look like I was enjoying myself.

So I spent a couple of hours out on the town. Everybody else seemed to be in families or couples. I ended up re-reading the local papers in the lobby of the El Paradiso where an insistent Cuban bellhop kept hissing familiarly in my ear that if what I was seeing on display wasn't to my liking, better fare could be arranged. I brushed him off and sat there until it was almost late enough to go respectably on up to bed and then I went into the bar for a nightcap. At the far end I spotted Confianca. He'd obviously already had a few of his own.

"Zhack," he cried embracing me. "You should have been there. A seess horse field. I say to Luis, knock out two, it's a cinch. Luis, he says, hol' everyt'ing. I give you the horse. So what happens? That dog — hee hee — he gives me the wrong horse."

"I thought the two of you were supposed to be out working for Art tonight," I said.

"Work? A man canno' be all the time workin', Zhack. We canno' all be so serious like Big Art Cooper up in his room." Confianca insisted on having a drink with me to celebrate my arrival; we'd just put it on Art's tab. Poor Big Art, he said. The important thing was for the rest of us to understand each other. We had to make sure Big Art had a good time, too, and above all to protect him from all the scavengers who cared only for a man's money and not for his principles, the ones who would try to take advantage of him just because he was a former football player.

I didn't see what Cooper's being an ex-football player had to do with his needing extra protection.

"You mean you don' know about Yankee foo'ball? Is no'

a man's game, thass for sure. Wha' you think? Wha' kind of a man play a game wit' little fish and birds and shit like that on the head? Wha' kind of a man wears a hat like that? Only one kind of a man and where I come from we run that man right out of the town. But worse of all," he said cackling to himself, "hee hee, the Rams and the Bikings and all the ones wit' little horns on the heads. These Yankees. Don' they know while they out grabbin' each other on the field wha' the bitch at home is doin' in fron' of the TB wit' the bess friend?"

I took the opportunity then to ask him what he thought of Cooper's belief that the game was fixed.

"Of course it was fixed. Wha' you think? You think they givin' all that shit away for free? Every game you see on the TB's fixed. Why else you think the quizmaster always wearin' such a big smile? Everyt'ing on the TB's fixed. Jus' take an example from history — take Oswald. They wan' you to think tha' Ruby plugs him right on the cameras. Bu' everybody knows you get shot on the TB it's no' for real. Tha' Oswald, hee, hee, he's probably over there in Cuba right now screwin' those bitches to his heart's content."

Confianca rose to his feet to toast the beauty of Cuban women, in the process managing to spill half his drink in my lap. He begged me to have another drink, but I had already heard more than enough.

On the way back through the lobby the bellhop I now realized was Luis greeted me like an old friend, with a big, obscene wink. "You should see the look on Big Art's face when I tell him jus' now you screwin' the cunts all over the place. Man is he ever jealous." I pushed my way past him. He laughed and shouted after me that he could set me up with a pair of real red-hot ones for the night. He'd put it all on Big Art's account. Unless, of course, he cackled, Big Art and I were having a better time by ourselves.

Upstairs Cooper lay in bed with his Dear D.A. letters, the TV on. He eyed my wet trousers coldly. "Well it's not too hard to deduce what you've been up to. I said to act natural, Rose, not revert to a sex fiend on an expense account."

I was too worked up to do anything but stand there and stare at him. Looking down at him and his battered nose I was sure I finally understood everything I needed to know about him. He had played in the time before there were face bars on the helmets; in the act of snapping the ball a center was defenseless. No doubt he had taken one shot too many to the head. It would explain everything: his wild suspicions, his idle boasts, his childish All-American optimism, his faith in those sad losers downstairs. He was simply nuts.

I locked myself in the bathroom and stood in the shower a good long time. What was the use of getting mad at him? His strong certainties, his daring plans — it seemed clear to me now they were only so many delusions. For all I knew the whole fix was the work of his imagination: the rumors about Kauffman, his paranoia about being followed, all of it. I didn't know exactly what I'd been expecting from him, but this brash, bossy, moody, money-blowing, manic imitation of a maiden aunt in menopause wasn't it. I'd been taken in was all. There was no point in hashing it out with him. People gave themselves all kinds of excuses for blowing their money. Who was to say that pretending to be on the trail of a gambling conspiracy was any less sensible than taking a trip, say, for the sake of your health. It was certainly a whole lot healthier than thinking a mere change of scenery could change your life in any significant way.

But whatever his problems were I'd had all I wanted. The thing to do now was try to get a good night's sleep, then take off first thing in the morning.

I came out of the bathroom to find him in a hot sweat, furiously propping the last of four chairs against the dressers that were now resting smack against the door.

"Something wrong with the lock?" I said, trying to sound calm.

"Locks don't stop these people, Rose."

"What people, Art?"

"Whoever the hell they just called to warn me about. Kauffman's back. They're coming for us."

"And just who called to tell you all this?"

"For chrissake, use your head, Rose. It was an anonymous call. It wouldn't be an anonymous call if they told you who they were, now would it?"

"You sure it wasn't an anonymous voice in your head?"

He stopped shoving furniture and stared at me. "Oh brother," he said. "Is that what you think? Or are you just sore because I know you've been chasing the broads up and down the beach all day long. If you've got a beef, Rose, you bring it straight to me. I won't have you moping around undermining the morale of this investigation."

"Morale?" I said. *"Investigation?"* This isn't an investigation, it's a farce. And there isn't anyone coming for us because even if there is anyone out there halfway interested in the first place, as far as they're concerned we're just a couple of closet queens on a spending spree. And as far as I'm concerned, you can just let those crazy Cuban characters fleece you until you don't have a cent left to your name. I've had it."

"Oh beautiful. I should've known better than to get involved with a goddamn Harvard kid. As soon as the big-time pressure's on the spoiled little Harvard kid wants out."

"Pressure?"

"OK, look, Jack," he said approaching me, "the first thing is — try not to get excited."

"I am *not* excited."

"All right, all right, you're perfectly normal. I'm the one that's excited. I'm the one that's hearing anonymous voices on the phone. Look, Jack, can't this wait till later? I mean — Jesus — they could be coming for us this very second."

"Oh they're coming for us all right," I said backing away

from him, "and let me tell you how we'll recognize them when they get here. They'll be the ones in the white coats. And we can tell them everything we know, and they can lock us up awhile, and when they finally let us back on the street again you can go and do whatever you want because I'm getting the hell out of here first thing in the morning." With that I shut off the lights and climbed into bed.

Then he was standing over me in the dark shouting that that was just fine with him, because his mind was made up, too, and if I thought that by making threats he was going to change one bit I was dead wrong. I said I wasn't asking him to change or to do anything else. I was through with him and that was that. Well thank God, he said. Thank God he had found out the truth about me before he had gotten into a fix where, heaven help him, he might have needed to count on me. He was still running this show, and he wasn't moving until he was good and ready and as far as he was concerned he'd be the happiest man in the world if when morning came I went out that door and he never had to see my face again. As far as he was concerned these were the last fucking words I was ever going to hear from him. Good night.

Cursing to himself in the dark he stumbled out onto the balcony and slammed the sliding glass door behind him. Some time went by, maybe ten minutes, maybe half an hour, and then he was back shouting and turning on all the lights. "All right," he barked, "you want to go. We're going."

"Fine. That's wonderful," I said pulling the pillow over my eyes.

"I mean we're moving out now."

"Oh Christ, Art, can't it wait till morning?"

"No it can't," he said, sitting down on the edge of my bed. "Don't you see, Jack? We can't just sit here and let them capture us before we've even had a chance to begin."

"And just where are we supposed to go in the middle of the night?"

"Wherever you say." He said I was right — it was crazy to think we could count on anybody else. We'd scrap his plan; we'd do it my way. We'd drive to Gladiola right away to investigate Murdock on our own before it was too late. If they were watching us we stood the best chance of giving them the slip right now.

"Art, Gladiola's all the way across the state."

"It's a thin state, Jack. And with that car we've got, are you kidding?"

"The way you drive?"

"You drive then. Just help me get out of this mess, Jack, that's all I'm asking. You can't just leave me here now like this."

He was looking me straight in the eye and I could see that he was truly afraid and I realized suddenly that whether I liked it or not I was at least partly responsible for his being here in the first place. If he had been deluded, I had helped make that delusion seem real. The least I could do was help him end this mad fixation with the investigation and see to it that he got out of here before those Cubans picked him clean. I could catch a plane back from the Gulf coast just as easily.

Twenty minutes later we were slipping out through the sleeping city, me at the wheel of the Chevy, Cooper alternately reading maps and keeping a lookout for pursuers. A full moon lit the bay and white clouds were piled high against the blue black sky. We went roaring down the expressway past the dark shell of the Orange Bowl and out along the edge of the airport. We swept down off one highway around and up onto another, the green and white signs floating into our lights and shooting past: ROUTE 41 WEST 1 MILE, then ½ MILE, then RIGHT LANE, then we were swinging off down around onto the road west, the city glowing behind us in the rearview mirror like it was on fire, the six lanes narrowing to four, and the four to two, and the two flying together undivided and straight as an arrow into the blackness of the Everglades.

This was more like it. With the sweet night air pouring in through the open windows the fumes and muffler weren't so bad, and there was even a nice, timeless feeling inside the high-domed vault of the old Chevy. Cooper folded his maps and turned his attention to the radio. It was an old tube radio with a rich sound but limited range. One by one we sunk the Miami stations, Cooper working the dial with the intensity of a navigator on whose delicate skills depended the life and welfare of the crew.

An hour later we could smell the sea again. We cruised into the predawn, locked-up center of the town of Naples, slowing down at the blinking red lights where the road turns north up the coast. Right after we crossed the Gladiola line we turned off at the first sign for a motel, went down a side road, popped up over a little bridge, and there suddenly spread out before us all silver and shimmering in the moonlight was the Gulf.

We pulled into the parking lot, rolled to a stop under a line of palms, and stepped right out onto the cool snow-white moonlit beach. Cooper was elated.

"Jesus, Jack, but this feels different, doesn't it though? Christ I don't blame you one bit for sounding off at me back there. I don't know what I was thinking." He said the sun must have got to his head: acting like a damn fool, throwing money away hand over fist, trying to play the big know-it-all hero for me. Well it was behind us now. We just had to get it going was all. We were on the right track now. All he wanted was just a couple of days to show me what he could really do. "For your own peace of mind, Jack," he said. "That's all I'm asking. You don't ever want to quit on somebody without giving them a fair chance."

Damned if he wasn't something else, though, with his Grade-B movie lines and his first-rate case of TV on the brain. He seemed so happy, I didn't have the heart to tell him that my mind was made up — that I wasn't going to encourage him anymore in his crazy ideas, that I was still pulling out.

I figured I'd save that little piece of news for the morning.

But in the morning the news was all his. He came charging into the room, waking me up with the announcement that we weren't going to be talking to Murdock after all. Half drugged with sleep I thought he meant he had finally decided to drop the whole crazy idea of the investigation. "Well I'm glad you've finally come to your senses about it," I said.

"The hell I have, Prince," he said, waving a newspaper in my face. "Here." He handed me the paper, a day-old copy of the weekly Gladiola *Gazette.* "I thought you might like to be among the first to read about my latest delusion."

The item was very brief. Two days earlier, in the middle of the night, a man identified as a local vacationer had been accidentally shot by a Gladiola farmer.

The dead man's name was John Murdock.

FIVE

Towards noon we drove into town to see what we could find out about Murdock's death.

It was the first time I'd been in that part of the state. Everything felt scaled-down and jumbled, like a model railroad layout. At first we were in real country, driving past fields and sandy intersections where women and kids sold fresh produce out of dusty flatbed trucks. A minute later the road shot up over a river, with people fishing off the sides of the bridge, and there was a view straight over the mangroves to a cluster of apartment buildings that rose like some great, distant metropolis against the blue disk of the Gulf. Then we bumped over the railroad tracks and drove on into the fashionable heart of the old town itself, the main street lined with elegant stores shaded by columns of stately royal palms. And floating over it all, dazzling in the midday sun, a great silver globe of a water tower with bold black letters: GLADIOLA.

We hung around the police station until the sheriff returned from lunch. We had cooked up a half-baked story about being free-lance writers, but the hearty young sheriff of Gladiola didn't seem to care who we were or what we wanted to know. Tan, cheerful, delighted to make our acquaintance, he ushered us into his office and sat us down in comfortable armchairs. A breeze from the open windows ruffled the loose papers on his desk, carrying the salty smell of the Gulf and the steady plop of tennis balls from the municipal courts across the street. The sheriff put his feet up on his desk and spent the better part of an hour going over the details of the case.

Murdock, he informed us, had been killed by James Shipley, an elderly farmer who lived with his wife up on the north side of town. For the last few months Shipley had been having some trouble with vandals. They'd shot one of his dogs, mutilated a calf — sick things like that, the sheriff said, done by people from who knows where, passing through along the highway. Three nights ago Shipley woke up because of his dog barking. Grabbing his pistol, he ran outside to discover the victim hiding in the dark behind a shed. At first the man acted drunk, refusing to show himself. Then he rushed Shipley and tried to wrestle the gun away. In the ensuing struggle the gun discharged.

The sheriff said that all the evidence was consistent with Shipley's account. Furthermore Shipley was one of the oldest residents of the area, a man of the highest integrity. There had been no reason to question his deposition. A clear case of justifiable homicide in self-defense. An unfortunate accident.

Cooper couldn't believe it. "You mean that's all there is to it? Some farmer tells you he just happened to shoot some guy in the middle of the night — a goddamn referee for chrissake — and that's it? You don't hear a word about it on the radio, on the TV, in the papers, nothing?"

The sheriff leaned back and smiled. "So you know that Murdock was a football ref?" he said softly.

"Is it such a top secret?" Cooper said.

The sheriff said that as a matter of fact it was. There had been no identification whatsoever on the body and it wasn't until the next day when they found his car in a ditch on a back road that they obtained Murdock's name and local address. He was a quiet bachelor with virtually no friends in the area, even though this was his second winter here. They didn't find out about his being a referee until they notified next of kin in Ohio. As for the lack of press, that wasn't exactly his department but he didn't suspect that a drunk ref getting himself shot while attacking an old man in the middle of the night was the kind of publicity either the city of Gladiola or the League was likely to kill itself trying to get out.

I asked the sheriff if he had any idea what Murdock had been doing on Shipley's property in the first place. He said as it so happened they had a pretty good idea. Because while Murdock evidently kept to himself, he wasn't a total recluse. It seemed he'd been enjoying the favors of a certain cocktail waitress, a gal by the name of Louise Boudreau down from Georgia, one chunk of a little lady, too, a real eyeful. She was living in a trailer park not far up the road from Shipley's, and Murdock had left her place late that night with his faculties somewhat impaired. He'd evidently driven off the road into the ditch, wandered onto Shipley's property and panicked at the sight of the gun. There was no accounting for what tourists and winter people were thinking half the time, judging by the messes they got themselves into. They'd all seen too many movies up north, the sheriff guessed.

"Well maybe some people haven't seen enough," Art said.

"Meanin'?" said the sheriff.

Art couldn't restrain himself any longer: "Meaning have you ever heard of a man named Morris Kauffman?"

The sheriff looked surprised. "What's he got to do with any of this?"

Cooper told the sheriff everything — about the game and our suspicions, Murdock's late arrival and his bad calls, Kauffman's last-minute bet and his reputation, that the real-estate company Murdock had worked for in Ohio as well as the motel he was staying at in Gladiola were both Kauffman's, that the two of us had resolved to find out the truth about it all.

The sheriff listened with an indulgent smile. "So what do you two figure now? Somebody get a little too worked up over one of his calls?"

"You've got to admit his death seems a bit strange," I said.

"That's right," he said turning to me. "But you spend a couple of weeks down here yourself and just see if the strange doesn't get to be the natural real fast. The strange thing in a place like this is that anything normal ever seems to happen anymore. Accidents, drownings, pills, booze — you name it — this isn't a city, it's a goddamn glorified traffic jam, everybody on the move, just passing through. Why the last time we had a nice, decent, old-fashioned straightforward murder case with a body and clues and the possibility of apprehending a suspect was a couple of years back when Frenchie Klinghoffer found his wife with a Mexican. Took us less than fifteen minutes to track him down, it being a Friday and one of the boys recalling that the Frog always had a tennis court reserved for five o'clock. I'll always remember Frenchie's words when we pulled up. 'Just three more points and I've got the match.' Actually it took him another three whole games to get that match, but everybody agreed they had never seen him play with such inspiration and that for once his temper didn't get in the way of his tennis. He put Judge Collins away six to one, six to two. Later, of course, the Judge had to put him away."

That was the Lord's own truth, it had happened right there across the street, and the sheriff wasn't saying it to discourage us, but just to make clear what kind of place this town was. The fact of what Murdock did elsewhere wasn't any concern of theirs here. Folks came to Gladiola to get away from all that, and it didn't serve any useful purpose to stir up resentments between residents and winter people. Things were already hard enough with the season being as slow as it was. Nor did the sheriff think it a good idea for us to bother James Shipley either: the old man wasn't likely to take too kindly to any more strangers just now. If we still insisted on fishing around while we were in Gladiola, the sheriff suggested we might have a lot better luck off the town pier.

"Jesus, Jack," Cooper said as we came out of the police station, "can you believe it? A goddamn ref for chrissake and that smooth-talking southern cop acts like it's nothing more than open season on zebras. After all it's only elementary detective logic: people get shot, zebras can be people, ipso presto they can get it too, right?"

"It's possible."

"That's right. Especially in the middle of nowhere at four in the morning by some trigger-happy farmer and you don't hear a word about it." Cooper was sure there had to be more to it than that, but it didn't seem too promising to me.

"Nonsense, these things always go this way at first, Rose. Look at any of your classic detective stories."

I said that was because they were stories: they built suspense by throwing obstacles in the hero's way. Cooper didn't see it that way; stories were like that, he thought, because they reflected the nature of things. You had to expect to poke and probe and shake things up before they broke. Why the hell did I always have to be so negative anyhow? I had to learn to take the bull by the horns, to put my shoulder to the grindstone. He was sure we'd get to the bottom of Murdock's death in no time at all and that when we did someone by the name of Morris Kauffman would be waiting there for us. "Unless, of course," he said, "you still think you might like to cut out, Prince."

"No," I said, "under the circumstances, if you don't mind, I think I'll stick around awhile longer."

So after a couple of quick cheeseburgers we got in the Chevy and drove to the place Murdock had stayed, a two-story motel in the heart of the tourist strip. Blazoned on the marquee, above the letters proclaiming plenty of excellent units still available on a weekly, monthly, or seasonal basis, was the logo of M. K. Realty.

As soon as the desk clerk figured out we weren't cops or insurance investigators or anybody he had to talk to, he refused to answer our questions. But then Cooper informed the guy that the real reason for our visit was that we'd heard so many nice things from our friend John Murdock about this place that we'd come by with the idea of perhaps renting something for the rest of the season, and if he was too busy to show us around, maybe we'd better speak with the manager.

Apologizing profusely, the clerk insisted on personally giving us the grand tour of the place, stopping at Murdock's room, which he assured us was one of their best and which, as it happened, was still vacant. Earlier in the year they would have had no trouble renting a room like this, for the entire season and at prime rates, too, not the discount Murdock received as a former Kauffman employee. Now with business the way it was it looked like they might be stuck with it, not that it wasn't a shame what had happened to our friend. He was such a quiet, private-type person, you hardly ever noticed he was around. Cooper asked if he'd ever seen Murdock with Kauffman himself, but the clerk said the only Kauffman they ever saw out here was the old man's son.

The room was a small cheerless space. It had already been cleared out, and there wasn't a trace of Murdock or anybody else in it. But Cooper made a big deal about how much he liked it and the clerk, urging him to take as much time as he needed, left us there to mull it over.

Telling me to cover the door, muttering to himself that every detail counted, Cooper swung into a Sherlock Holmes act, opening drawers, lifting the corners of the carpet, inspecting closets, looking under the bed and behind the curtains,

in short leaving no stone unturned in his search for the tell-
tale word scrawled in blood, or the neatly typed double-
spaced, fully notarized letter of confession addressed to whom
it may concern, containing the names and numbers of everybody involved in the fix.

I went outside to wait and ran into the cleaning lady, a
sweet old thing who said how very sad she felt for poor Mr.
Murdock. Such a neat man, such a clean man — but funny,
too, about his privacy. He didn't even like her to come in to
clean. She used to sneak in when he was out just to make
sure, but the room was always as spotless as if he never even
used it.

Next Art and I drove over to the lounge where the sheriff
said that Louise Boudreau, Murdock's girlfriend, had worked,
but they told us she hadn't been in for weeks. One of the
waitresses gave us directions to the trailer park where she
lived. There wasn't any number.

The day had turned cloudy and muggy, but on the way
over Cooper's spirits were sailing high. As far as he was
concerned this Boudreau woman was herself a prime suspect
and he was eager to have at her. Since this would be our first
major joint interrogation he thought we should discuss general strategy. Every professional investigative team, he said,
employed some sort of technique to subtly manipulate key
suspects — like one of us should play it tough and ask all
the hard questions, while the other should be gentle and sym-
pathetic. That was fine with me, he could act as tough as he
wanted. But Art shook his head. The whole point was to
disorient the suspect. Who the hell would be disoriented if
he acted tough? Obviously he was the tough one; could I
imagine the effect of him deliberately trying to act even
tougher? We wanted to manipulate the suspect, not terrorize
the poor thing. And another thing, as long as we were on
the subject. Although he personally doubted that any referee
could make it with a broad that was halfway decent, I should

nevertheless be on my guard. No offense, but from what he'd seen so far I had little or no resistance where broads were concerned. As a female this one might attempt to use her charms on us, and we had better keep on the balls of our feet. We'd make out fine if we remembered that they were basically no different than anybody else. All we had to do was stay on our toes and use a little psychology.

In the case of Louise Boudreau we could have been the national psychology tag team champions for all the good it would have done us; we still would have been lightweights in the main event. Louise didn't play at psychology, she was one of those women who live it. There was more psychology in one of her itsy-bitsy, curled-up, red-lacquered Confederate toes than in our combined 400-plus pounds of mesmerized Yankee beef. In her prime she may not have been the classic wholesome beauty contest winner, but she sure as hell was the one loser you'd have most wanted to console. Not that time appeared to be slowing her down any. For someone on the far side of forty she still had all the moves of an impetuous Teen Queen. She was a compact, busty, dark-haired jungle of a woman, a hot-blooded southern melting pot spiced with Indian and black.

From the start she blew hot and cold, first screaming like a wildcat from the dark lair of her trailer, yelling that we had a nerve waking a girl up at this time of day, that we had to be out of our minds if we thought for a second that she was going to talk to a pair of perfect strangers about something as upsetting to her as poor John Murdock's death, that if we insisted on hanging around like a couple of long-faced dogs we could at least have the decency to do it out of sight of the neighbors and then sending us around back where as far as I could tell the neighbors couldn't help but see us.

When Louise finally did open up the door, though, she was all sugar and honey and full of apologies about how long it took these days for a girl to make herself presentable. One thing was for sure — whatever she'd been doing in the quarter of an hour she'd kept us cooling our heels wasn't in the general area of putting on clothes. She wore nothing but a tight T-shirt that climbed right up her thighs to her panties the instant she sat back on the couch, folding her legs up under her. Sitting practically in her lap as we were in the narrow trailer you couldn't help but pick up her heavy, musky scent. That and the overripe odor of rotting garbage from the kitchen. There was no air in that tight tin box of a trailer and it was oppressively hot. The only light to speak of came from the blue gray screen of the television where soap opera characters with pained expressions flickered silently. Everywhere you looked there were pieces of clothing and empty Chinese food containers. But you couldn't really make out all that much in the dark.

One thing we couldn't miss, however, light or no light, was spread out on the coffee table at our knees. It drew our eyes like heat draws missiles. "Oh that," Louise drawled. "Now what's that doin' out here?" That was nothing at all, just her professional portfolio. She doubted, she said, turning the pages slowly, whether that was of any particular interest to us. The portfolio consisted of large glossy photographs of Louise in various lively poses, with here and there an occasional feather or rhinestone for decoration. But that was just the showgirl stuff she'd done for money in clubs. Her real ambition was to be an "artiste." The artistic shots were in the back of the book. Here she did away with the artificial encumbrances of pasties, G-strings and cottontail rumps. As an artiste Louise wore only the purity of her emotions as expressed through the medium of her body.

Cooper barely glanced at the portfolio. In fact he had hardly uttered a word since Louise let us in. He just sat there on the couch gazing at her with a goofy, sheepish grin, nodding at everything she said like a big bear struck dumb by the sugary sound of her voice. I didn't know whether the heat had gone to his head, or if this was his idea of playing it soft. But as soon as I steered the conversation around to Murdock, Art began what seemed to me a systematic attempt to sabotage the interview, playing the passionate defense attorney whose every objection on behalf of his beautiful, fragile and falsely accused client was sustained by the judge. Cooper also played the judge.

"Mistah Coopah's" performance quickly earned him the full brunt of Miss Boudreau's attention. I was demoted to "that boy," and got nothing but the back of her shoulder and an occasional glimpse of her pouting lips as she dreamily lifted her head and chest to formulate each answer. Somehow we managed nevertheless to establish the basic outline of her relationship with Murdock, from their meeting the previous winter to their growing involvement prior to his return north for the start of the football season. Could she tell us what happened next?

She sighed and reached back to smooth down her hair and in so doing caused her T-shirt to break new ground in its advance up the slopes of her thighs.

"Don't answer that if you don't want to," Art advised.

She smiled at him gratefully, then wistfully shook her head. "Mistah Coopah, you must think it heartless of me to have put all this business behind me the way I have."

"Oh not at all. From what I've seen I'd say you had to have the biggest heart of any lady I've ever known."

"Why Mistah Coopah," she exclaimed, "I believe you did enjoy my pictures."

Even in the dark I could see Art flush a shade deeper. "Don't get me wrong, Miss Boudreau. I merely deduced a broad's got to have a very big heart to expose her emotions the way you do."

Patting his arm she cooed that she was only teasing. Her life with John had been strained for some time, though that didn't mean she didn't feel just awful about what had hap-

pened the other night. That didn't mean she didn't feel as
if she was afflicted with some terrible sort of curse. She looked
at Art meaningfully and asked if he wasn't interested in knowing what kind of a curse. Art waved his hand feebly and said
there were some things you just didn't ask a lady about.

But I didn't mind asking.

"Boy now," she said turning on me, "if that ain't the
dumbest question I ever heard. What kind of a curse do you
think it was? Ain't but one kind of a curse and that's a bad
one."

"Rose, for chrissake, will you try to ask intelligent questions? Can't you see Miss Boudreau here's an artiste?"

Well that did it. That was all he had to say. It was as if
he had pressed the magic button. She laid her head back on
the couch near his shoulder and gazed up at him with this
creamy rapturous look as if he were the Second Coming.
Why, she declared, if she didn't feel all soft and buttery on
the inside in a way she had never felt with a man before.
She felt purely naked in his presence, as if he could look right
through her clothes to the secret truth within her. She felt
as if she could tell him anything and he would understand.
"Most any other girl would have been thrilled to death just
to meet someone like John Murdock, much less go with him.
Like John used to call me up special just to let me know when
he was going to be on, and then sure enough, there he'd be
on the TV lookin' so smart and elegant in his uniform, bossin'
around all those big dumb ballplayers who thought they were
such hot stuff. A lot of girls would've let somethin' like that
go to their heads. They would've thought that put them on a
pedestal a cut above everybody else just because he was on
television. Of course that didn't matter none to me. Men
were always beggin' for the chance to put me into pictures
or TV or one thing or another. An Arabian sheik wanted
to take me back to his country and make me a queen, and
there was a New York executive who was planning to build

an entire national advertising campaign for foot powder around me, and there were more men willin' to leave their wives and li'l babies for me than I could count, though I never was one for breakin' up families. It's been that way ever since I was a little girl, one damn fool boy after another losin' his head over me."

It wasn't her fault if men were always coming to grief over her. How could she be blamed for trying to save herself for that one true love? How could she be blamed if John Murdock, despite his being a big-time football official and all, wasn't that love? Maybe she was crazy. Other girls would've snatched up a man like that quick as they could've dropped their drawers. Not that he would ever have trusted those kinds of girls in the first place with the secret of who he really was. In all of Gladiola she was the only one who had known.

"Why was he so secretive?" I asked. "Didn't that seem strange?"

"Strange for you maybe. Strange for them that's got to run around impressin' others. John came down here to get away from all that. With me he could be his real self."

"Was he ever in any trouble that you knew about?" I asked.

She smirked and gave me the back of her head. "John Murdock wasn't the type for trouble. He wasn't the type to ever dare do one single thing to jeopardize his career."

"Well with all due respect, Miss Boudreau," Art said, "he apparently almost did miss the New York–Boston game on the seventeenth of December."

"Well if he had, Mistah Coopah, I can assure you I'd have heard all about it when he came down to see me for New Year's."

"He hadn't been down here before that?" I said.

"I didn't say he had and I didn't say he hadn't and I'm not sayin' no more about it than that."

"Well I was only asking, because according to what we've

been able to find out he was in Gladiola before that game."

"I already told you," she snapped, her voice on the edge of cracking, "I'm not sayin' no more. Why should I? You want to go bothering somebody with your dumb questions why don't you go ask that farmer why he really did what he done. He's the one that done that horrible thing to John," she sniffled, "not me." Then she burst out crying.

To see Louise Boudreau cry was to understand why they named hurricanes after women. She went at it with a positive passion, an active joy. You would have thought she was having some kind of ecstatic fit the way she was wailing and flailing around on the couch. I'm sure that's what Cooper must have thought, judging by the way he panicked, but then he was catching the worst of it. She was all over him and he was beside himself, begging her to stop and threatening to knock my block off for making her cry, asking her if she wouldn't like to see him do that to me. But each time he made a move in my direction it only made her cry all the louder and hang on tighter, pulling him back down to her. They were tangled up in each other like two wrestlers working for an advantage, Cooper fighting a losing battle in which, to his evident discomfort, every gesture of tenderness and concern only seemed to further unleash the floodwaters of her emotions. It was all he could do just to keep pulling her T-shirt back down over her panties.

When it was all over she sat calmly by his side. She said he was one of the kindest, tenderest, most gentle men she had ever met. She said she hadn't ever meant to lie to him. "John might have come down earlier than I knew. I didn't tell the sheriff but the truth was I didn't hear from John during the last part of the season: he had gotten stuck on me and I had done my best to break it off. Then the other night he suddenly showed up drunk at my place threatenin' to kill himself if I didn't marry him. Maybe it was the wrong thing to do, but I wanted to make it as easy for him as possible, so I told him there was somebody else. He went runnin' off

half out of his mind. It was the first time he had actually
been out here — him bein' too much of a gentleman for seein'
a girl at her own place or for motels and the like — and he
must have gotten lost."

She didn't see how she could be blamed for what had happened. And one thing she was sure of — John Murdock was
too decent and proper a man ever to attack anybody the way
the sheriff and that farmer said he did.

"Jesus Christ," Cooper said when he had finally managed to
tear himself away from her and drag himself out to the car
where I was waiting. "I said to play it hard, Rose, not torture
the poor broad."

"Me? What about you? Playing it soft is one thing; fon-
dling everything in sight is something else."

"Don't think I enjoyed deceiving that poor broad for one
second."

"Oh, on the contrary, Miss Boudreau. You've got the biggest heart of any broad I've ever felt up."

"I'm telling you, Rose, right now, you can just knock it
off."

"And if she was lying?"

"Tears don't lie, Rose. Those were real tears, real hot,
wet ones. I don't know what it is when a woman cries," he
said sitting back with a sappy, punch-drunk smile on his face,
"it just does something to you, you know?"

The day had turned darker and it looked as though it was
going to rain soon. Cooper said that we had no choice now
but to go talk to Shipley. Louise was obviously as innocent
as they came; she hadn't even heard of Kauffman. But just
because Murdock had left her place in a drunken fit didn't
necessarily explain what he was doing at this so-called farmer's place in the middle of the night. For all we knew this
trigger-happy Farmer Brown guy was Murdock's bagman.
There had to be some connection to Kauffman.

I recalled the sheriff's request that we leave Shipley alone, and suggested that we at least show the old man the consideration of calling him in advance, but Art said you just didn't spring a surprise visit on your prime suspect by calling up to make an appointment.

Halfway over to Shipley's the sky turned an ominous, sullen black. A couple of heavy raindrops splattered on the hood: a minute later the storm broke, the rain lashing in sheets that made an instant blur of the windshield and forced us to the side of the road. We waited it out in the vaulted gloom of the Chevy, lightning crackling all around us, thunder booming and the rain hammering at the roof, splashing and dripping its way through a dozen leaks. Cooper, still wearing his sappy smile, thought the thunderstorm was one of the most beautiful things he'd ever seen. It reminded him somehow of Louise.

The storm passed as suddenly as it had broken. We continued on inland, the wet woods shining on either side of the road and delicate stretches of clean, pale blue sky showing through rifts in the clouds. We crossed a narrow wooden bridge, the creek below muddy and swollen with the rain, and came to the road to the Shipley place, called, appropriately enough, Shipley Road. The woods opened up to reveal a strange sight.

On the far side of Shipley Road, as far as you could see, the land had been razed and asphalt streets had been neatly laid out, with fire hydrants sticking up everywhere like half-buried tree stumps. The asphalt was already cracking in places, and the bulldozed earth was overgrown with weeds. Here and there in the distance, like archeological relics in the rubbled midst of an ancient civilization, stood split-level suburban houses, each on its own quarter-acre oasis of grass, with a two-car garage, a television aerial and a little walk leading up to the front door.

On the near side of the road the woods were intact, and set back from the road was Shipley's farm. It wasn't much of a place to look at: a small, old house, with a weather-beaten porch, a few low sheds and some cattle grazing in a field. As we bumped up the dirt driveway a yellow bitch ran out barking. Then a tall bony woman came to the door, wiping her hands on her apron. We pulled up beside the rusted remains of an old pickup truck on blocks, the bitch running in circles around our car, yapping excitedly. Cooper, rolling up his window, advised me to wait until they called him off. I said I'd take my chances. "Well for God's sake be careful, Rose. He looks like he means business."

The bitch jumped up and licked me, then bounded off towards the house. I followed her. The woman stood shielding her eyes with one hand, polite but distant. She had a strong nasal twang, a heavy rural accent that sounded more like the West to me than the South. She said her husband was sick and the doctor didn't want him pestered none. He'd already answered enough questions and if we weren't from the sheriff's she wasn't about to pester him no more on our account.

Just then, from behind the house, with a rifle slung over his shoulder and the dawdling air of a schoolboy playing hookey, came Shipley himself. He was a small, wiry, leather-skinned old man, hardly more than bone and gristle. He nodded at me in greeting and asked why I had my friend locked up tight inside the car. "Ain't got the pox, has he?" I said he was worried about the dog, who was now planted right under Cooper's window chewing away on a stick. Shipley called her over and waved at Cooper to come on out. His wife said then that if he didn't get right back in bed where he belonged that instant she was going to get on the telephone and call the doctor.

"Hang that doctor, hon," Shipley said. "He don't know the half of it." Shipley asked me just what it was we wanted to talk with him about. John Murdock, I said. Shipley nodded, lowering his eyes, but his wife broke in saying she wouldn't hear of it, wouldn't allow it, she was sorry but the doctor . . . The old man stopped her with a touch of his hand. "Now, Ma," he said, "I reckon that's the least we owe the man." She looked at him, then turned away, biting her lip, and disappeared into the house.

Shipley asked us to excuse his wife. He hoped we didn't mind doing our talking out-of-doors, but he did love this hour so, especially on a day like this after the rain, out back by his citrus grove.

Cooper asked if it was necessary to carry the gun while we talked. "No it ain't necessary a-tall," Shipley said. "That is if you got a better way of your own of stoppin' a rattler."

We walked down a grassy lane between rows of trees laden with fruit. The early evening air was cool and fragrant with the scent of oranges. Shipley told us his roots in the land here went back to the earliest times. His maternal great-grandmother had been half Seminole. The road out front was named for his grandfather, and Shipley himself had been born in a shack not far from this very spot. As a young man he'd traveled — Tallahassee, Jacksonville, Mobile, he'd seen them all, but no place else had ever quite suited him right.

Of course that was back before all the strangers started coming, men you didn't know and who didn't know you, bulldozing, banker men. One by one the other old-timers sold out. He supposed this wasn't really any concern of ours, maybe he was just a damned old fool who deserved what he got for going against the nature of the times, but for what it was worth he had always had this idea, that he would stay on and see it through, no matter what.

"Mind now, I ain't sayin' the thought never crossed my mind, but as for actually shootin' a man, that I hadn't ever done before. Now I ain't settin' to make excuses, but I am sayin' I don't see as how I could've done other'n I did. There was no time to think, you see; just plenty of time to worry myself sick about it ever since. He just came at me — hard to say which of us was the more frightened. Then when I seen 'im layin' there in his party clothes, smellin' of liquor, I knew what an awful thing I'd done."

"Did he die right away?" Cooper asked.

"No. It took him a piece."

"Well did he say anything? Anything at all?"

Shipley gave a little laugh. "You mean like where he'd buried his pot of gold? No, I'm afraid he was beyond talking at that point."

Both of us were suddenly without any more questions and it seemed to me we had imposed on him enough, but Cooper hesitated. "I was just wondering," he said, looking around at the grove, "are these the same kind of oranges you get in a store?"

"I'm glad you asked me that. You won't never see oranges like these in no store. Them little oranges 'air is an early orange. Now I may be biased, but I do believe you won't find a sweeter eatin' orange in all of Floradee." Shipley insisted we take a bushel or two with us. We wouldn't go wrong and we'd be doing him a favor besides; it didn't pay to try to sell them anymore — the big companies preferred the ones that were all painted the same color over a natural-looking orange.

Well the last thing we needed was a bushel of fresh fruit, but Art was taken with the idea of picking his own oranges from an actual tree. He turned out to be an eager student, too, fetching the ladder and positioning it just the way Shipley instructed, then climbing up ever so carefully, like a big cat stalking his prey. "That a way," Shipley called out as the boughs began to bend under Cooper's weight. "Now, just remember. If it breaks on yer, don't get hurt."

Tentatively, as if reaching for a wild bird, Cooper's hand hovered over the unsuspecting piece of fruit. With a sudden lunge he seized it, twisted it off the stem and tossed it down to me. Shipley quartered it with his knife right there on the spot and we sunk our teeth into the sun-warmed flesh, juicy and sweet beyond belief. Then Art went at it for real, raining oranges on us. Shipley said he had the makings of a first-rate farmhand. "I do believe, we ain't yet begun to see just what this man can do in a tree."

Later, with the sherbet-colored clouds of the sunset ranging from lemon to raspberry, we lugged the heavy baskets of fruit around out front to the car. Shipley said he was glad we'd come. The whole thing had been weighing on him more than we could know. There was something he hadn't told anybody except his wife, because it wouldn't have seemed right for him to be the one saying it, but he thought we might understand. While Murdock lay dying Shipley stayed with him alone, his wife having gone out front with a passerby who'd stopped to help, to await the police and the ambulance. He said that while Murdock lived he kept his eyes on Shipley the whole time until Shipley had the strange feeling that Murdock knew him, that he knew it was an accident, and that he forgave him.

"Strange, ain't it? Me killin' some drunk Yankee tourist by mistake over a piece of land that don't have no value any-more, except as something for somebody to build a super-market on someday." He gestured across the road to the miles of razed, asphalted land. "Makes me heartsick just to look on it. Well I seen it comin' and I said what the rest of 'em did was no concern of mine. Ain't nothin' more to do now but set here and watch it come."

Shipley said he had half a mind to just go ahead and sell out — that's what the ones who'd been vandalizing his farm wanted to push him into doing.

"Hell," Art said, "you shouldn't let that get to you; the sheriff told us that was probably just the work of people passing through."

"The sheriff is nobody's fool. He knows where his bread is buttered."

"What do you mean?" I said.

"The people who want my land is what I mean. Saw him

myself at the sheriff's the morning of the shootin'. Name wouldn't probably mean nothin' to you. Some big money man from Miami, name of Kauffman."

When I came out of the shower he was still lying there in his shorts, just the way I'd left him.

"All right," he said. "Maybe I was wrong about Shipley. Maybe it was an accident. But that doesn't mean there aren't a whole bunch of questions, about Murdock, about what Kauffman was doing here in Gladiola the morning of the shooting and why that sheriff didn't admit as much. And there's still the whole question of that lousy game itself and Kauffman's bet."

"Art," I said climbing into my bed, "we've been over it. Without a murder — without a more direct connection to Kauffman — we haven't got a case at all."

"But there's just got to be some link, Jack. So what if the pieces don't quite fit yet. A good detective doesn't expect too smooth a fit too fast. In fact he'd be outright suspicious if he got too smooth a fit. You follow?"

"Vaguely."

"For instance, now how do we know they're all telling the truth anyhow?"

"They're all in it together lying?"

"No, not *lying* lying, not necessarily, not on purpose. But just suppose," he said raising himself on one elbow, "suppose they themselves didn't know what was really going on. Suppose they were all deceived. I mean how do we know, you know?"

"Sure," I said, "and how do I know you're real and how do you know I am and how do we know any of this is really happening anyhow and not just something somebody dreamed up? And as long as you're taking on all the big ones, how many angels can fit on the head of a pin, and if a tree falls in a forest does it make a sound?"

"Of course it does."

"Even if there's nobody there to hear it?"

"The question, Rose, is not whether the goddamn tree makes a sound; the question is whether you'd be willing to take a chance standing under it." He lay back staring up at the ceiling. "Something'll break," he said.

"Like a date with Louise Boudreau," I said.

Cooper folded his hands behind his head and smiled at the ceiling. "I was kind of thinking I might just take her a basket of fruit. What the hell, you know? We can't eat half a ton of oranges by ourselves. Think she'd like that?"

"She's a man-eater. You set foot in that trailer again and she's going to eat you and your fruit."

"You're wrong about her, Jack. Guys like you think just because a broad takes off her clothes in public that makes her a tramp. Well it's different when it's for art."

"If my name were Art I'd probably feel the same way."

"Aaah, what's the use of talking about it anyhow." He said it wouldn't be right to take advantage of her when he was on an investigation, though it was just his typical luck to meet a broad like that at a time like this. But why she wasted time on a guy like Murdock he'd never understand. He just couldn't see it. A lousy zebra for chrissake with a fabulous broad like that.

I knew then he would lie there for a long time like that, and we would have to sleep with the light on, too. Cooper said if Kauffman and his boys came for us in the night the slightest change in shadow might be the warning we needed. He said all great investigators slept with a light on, evidently forgetting that he had once told me he always slept with a light on, because of his insomnia.

So I lay there pretending to sleep but actually looking at him, his bad leg extended straight out, the knee the size of a swollen, pulpy grapefruit. And I thought what a strange thing it was to actually live with another person; to go behind the image the self brought to the world and the standing the world gave it back. To see the way someone like Cooper dressed and undressed and went about his bodily business. To see the tufts of hair sprouting from the ears, the yellowed toenails, the momentary lack of purpose. Just a sack of bones and breath lying there on a bed. And the fact that he was such a big man making it even stranger, as if something inside you would still have it that a man, a very big man, at least, need never lie down.

I rolled over then, but I couldn't sleep. Louise Boudreau kept beckoning to me from the door of her trailer. I tried to put her out of my mind, but she kept creeping back in, each time with a warmer smile, and her shirt pulled up a little higher on her thighs. I tried to take her in her trailer but it was too hot and airless there, and I couldn't hold her in my mind. I tried to take her here in my bed, but that meant re-moving Cooper from the next bed, and somehow he wouldn't go. The hell with it. That was no way to fall asleep in peace, though times were surely hard when you couldn't even find a place for your fantasies.

And shy, quiet Murdock? Where had he taken her? He wasn't the kind, she'd said, for motels and the like. Then what kind was he? Where had he taken her if not to his place or hers? The man just made no sense. By day a drab, retiring guy who wanted to keep his identity secret and avoid public notice; by night, a secret swinger with a taste for a flamboyant hotbed of trouble like Louise Boudreau. The two images didn't mesh. I couldn't see the flesh and blood guy. And a flesh and blood guy had to have a place to take a woman like Louise.

And on those other nights when she hadn't known he was in town? Where had he gone then? What he was up to?

Art was right. When you put your mind to it, there were a lot of questions you could ask.

SIX

I sat in the oven of the Chevy watching the afternoon heat waves rise from the asphalt of the shopping center parking lot. When Cooper finally came out he was really peg-legging it.

"Jack," he said climbing in, "I found Taylor."

"You're kidding. Where?"

"In one of the places she mentioned. That lounge. I went back a second time. You were right, Prince, God you were right. She didn't tell us half of it. This guy Taylor knew Murdock, all right. Murdock practically lived at Taylor's place. The guy knows everything. He's going to tell us all about it tonight.

"It was the most amazing thing," Art said. "The minute I walked in he came right up to me."

"Maybe Louise called him."

"No, she says she's not even on speaking terms with him now. He recognized me by my size. He thinks I'm some kind of football player."

"So?"

"I mean he thinks I play now."

"Oh Christ, Art. Any moron can see you were conceived before the forward pass."

"Not this one, Jack. He's some kind of pervert — compared to this horny bastard, you're almost a saint." Cooper said Taylor seemed to think we were friends of Murdock's down for a good time. He was going to show us the town. All we had to do was string him along. Art could handle him all right if I just backed him up for once.

"Am I supposed to be a ballplayer, too?"

"Jack, be serious will you? The guy may be weird but he's still got eyes."

Randy Taylor did have eyes, although in the darkness of the lounge where we met him that night that fact was not immediately apparent. He wore mirror-finished wraparound shades, and all you saw in them were dozens of lights and fragments of yourself glittering on the surface as his head whipped around from side to side. He was a hyped-up, turned-on, spaced-out dynamo, fueled on booze, cigarettes and God knows what else, with spindly little Martian arms and a mop of hair that looked as though he'd styled it with ten thousand volts of raw juice. His face, the long-nosed, slack-lipped, ferretlike face of a born lecher, blazed like a spotlight.

"Artie *baby*," he cried squeezing Cooper's arm, "you got me so excited I can hardly stand it. I can't believe it. Me — out on the town with a real honest-to-god professional football player. Man," Taylor said snapping his head around to me, "I bet you have your hands full managing this stud on the road. I bet when this hunk of beef wants something he doesn't even have to ask — he just takes."

"Naaah," Art said with a modest wave of his hand. "That's just a lot of baloney."

"I love him," Taylor squealed, slapping Art's back. "Don't you just love him? What a sense of humor." Taylor took a gulp of his drink, a deep drag on his cigarette. Smoke streamed from his nostrils. He leaned lasciviously towards Cooper. "Come on you hot shit, you," Taylor said, draping an arm around Art's neck. "Are you for real or what? Everybody knows about you guys. Give me the inside story. What's it really like?"

"Jeez," Art said, "off the top of my head like this — it's a little hard." He cast me an imploring look.

"What the big guy means to say," I said, "is that when you get as much as he does it all tends to become one big blur." Of course, to tell the truth, I had to admit to Taylor that as an offensive lineman Art personally didn't score as much as some of the people who played the more glamorous positions; but then there were always the old standbys, the cheerleaders, the pompom girls, and the groupies giving out quickies in back of the stands, the wives of big boosters at parties, stewardesses, waitresses and barmaids on the road, not to mention all the dancers, models, actresses and other assorted nymphomaniacs one tended to meet these days at the various orgies.

"Goddamn," squealed Taylor hugging Cooper, "if you aren't every bit one-hundred-percent pure hot shit." He didn't know how much of that big-time stuff he could offer us on such short notice, but he did, if he didn't mind saying so himself, regard himself as something of a student of the art of conquest, and he looked on the opportunity to please Cooper as a special test of his powers. Now if Art could just help out a little with a hint as to the particular type of woman he had a special hankering for at the moment.

Art said that if that was what Taylor had in mind he could stop right there. As far as that went he had recently met a dream of a woman; unfortunately their union was not destined to be, and he had to content himself with loving her from afar in purity. For the time being therefore Cooper was temporarily off broads altogether; but that wasn't any reason why the three of us couldn't have a nice time by ourselves discussing our friend Murdock.

"Sure, all right," Taylor said, "whatever you want Artie." But first he had to make a couple of quick phone calls, then we could all go back to his place and talk. He jumped up and grabbed the check, but it seemed he was temporarily out of cash. Art whipped out his roll of bills, not bothering to mention that it was the last of our money. "You stud, you," Taylor cried with delight, a thousand lights dancing maniacally in his shades. "We're going to have one hell of a time together."

While Taylor made his calls Cooper and I waited out front. "Way to go, Jack," Art said. "Way to back me up. Way to come through in the clutch. Have you ever seen such a fruitcake in your life? I told you we could take him."

"Seems to me he might be taking us," I said.

"*Might*, Rose? What do you mean, *might*? You bet your sweet ass he is. He's hustling the pants off us."

"Well you're being an awful good sport about it."

"Because I can afford to be is why." Cooper said he'd been around hustlers all his life, the real thing, too, not some small-time queer with would-be pimp written all over him. Cooper didn't especially enjoy associating with phonies, or being pawed all over the place and called "Artie" by any weirdo, but when it came to the success of the investigation there were just some things we had to do, however personally distasteful. Let Taylor think we were out for a hot time; as soon as we got to his place we'd put it to him about Murdock.

Taylor's bachelor pad was on the eleventh floor of a beachside high-rise. He put some jazz on the stereo, brought us a couple of beers and told us to make ourselves at home while he took care of one last phone call. Cooper cast a suspicious eye over the leather furniture, animal skins and stacks of girlie magazines. He said we'd better get tough now, and be on guard for any fast moves.

A minute later Taylor danced back into the room wearing an oriental-looking robe. He boogied around the room, dimming all the lights, then sidestepped up to us with an electric grin and produced, with a snap of a magician's wrist, a huge, perfectly rounded cigar of a joint. He drew it under my nose for my approval.

"What are you doing to him?" Art said. "That's narcotics you're using on him, isn't it?"

"God I love him," Taylor laughed pinching Art's cheek. "What a comic gift." Taylor said he was really sorry he couldn't score anything heavier on such short notice, but he thought this stuff might do the trick. Cooper, however, wasn't interested in any tricks. He wanted to talk.

"Sure we'll talk," Taylor said. "But first we've got to un-clutter our minds."

Cooper said he preferred to keep his the way it was. Taylor refused. If Cooper was going to insist on talking about something as depressing as John Murdock then we'd all better do some dope or there wouldn't be much of a party left. Besides, who was Cooper trying to kid anyhow? Everybody knew that pro football players were some of the biggest heads going. Taylor asked Cooper's road manager if he didn't feel like smoking a little. Well the tips of the manager's toes were still tingling from that first sweet sniff and he didn't see what harm it could do.

Cooper wanted to talk to me right away out in the hall.

"All right," he exploded. "Just what in hell are you trying to prove?"

"For chrissake, Art, what are you making such a big deal about?"

"*Drugs*. Drugs is what I'm making such a big deal about. Are you actually going to just sit by and let that pervert ply us with drugs?"

"Not *drugs*, you idiot: dope. I can't believe you're getting so worked up over a lousy joint. Haven't you ever turned on before?"

"Oh is that what you think, Rose? That is just what you would think, isn't it?" Well just for the record, he told me, it so happened that before I'd even been born he'd already taken so many fixes he'd practically gotten himself addicted and he wasn't about to start up now again at his age on my account. Not to mention the security factor. What if it was a frame-up? What if Taylor zapped us while we were unconscious?

Well this wasn't narcotics dope, I told him, it was just marijuana dope, and the only dope undermining the situation was him. To refuse to smoke would only offend someone like Taylor. Since Cooper knew so much about it anyhow he obviously realized that a little pot couldn't possibly have any effect on him. All he had to do if he was worried about it was fake a drag or two to be sociable. He had said it himself: there were certain things we just had to do for the sake of the investigation.

We trooped back inside and Cooper sank into a tigerskin armchair, clinging to the arms like a condemned man. Taylor lit the joint and handed it to Art, who stared at it for what seemed an eternity, before he finally puckered his lips and, closing his eyes, took one shallow, painful little toke. Then he passed it on like a hot potato, declaring that this stuff never had any effect on him anyhow, and the two of us might as well go ahead and finish up what was left rather than wasting it on him.

Taylor and I passed the joint back and forth and the beautiful blue white smoke began to fill the alcove. It was incredible stuff. By the third hit warm streams of pleasure rippled through my arms and legs. With the next my kneecaps started sizzling like a couple of sunny-side up eggs in a skillet. I lay back on the rug and heard Cooper's voice over what sounded like a loudspeaker, saying he didn't see what all the big fuss was about and asking for another puff. Taylor and I giggled in unison.

Then, true to his word, Taylor told us all about Murdock. They had met when Murdock first came to town, about a year earlier, and Taylor had never seen a worse case of what an up-tight, straight, puritanical society could do to someone. But he sensed that Murdock was searching for something more out of life. Under Taylor's guidance Murdock came out of his shell like a starved man. Sex, dope, booze — Murdock couldn't get enough. He lived a secret life at Taylor's.

But then he got hung up on the two sides of himself. Murdock knew Taylor didn't give a damn about football or his career as a referee, but he became paranoid about people watching and following him. He was terrified that they would report him and he'd be kicked out of the League.

When Murdock flew down in December, before the football season was even over, Taylor knew he was in real trouble. The guy was a walking zombie. One weekend he almost didn't make it to his game, he just sat around Taylor's place missing plane after plane, saying his whole life was a fraud, that he couldn't face it, that he couldn't go back up north again. Taylor finally had to pick up the phone and make the call to say that Murdock would be arriving a little late.

After almost missing that game Murdock freaked out entirely. He was afraid that the League would investigate him and find out everything. But he couldn't make himself cut the cord and quit. Instead he got wild and reckless, staying stoned day and night, fucking everything in sight, throwing his money away as if there were no tomorrow. Taylor tried to make him cool it, but the guy was just hell-bent on self-destruction.

That's why Taylor figured Murdock's death was no accident, at least not like the sheriff made it seem. He figured Murdock took one look at that farmer's gun and saw his ticket out. He figured it was a kind of suicide.

Taylor had considered setting the record straight, but unfortunately he'd already had a few misunderstandings of his own with the sheriff. Taylor doubted that anybody else was involved. Hell, he was just about the only one in Gladiola who even knew who John was.

"You and Murdock's girl," I said.

If Taylor was surprised to learn that we knew about Louise, he didn't show it. "In her case I broke my own rules. Normally a guy like John wouldn't have had a prayer with a girl like Louise. But I happened to know that she has this thing for people on TV; setting John up with her was a snap." Taylor said they saw a lot of each other for a while. He didn't know why Murdock had gone out to her place the night he was shot. They had always met at Taylor's.

For Taylor, Murdock's death was a suicide, and the story behind it was a simple one: it was the story of a little man who lived by the rules at the expense of his deepest longings. The little man tried to tell himself he was happy, that his career was everything. He lived for an image he knew to be a lie, and in the end he died for it.

Lying there in the dark I was filled with a sudden deep sadness for Murdock, and Shipley, and Louise, and for Taylor, too; for everyone I had ever known, for every poor soul who, given free rein in this circus sideshow of a country to make and remake himself in his own image, had stumbled into self-parody. But most of all I felt it then for Cooper and myself. We had tried to escape the logjam of our lives by going off on a wild-goose chase after some farfetched conspiracy; and we had found only ordinary people, each of them struggling alone with the ultimate fix of his own life.

"Do we," Cooper said, breaking the silence, his voice slow and heavy as if coming through water, "have anything to eat?"

"Stuff getting to you, stud?" said Taylor.

Cooper laughed. "That stuff doesn't have any effect on me. I'm just hungry is all. And thirsty. Very thirsty."

"Some get hungry," Taylor said, "others get horny, others see things."

"What kind of things," asked Art.

"Whatever they most crave," Taylor replied. Art said the only thing he wanted to see right then was a well-stocked fridge, but his departure for the kitchen was temporarily impeded by his chair, which seemed reluctant to let him go. Thwacking hard at the tigerskin cushions, and muttering to himself about modern furniture, he finally made it to his feet, setting off for the kitchen with the slow-motion, high-stepping gait of a man walking on the ocean bottom.

He was back an instant later in a cold sweat, one hand clamped tight over his eyes, the other groping in front of him like a blind man for his chair.

"Something wrong?" Taylor asked.

"It's happening," Art cried in a high-pitched panicky voice. "I'm seeing things."

"What kind of things are you seeing?"

"Not *seeing*," Art said. "*Saw*. In the bedroom," he whispered, pointing urgently. "Broads."

"What did they look like?" Taylor asked.

"For chrissake, haven't you ever seen a broad before?" Cooper said they were hardly wearing any clothes at all. How the hell could you tell what they looked like when they weren't wearing any clothes? "Oh my God," he moaned, clamping both hands tight over his eyes. "This is it. I'm going. I'm addicted."

In a reassuring, hypnotic voice Taylor told him to stay calm, that there was nothing to worry about, that it hit lots of highly susceptible people this way. He guided Cooper over to the couch and made him stretch out. Taylor was sure a little food would alleviate Art's condition right away, and with a gleeful thumbs-up nod at me he hurried off, grinning to himself like a cat that swallowed a hundred-watt bulb.

Cooper said he supposed now that Taylor was gone I was going to try and tell him he hadn't really seen any hallucinations at all, that it was only his imagination. I said I wasn't going to tell him anything anymore. That was just fine with him. What did I know, anyway? Hadn't I realized I was dealing with a highly susceptible personality? After what

I'd done to him tonight he wasn't listening to anything I had to say ever again.

Frankly I was too stoned to care. I sat there staring at him stretched out on the couch, both hands still pressed over his eyes. It seemed to me I was seeing him very clearly, as if he were a specimen under glass, with the edges of him standing out sharp and detached from the place we were in. And what I saw was nothing but an outsized, fifty-year-old, cliche-spouting ex-jock, with his Boston working-class bravado about whatever he knew, and his absolute Irish Catholic certainty about whatever he didn't. And I didn't care. What did it matter now anyhow? I was more stoned than I'd been in a long time and none of it had anything to do with me anymore.

Taylor came back carrying a tray heaped with food, and Art went at it like a machine, gobbling and crunching his way through the assorted offerings. He became very talkative. Everything tasted fantastic. Never in his life had he tasted crackers so crisp and wheaty, cheese so creamy and nutty, or juice so rich you could feel it coating your throat and turning your stomach a nice happy orange. Where the hell did Taylor do his shopping anyhow? This food was making him feel better already. Stupid to drink so much beer on an empty stomach. This was really a helluva pad Taylor had here. Cooper was thinking of moving down to a place just like this himself when he retired. He could always manage an orange farm, or just hang out on the beach in his Chevy and catch fish and take life as it came.

He was chatting merrily on about his future and munching his way like a typewriter through a cold ear of corn when suddenly he froze. Louise Boudreau, wearing a flimsy black nightie and a red ribbon in her hair, was standing at the foot of the couch, beaming down at him with a look of benign adoration. The corncob slipped from Cooper's fingers.

"Something wrong with the food?" Taylor said.

Art smiled weakly. "Nah. I think I just ate too fast." He

eased himself back down onto the pillows. "You guys," he stammered, clamping a pillow over his eyes, "when you look around . . . You don't by any chance . . ."

"What?" said Taylor.

"Aaah, forget it."

Well I was pretty stoned myself but I could still tell the difference between a hallucination and a real woman when I saw one, even if she had just emerged from nowhere half-naked, unbelievably built, and obviously more than a little spaced-out herself. But it wasn't Louise who held my eye. Lounging in the doorway on the far side of the room was a young blonde wearing tight jean shorts and a tiny pink halter. She was beautifully packed into her body and she knew it. She shot me a sizzling smile that dropped me through the pit of my stomach like a parachutist.

Taylor was soothing Cooper again in his hypnotic, theatrical voice. Louise, in a trance, stared at Taylor as if waiting for a cue. Taylor said that the woman Art was seeing was probably his dream woman, the one he had told Taylor about, and that he had conjured her up because she was of his deepest longing. "You are now on the frontier of consciousness where few men have the power or courage to go. You are poised on the brink of unlocking the secret of one of mankind's greatest dreams: the transmutation of fantasy into reality. All you need do now to make her real is to extend yourself."

"I don't want to extend myself," Art murmured through his pillow. "I'm having enough trouble already the size I am. And I don't want to have to be on any fucking brink either. I just want to be back in my motel room with a bag of burgers and the late news and if I have all this power why can't I transmit myself over there this very instant?"

"Because," Taylor said, "you are now beyond such crass cravings. You have summoned forth this vision of female beauty from your deepest inner longings, and the one thing you must not do at any cost, the one thing that could prove disastrous at this point, is to turn your back on your truest secret desire."

Cooper lay completely rigid as if stricken with the truth of what Taylor was saying. Stiff as a mummy he listened to Taylor's hypnotic promptings to relax, to go with the flow, to speak to her, to command her to be real.

In the silence that followed there was no sound except for Cooper's heavy breathing. He cleared his throat and swallowed so hard I heard the gulp. "Hello," he whimpered. "Miss Boudreau?"

Taylor nodded to Louise. Her one word hung on the air like a puff of perfume. "Darlin'."

"Oh Jesus!"

"Speak to her," Taylor prompted. "Tell her what you want."

Cooper gulped more air. "Miss Boudreau? You still there?"

"Darlin'. Call me Looloo."

"Whatever. Look, there's something I got to tell you. I think back in your trailer there yesterday you got the wrong idea about me."

"You didn't tell the truth about yourself, did you?"

"You know that?"

"Oh yes, sugah. And I understand. You were too good and strong to take advantage of me. And all along not even lettin' on you was a big professional football star."

"Well now that's something else we should clear up right away, too, as long as we're at it. I mean — the truth is — I'm not really that big of a star or anything."

"To me you are. To me you're the kindest, gentlest, purest man I've ever met. And I'll be so good to you, baby. I'll do whatever you say and I won't never give you cause to be one bit sorry."

"OK, hold on a second, Looloo, will you? Rose? Taylor?"

he called with a little hysterical laugh. "You guys still there? You won't believe this. I think this broad is really stuck on me."

"Sure she is," Taylor squealed. "She's crazy for you, you hot shit you. Take her. Make her yours."

But Art said he couldn't do that. In the first place it wouldn't be right to take advantage of a delusion like that; in the second, this delusion obviously didn't know the first thing about him. He had only pretended to like her to get the truth about Murdock. He'd temporarily deceived himself into thinking he loved her, but now that he had the opportunity for a second look what he really wanted was for her just to go away and leave him alone.

For the first time that day, Taylor was at a loss for words. The slack, however, was immediately taken up by Louise, who fell to her knees at Cooper's feet, weeping.

"Oh Jesus no," Art said. "Now I've made her go and start crying on me again. If there's one thing I can't stand it's a crying broad."

"I can't help it," wailed Louise. "You don't want me because I haven't told you the truth, the real reason John visited me that night and ran off the way he did. I swear to you if you only send everyone away and hold me in your arms again I'll tell you everything."

After a long moment's hesitation Cooper announced through his pillow that the last thing a man in his condition needed was to be left alone with a half-naked delusion, but that sometimes a man just had to do certain things for the sake of a higher goal.

"Sure we do stud," squealed Taylor, giving him a parting hug. "Go to it you hot shit you." If I had any second thoughts then about leaving Cooper in that condition they were instantly dispelled by one impatient, tight little tug of the blonde's hand.

In the kitchen Taylor was beside himself with the thrill of

it all. To set someone up was one thing, but to shape their reality, to direct the content of their experience, that was something else. "When that lucky stiff wakes up to find himself in that floozy's arms — oh Jesus, it'll blow his fucking mind." The thought of it excited him so much he needed to be by himself for a while.

I was pretty excited myself. My blonde had her arms tight around my waist and her hand was stirring waves of molten lava. Her name was Marcia. She lived just across the hall from Randy. I didn't know it but she had seen me in the lounge earlier that evening. Randy was okay, but he got too carried away with his little head games. She said the two things she liked best in all the world were to smoke and to fuck. She asked me if I wouldn't like to come across the hall to her place. My teeth were chattering so hard I couldn't talk.

Once at her place there was no holding her back. She was crazy for it, that girl. I tried to slow her down, but there was no slowing her down, and after a while I saw that it didn't matter who I was or what I wanted anyhow. But as fast as she took us it wasn't fast enough because almost immediately there were shouts and screams in the hall and I was startled to hear someone — Cooper — yelling my name. He sounded scared half out of his mind. I guess it hit me then. Nothing seemed more important than making sure he was all right. Instantly I was switching on lights and throwing on clothes. I told the blonde I'd be back as soon as I could; she said if I dared walk out on her like that I could go fuck myself. I told her she could do the same.

But when I stumbled out into the hallway, Cooper was nowhere in sight. Taylor was lying in the middle of his living room, blood streaming from his nose; Louise, her nightgown ripped open, was standing over him screaming hysterically that Taylor was sick, that he was a parasite who got his kicks fucking with other people's lives because he had no life of his own. Taylor just lay there smiling happily up at us through the blood. He didn't see what everybody was getting so worked up about. "I only wanted to take us all on a little trip. I only wanted for everybody to have a good time."

It took me close to an hour to find him. He was down on the beach, as far down as you could go, at the pass where the fresh water ran shimmering in the moonlight into the Gulf. He was sitting on the wet sand at the edge of the surf. Under the huge vault of starry sky he looked very small.

I sat down beside him and started fumbling for words.

"Shhhh," he said putting a finger to his lips. "Listen," he said. "The seeeeee." He said if you listened carefully it sounded as if it were breathing. He thought the waves sweeping up the beach were like fingers reaching to touch us. He asked me if I thought it knew we were here. I said I didn't know.

"What do you know then?" he said softly, too softly.

"Art, I'm sorry."

"Nah, what have you got to be sorry about? You get an opportunity like that to screw your best friend — how can you pass it up? You can't make an ass out of someone who doesn't have the raw talent for it to begin with. Me the big stud, me the superstar. I take the one thing in my life I can honestly be proud of and I muck it up."

"So you stretched things a little about the football. So you bluffed about the dope and it went to your head."

"I'm no bluffer, Jack," he said looking away up the beach. "I couldn't even do it with her."

"So what? Those weren't exactly ideal conditions."

He shook his head. "I mean ever," he said flatly.

I still didn't understand.

Cooper said there wasn't much to understand. His dad had been laid up sick the last years of his life; his mom had worked two jobs. There was the house and his father to take care of, and after school Art had worked, too. He was a big, awkward, shy sort of a kid and there had just never been much time for girls or anything else. Except football. He could block and he could play ball and it was the only thing that made the rest of it make sense and he made it his life. It was a pure thing, the realest thing ever, and when he lost it by getting hurt, when suddenly he had all that time on his hands, he no longer felt right about himself, he no longer felt whole. All his big talk about broads. It had been nothing more than that. Just a big act, like everything else about him, to try to impress me. He wasn't any hero. He wasn't even a real man. The only thing I had to be sorry about was getting hooked up with a chump like him in the first place.

The surf washed up the beach and slid back down. He had just told me something important, something very serious, but I couldn't think of anything to say to him. All I could feel was how sorry I was. And sitting there on the beach I realized that I had betrayed him, and that it went a lot deeper than a practical joke. I had deceived him by deceiving my-self — by acting as if nothing mattered to me. But I knew now that something did matter. And I tried to tell him so.

"Jesus Christ, Rose," he said wiping at the corners of his eyes. "What the hell's wrong with you anyhow. You couldn't tell a lost cause if they locked you in a padded cell with him. You want to know what I'm like — I'm like an onion. Strip off one layer and there's more of the same, only the stink keeps getting a little worse. To tell you the truth I don't really know what the hell I am anymore. I'm bits and pieces of lines and junk I get out of bad books and movies. It's like I'm just some kind of human phantom."

"And the guy who threw that block against New York in nineteen fifty. Was he a phantom, too?"

"That block blew two Giants off the line, Jack. Phantoms don't block like that. But I'm no hero, Prince."

"I forgot. You're an onion."

"That's right. A lousy scrambled onion of a hero."

"With maybe just a little ham thrown in," I said.

He laughed. "Why not? And some cheese, and some baloney, and some green peppers and mustard and Jesus, Jack, I'm starved though. I'd eat a horse if you could coax him between two slices of bread."

We began the long trek back up the beach. Art told me that at least for all his trouble he finally got the truth out of Louise, for what it was worth now. I was right about her from the start — she lied to us about everything. It wasn't Louise who ended their affair, but Murdock. He had promised to marry her as soon as the season was over, but then he showed up in Gladiola without telling her. When she called him up he said he was through with her. She threatened to report him to the League if he didn't at least come out to her place and talk it over. He showed up at her trailer drunk, laughing in her face when she brought up all his promises. He said she had to be crazy to think a man in his position would ever marry someone like her. He had an image to uphold. Then he passed out on her sofa. She looked at him until she couldn't stand the sight of him any longer. Then she noticed someone parked across the street in front of her girlfriend's. Waking Murdock out of his stupor she told him to run for it, that she'd reported him to the League and that they'd sent someone out to get him.

She never meant for it to end the way it did.

Art and I didn't talk about it anymore then, or about what would happen in the morning.

We thought we had come to the end. We thought it was all a waste.

And if we saw the black car waiting in the shadows, we never gave it a second thought.

SEVEN

Through a deep stoned sleep I heard Cooper. "Jack," he kept insisting. "There are men here."

"Tell them to come back later," I mumbled.

The sting of his slap popped my eyes open. The room blurred, then swam into focus. There were men, all right, four of them. In their black suits they looked like a committee of undertakers — except for the guns. And the warning that the next word out of either of us would be our fuckin' last.

They made us get dressed and rushed us out to their car, shoving Cooper into the front seat, me in the back. Two of them jumped in front with Art, two in the back with me, and we pulled out into a thick morning ground fog and headed inland. After a couple of minutes the fog broke and I could see what was left of the mist floating in patches on the fields, clinging to the low line of the pines. Then we were back on the straight flat road to Miami.

Halfway to Miami they stopped for gas. Two of them went inside to use the phone; the others got out to stretch.

"Rose," Cooper whispered, keeping his head straight ahead, "you all right?" I grunted. "Listen, Prince, go ahead and let me hear you talk your way out of my latest delusion. Tell me I made these hoods up."

"There's got to be some mistake."

"Make no mistake — they don't send carloads of hard guys hundreds of miles for nothing. From here on in we'd better start playing our hand a hell of a lot smarter."

"*Hand?* For chrissake, Art, what hand?"

"For the love of Jesus, Jack, this is no time to be looking on the negative side. If you had only let me send that letter to the D.A. like I wanted, things might not be so bad. But for now we've got to make the most of what we have."

"Art for God's sake we don't have a goddamn thing. We'll just tell them that."

"Sure, and write ourselves a one-way ticket to Fuckedville, U.S.A. Our only strength is they don't know how much we know. Until we find out what this is all about we don't give them a thing."

Nothing like this had ever happened to me before. My insides were churning away. As far as I knew nothing like this had ever happened to Art either, but that didn't seem to be bothering him. He sat there straight and calm as a martyr on the way to meet his maker. Despite our predicament, he seemed almost relieved that reality had finally confirmed his suspicions. But there wasn't time to talk about it because they were already piling back into the car. Spraying gravel, we hit the road.

We cruised through Miami and up Miami Beach, past the El Paradiso and along the edge of the green Atlantic. Then we turned off at a luxury apartment building, shooting down into an underground garage. They pulled us out of the car and into a service elevator. On the way up they frisked us roughly from head to toe. They hurried us down a back corridor to an unmarked door and shoved us inside. "Remember, Rose," Cooper murmured. "We admit nothing. We volunteer nothing. Above all we don't let them intimidate us."

At the far end of the vast living room, perched on a velvet sofa like two tiny China dolls, their feet barely touching the floor, an elderly Jewish couple waited for us. He was elegant and silver-haired; she wore ropes of diamonds and smelled at ten paces like Bloomingdale's entire perfume department. The gentleman was Morris Kauffman; the lady, his wife, Ida.

"Don't anybody make a fuss," she said. "Just go ahead with the business as usual. I'm not even here." She smiled sweetly at me. "Young man, if you don't mind my asking, what kind of Rose are you?"

"You don't have to put up with that kind of talk, Jack," Cooper said.

"Well," she said, "it could be an Italian Rose. Or an Irish one."

"My father was Jewish," I said.

"Morris!" she squealed. "What did I tell you?"

"I heard," Kauffman said, but he didn't seem as pleased about it as she was.

"Boys," she said, "you must be tired from your long ride." She tilted her head coquettishly. "A little cake maybe. A little coffee?"

"We're not touching anything," Art said.

"I've got some eclairs — fresh from Noodleman's."

"Ida, don't force-feed," Kauffman said.

"So who's forcing, Morris? I was just offering. They look like such sweet boys."

"Appearances can be deceiving," Art said.

"Not to a mother, big boy. A mother knows from bad boys."

"All right Ida, please," Kauffman said. "He wants to be tough — so what's the harm? So what's tough anyhow? You take the tough ones, Mr. Cooper, I'm talking now legendary names like Meyer and Bugsy and the rest of that crazy, meshugge bunch — the so-called Jewish Mafia. I dealt with all of them in the old days. You want to know a little secret, gentlemen? The ones that basked in the limelight never worried me. It was the ones who didn't, that did."

"Everybody knows what a big shot you are, Morris."

"Ida, I told you to stay out of this."

"Yes, you told me. I have a memory, don't I? And I remember who got us into this mess in the first place, I remember that, too."

"Gentlemen," Kauffman said, "please excuse my wife, she's a little crazy with worry right now."

"Crazy you call it, Morris? You're dragging these poor boys all over the place and I'm the one that's crazy?"

"Ida, will you please stop butting in."

"Let me tell you something, Mr. Jack Webb. When you're broadcasting an all-points bulletin on my faults I don't have to be butting in to hear. Just remember, if you please, just who happens to be the mother of your children," she sniffled. "The mother of your own . . ." Suddenly she burst into tears.

"Oy vay! That's it," said Kauffman, reaching for his walking stick.

"Morris?" she cried. "Where are you taking them now, Morris?"

"Out. Out where I can talk business in peace."

"Out to that swamp you mean. All right," she shrieked. "You won't let me try it a mother's way. Go on then, do it your way. Twist arms, break bones, crucify them for all I care."

"That's enough, Ida," said Kauffman. He got to his feet and motioned to us with his stick. "This way boys."

We followed him into the hall where his men were waiting. "Hang in there, Jack," Art whispered. "Try not to let them get to you."

"I don't know, they don't seem all that bad to me."

"Are you crazy? Don't you hear the way they talk? They'd just as soon cut us to ribbons as give us the time of day."

We all piled into the elevator and rode down to the garage. Kauffman's chauffeur rolled out a limousine and Kauffman signaled for us to get in the back with him. The other men got in their car and followed.

"Gentlemen," said Kauffman, leaning back against the soft suede upholstery as we sped up Collins Avenue, "why don't we come directly to the point. You have an interest in a certain affair of mine, a little wager."

"If that's what you call a two-hundred-thousand-dollar bet," Art said.

Kauffman said he wasn't going to quibble. He understood that we had been trying to find out the full story of his bet. He would level with us first and expect no less in return when the time came. He would tell us the story. We might even enjoy it. It was an amusing story about a foolish old man.

"To begin from the beginning, I don't know how much you know about me. Undoubtedly you know that I have a certain reputation: well, much as I hate to undercut my own glamor, basically I'm just an ordinary businessman. With certain contacts, it's true, but basically a legitimate businessman. If I've done less than everything in my power to dispel certain rumors, well in America a little free advertising never hurt anyone. In America any image is better than none. And I've done what I had to do to survive and prosper.

"Now as a young man in the old days it's true that I was a great gambler. My luck was famous from Brooklyn to the Bronx. Of all the sports I took an interest in, my specialty was football, a game about which I took pride in knowing as little as possible. It used to drive the wise guys nuts. But the way I always figured it, if a bunch of goyim were going to run into each other at terrific speeds and all fall down, how much logic could be involved?

"I was something of a playboy at the time, too; that is, until I met Ida. Then I sobered up. I began to realize that having arrived penniless in America at age thirteen, trying to build a secure future for myself and my family was enough of a gamble for one lifetime.

"From that time on I stopped gambling, but my good luck in business and life continued. I'm not bragging idly now. In this country I've been thrice blessed, with health, wealth and a wonderful family. You shouldn't judge my wife by what you've seen today. Three gorgeous daughters she's given me. Eleven beautiful grandchildren. Seven wonderful great-grandchildren already, and at least two more that I know of in the works. Yes, in every aspect of my life in America I've been blessed and doubly blessed. Except one. The baby. My son. My only son. Martin.

"He's not a bad boy really. Something of a shlimazel, if you know what I mean, but basically a good boy. A good boy with certain gaps in his dictionary. The word 'work' — that's one gap. The word 'plans' — there the whole page is missing. His only plan as far as I can tell is to wait around until his father drops dead. Not such a bad plan actually for a boy with a loaded father.

"Poor Martin. Everything he tries fails. He doesn't understand that luck is only your reward for hard work — provided of course God gives you a few talents to begin with. But the only talent that boy has is devising new ways to throw away his father's money — always running around with bad crowds, always getting into one kind of trouble or another. Maybe I've spoiled him. But when you start life at the bottom, the way I did, maybe you can be forgiven for lavishing a few luxuries on your only son."

Kauffman sighed. He reached into his jacket and pulled out a snapshot of his son. He was a small, thin guy with mournful eyes and a sad smile.

We were turning onto the expressway now, heading inland.

"Where are you taking us?" Cooper said.

"Don't interrupt. Just listen.

"The week of the bet he calls me. Not a word from him in four months — not even so much as to pick up the phone and say hello — but now he's got to see me in a big hurry.

So he comes up to the apartment all excited with a 'Pop, how are you; Pop, how're you feeling; How've you been, Pop; Pop, I've missed you' — Pop this, Pop that. Each Pop, I'm estimating conservatively, is costing me a thousand dollars a crack. Then he really floors me. 'Pop,' he says, 'I want to change my life. I want to model myself after you, Pop. I want to be exactly like you.'

"I'm stunned. I can't believe my ears. With all the nonsense I've heard from him over the years, I think maybe now he's Popped my eardrums once and for good. He doesn't even sound like himself. 'Moe,' I say to myself, 'careful. The boy's talking four, maybe five figures now at least.'

"Suddenly he wants to be exactly like me. Can you imagine it? A thirty-five-year-old man already and he wants to be like me when he grows up. I was more of a mensh at three than he'll ever be. But all that put aside, here is this boy, this person for which they gave me a piece of paper I bother to keep locked up in the safe alleging that he is — God knows for what reason — my own flesh and blood, my boy. He says he needs my help for a big business deal.

" 'Wonderful. Very good, Martin. What kind of business?'

" 'Pop, don't pry.'

"Now this at least sounds like my son. 'All right, Martin,' I said. 'How much?'

" 'I don't want your money, Pop,' he says. And that's when I really begin to worry. Because do you know what it was, this big business deal that was such a top secret? A bet on a football game. He and his partners have been betting and winning all year, he tells me, and now they're ready to move into the big time. They want to bet two hundred thousand dollars, but they're afraid of attracting too much attention. They want to use my name to get it down for them. My son tells me there's absolutely nothing to worry about. One of his pals is an insider — they have some kind of a hot tip that the game is in the bag. I shouldn't ask him any more, he can't say anything more about it; but at this point I'm not even listening anyhow. Much better he should have just called up and said, 'Hello Mr. Kauffman, remember me, this is your son, Martin, listen, can I have a few grand quick to flush down the toilet?' Just between the three of us, if he had tried that I would have been impressed. But no, he comes to me Popping my head off in the same breath with being a big-time gambler like me and taking a tip. In all my gambling life I never took a tip. You need a tip, you need a tout, you want to fix things nice and tight — go into business. Gambling on games is for when you want to have a little clean honest fun."

We were coming down off the highway, the countryside around us scrubby and desolate. Kauffman leaned forward, lowering his voice almost to a whisper, as if he were about to let us in on a terrible secret.

"For myself, I was willing to drop the whole matter. But my son wouldn't let me drop it. He attacked me, saying I was against him, had always been against him, had done everything I could to hold him back all his life."

Kauffman stopped, his tiny hands like bird claws clutching his cane. He said he was not a violent man but if this stick had been in his hand at that instant he believed he would have struck his son dead on the spot — his own boy for whom he had so much hope. Then all of a sudden a terrible pain had shot through his arm and he'd collapsed.

"Let me tell you," Kauffman said, "for all I know I'm dying there and then on the floor, but I'm not yet so far gone I don't have the presence of mind to search his face for a sign that this is what he's after, that with these words he's come to kill me. Had I seen such a sign in that moment, so great was my pain and my heartache, I believe I would have died, too. But no. Instead I see only a frightened little boy. 'Poppa are you all right, speak to me,' he's crying. He says he didn't mean it, he says it wasn't me who failed him, but him who's failed and disappointed me all his life. 'Please, Poppa,' he says, 'say something.' And I saw him standing there over me and I thought to myself, 'He's my boy and he can't help being what he is any more than I can help being what I am.'

"All at once the pain subsided and I realized that maybe I had failed him by holding back on him, not money or favors, but by shielding him too much from life, by never demanding that he become a man. In short, not by being too much of a father, but by being too little of one. At that moment I had an inspired idea.

"I took my son up to the roof. At the far edge of the sun deck there was a pay phone.

" 'Martin,' I said, 'come stand close by me.'

" 'No. Why?'

" 'Genius — why else? So you can hear what I'm going to say.'

" 'It's a trick. You're going to do something to me.'

" 'You bet I am, buster.' Picking up the phone and dialing, I said I was going to show him once and for all what his father was. And I was going to show him what gambling was, too, and what I thought of his hot tip and his friends. I asked him what team he wanted with his hot tip — because whichever one it was, I was taking the other side.

"You should have seen the look on that face. Such a look. The big wheel who wants to be like me. His tongue won't move, his voice won't work. Well which team is it? He can't even think straight. First one, then the other, then the first. 'C'mon, c'mon,' I say. 'This is a busy man on the line. I can't keep him waiting forever.'

" 'Boston,' he says finally.

"Good. I get to take my old hometown team. 'Herb,' I say into the phone, 'I want to make a bet. A big one. Two hundred thousand dollars' worth on New York.' Martin's mouth falls open. Such a look of respect as few fathers will ever see on the face of a son."

But Kauffman's joy was short-lived. When he finished placing the bet and hanging up, his son turned and fled. "My poor baby boy," Kauffman said, shaking his head mournfully. "I tried to show him what I am, to bring him close, but I only drove him away."

The old man ran his fingers slowly through his silver hair. Sitting there in the broad back seat of the speeding limo he looked very sad and vulnerable to me. But Cooper wasn't about to be taken in by him. Just who the hell did Kauffman think he was, scaring the living shit out of us with his goons, dragging us two hundred miles to the middle of nowhere to listen to a crock-of-bull story. Art was furious. I had never seen him so mad. He was literally twice the old man's size and for an instant I was half afraid he would hurl Kauffman out of the car. But the old man just sat there perfectly calm, nodding thoughtfully at everything Cooper had to say, as if he couldn't agree more. Art told him he could nod to himself all he wanted; he, Cooper, wasn't buying one word of it.

"So who's twisting your arm, big boy? You came for a story, right?"

"I came for the truth."

Kauffman smiled. We pulled off the road into a stand of tall trees beside a canal. The other car pulled up behind us a few seconds later. Kauffman tapped on the glass and we bounced down a dirt road for about a mile and came to a dead-end stop at a gate. An armed guard waved us on through into the middle of an enormous construction site where the steel and concrete skeletons of three tall towers rose straight up out of the raw red earth.

We got out of the car. Kauffman spoke to his men, then signaled for the two of us to follow him. He led the way into one of the buildings, picking his way carefully over and around boards and bricks, apologizing for the confusion and clutter. "Every four years, like a pestilence or a drought, you can count on a scandal in the construction industry. It's all politics. Politics when they want you to build; politics when they try to close you down. At least it's not such a bad place to talk alone man to man." He sat down on a stack of lumber.

"If you're planning on telling us any more tall stories," Cooper said, "you can just forget it. A two-hundred-thousand-dollar bet at the last minute, and you expect us to believe you placed it just to teach your kid a lesson. Just who the hell do you think you're dealing with anyhow?"

"My friend," said Kauffman, "that is exactly what I would like you to tell me. And more to the point — how and why do you know so much about my little gamble? You said before that I didn't tell you the truth: you are right. As it so happens I neglected to include one little fact. You see, the truth is that I never actually placed that bet. It was just something I made up into the phone to impress my son."

"But that's impossible," Art stammered, looking from Kauffman to me. "That bet was . . ."

Kauffman sat twirling his cane in his hands, a sphinxlike smile at the corners of his mouth.

"Mr. Kauffman," I said then, "you didn't bring us all the way out here just to tell us stories."

"Ah, so our young Rose has a voice of his own after all. You're absolutely right. I've brought you here because I'm as baffled as you two claim to be. That bet was made, yes; but not by me. Why that bet was made in my name, and by whom, I would like to know. Why the two of you are so interested in a bet that was never made by me, I would also like to know. Most importantly, I'm afraid for my boy. Since that night nearly two months ago I haven't heard a word from him or been able to uncover any trace of him. I have reason to believe my son has fallen in with very dangerous people."

Art smiled a sickly half-smile. "Oh I get it now. This is all some clever frame-up, isn't it? Either we deal with you or you dump us into the swamp and put it out that we were involved in some underworld kidnapping scheme."

"Mr. Cooper," Kauffman sighed, rubbing his temples, "will

you just calm down, please. Ten minutes in the house with my wife and you're jumping at conclusions worse than her. Sure, I considered the possibility that you were the kidnappers. You had been making inquiries about me all over the state, you'd had my place watched, and so forth. But the minute I laid eyes on you I knew my wife was right: you're good boys. For whatever inconvenience I have caused you I am sorry. You have to try to understand my position. I am a desperate man. I will reward you handsomely, guarantee you whatever protection you require, do whatever you ask of me, but if you have any information that might help me find my boy, you must tell me."

"I'm sorry," I said, "but we don't know a thing about your son."

"Then you must tell me what you do know," Kauffman pleaded.

"Jesus, Jack," Art said, "I don't know . . ."

"It's all right, Art," I said.

So we told him everything, right from the beginning: about how Cooper and I had met, about how we'd learned of Kauffman's bet and his connection to Murdock, about Murdock's death and the fact that Kauffman himself had been in Gladiola on the morning of the shooting.

"Of course I was there," Kauffman said. He'd had his boy working in Gladiola off and on the last couple of years and he'd gone to ask the sheriff for his help. Kauffman said he had never heard of Murdock. Thousands of people had worked for his companies at one time or another. He made us tell him what we'd been able to find out: how we'd discovered Murdock had been on the verge of a nervous breakdown that had caused both his poor performance in that game and, apparently, his death; and how the trail had turned cold and we'd come to the end of our money; and how we'd thought that Kauffman's summons meant something had finally broken.

After a while Kauffman looked up at the skeleton of the
tower above us. "Do you know what my dream was? One
day I was going to build a building just for myself. In it I was
going to put my children and all their children and all their
children's children. Around it I was going to make beautiful
lakes and ponds, fountains and gardens, and trees — everywhere lots of trees. Then everything I looked out on in the
end would be familiar and of my own making. Can you
imagine such a dream?

"But enough of an old man's regrets. I want to make you
an offer. I don't know what was going on in that game, but
I'm convinced now that that game was tampered with and
that my son is somehow involved. Find out the truth about
that game and you might find my boy." Kauffman wasn't
asking us to go one step out of our way for his sake; he
would continue with his own private search. All he was
asking us for was the opportunity to support our investigation. He wouldn't interfere in any way except to suggest that
perhaps Cooper had been barking up the wrong tree in fixing
on the refs. On the basis of the little his son had hinted at,
Kauffman's guess was that it was players they had gotten to.

"Christ," Cooper said. "I was so set on Murdock I never
considered that. But if one or more of them were taking a
dive they could easily have forced the refs to make half those
calls." Art stopped suddenly. "One thing I don't get. Why
did your son tell you he was taking Boston when the bet in
your name was on New York?"

Kauffman said that was what hurt him most of all right
now. "Obviously Martin was only a cover for the placing of
a large bet once the fix was in. He must have promised them
he could get his father's cooperation if necessary. Why not?
— I've never denied him anything in his life. But then I was
seized by my crazy idea, and Martin, my poor son, in his one
confused act of manhood had refused to make his father a
loser.

"I beg of you. You must do what you can to help me find my boy."

Two days later, the Chevy returned, our stomachs stuffed with Ida's cooking and our wallets bulging with Kauffman's cash, we left Miami. I watched the plane's winged shadow sweep over the red tile roofs and turquoise swimming pools, the yellow strip of beach, the green shallow water and then the ink-blue hide of the ocean. Cooper, grinning at me from a Dramamine fog, fell almost immediately to sleep.

I thought about what we might be up against now. Burke's face came back to me as I had seen it the day of the game, staring out through the screen with the intensity of his private knowledge. Were his own players the "they" he had really meant, the "they" who robbed him of that last game? Had he known?

Art had said no. Bill couldn't have known for sure, because he would never have stood for it. Bill was different from other men. Bill, Art said, was an actor.

That's what Art had said, Art who now slept peacefully by my side, Art who believed that someone had to make the fast guys pay for what they had done and that we were the ones to do it.

High over Norfolk there was a glimpse of the line of the Chesapeake Bay, then the ground vanished in the haze. The clouds thickened, and the day grew darker and the yellow cabin lights glowed against the winter dusk outside.

I felt then the loss you feel at the end of the summer, and the sudden cold doubt you get in the pit of your stomach as you near a new destination.

Because Art was right. He had been right all along. There was something real out there.

PART THREE

EIGHT

We spent a couple of days in New York, then took the train up to Boston. Cooper found us a room in his old neighborhood in Somerville — the landlady had been a friend of his mother's — and we bought a used car, this time a reliable one, and set to work. For the most part I holed up in the library piecing together the public record of the season while Art chased down old friends and contacts and showed around a snapshot of Kauffman's son. The town, Art reported, was still jumping with rumors — you could find someone willing to say almost anything about that game. Art was particularly interested in a big local sports bookmaker, Victor Calabrese, who was supposed to have made out like a bandit on Boston's collapse, and who was known for cultivating the company of pro ballplayers. We hoped to get hold of someone who could fill us in on Calabrese, but Cooper had been away a long time and it was tough getting back in touch.

Meanwhile he didn't see much point in rehashing that game for the thousandth time and trying to guess what form the fix had taken. What we really needed now, he argued, was someone inside the team who could steer us in the right direction.

But there too we weren't making any progress. All of Cooper's initial feelers had fizzled out, and his surprise visit to the one team guy he knew from the old days, an equipment man, had been outright discouraging.

Art had driven alone to the team's offices in the stadium down in suburban Saxton. By then we'd figured out that the inside story of Boston's season boiled down to a power struggle between Burke and the new general manager, Greenley. Cooper couldn't believe the way Greenley was running the place. Just getting inside was like cracking the Pentagon, complete with security guards and stuck-up secretaries.

And Greenley. The guy had to be the biggest prick in captivity. He came across Cooper in the hallway and demanded to know what he was doing there. All right, admittedly Art might have been loitering a little, trying to scare up somebody to shoot the breeze with, but what the hell kind of a way was that to run a football organization anyhow? How the hell did they know Cooper didn't have a tip to peddle on some hot prospect? And besides — was that any way to treat an ex-player?

And Cooper's friend — Art couldn't believe it. OK, so maybe he and Frank had never been bosom buddies to begin with, but either the old days mean something or they don't. Cooper walks in through the door after half a lifetime and the guy acts like he's tracking in the plague. Hardly seems to remember him. Says he can't talk about the past season. Not that he doesn't know anything, or that he doesn't feel like it, or even that he's too busy. He just can't talk about it. Period.

Cooper didn't know what to make of it. Football people were a pretty sociable bunch, but this guy Greenley had everybody quaking in their shoes. Until we found somebody on the inside willing to talk, we'd just be revolving in circles.

A full week passed before we got our first real break.

That night I came back late from dinner with an old college friend, who was now a lawyer in Boston. It was freezing out and Cooper wasn't in yet. I read in bed until almost two before I heard the car. Half a minute later he came pounding up the stairs. "Jackie," he said bursting into the room, breathless with excitement, "how would you like to come for a little ride with me?"

"Where to?"

"A broad."

"And here I was beginning to think I was never going to get laid on this investigation."

"It's not that kind of a broad, you jerk."

"Art, at two o'clock in the morning what other kind is there?"

"The kind that's two hundred and sixty-six miles north of here, you one-track-minded pervert. *Abroad* abroad. We've got to be in Montreal by seven o'clock."

He told me all about it as I raced the car out through the slush-frozen back streets of Somerville.

He'd gotten in ahead of me, around eleven, to find a message that he was supposed to call Frank, that equipment man, no matter how late. Art, Frank says, you want to know about your pal Bill Burke's last season bad enough to be at my place in half an hour? His place being all the way the hell out in Framingham. He's waiting on the stoop, all apologies about the other day: Greenley's been watching them all like a hawk. Says Greenley has laid down a rule against any talk about the past season and the sonofabitch is sneaky enough to think up special ways of testing you. Says he can't tell Cooper much of anything anyhow, but he knows someone who might. He dials a number and hands Cooper the phone.

"Art Cooper?" says a voice, high-pitched, nervous.

"Yes?"

"Prove it?"

"Jeez," Art says, "over the phone? I mean — how can I?"

"Tell me about that game."

"Which game?"

"You know," says the voice. "The Giants, the snow."

"Oh," says Art. "That game."

So Art starts: December 3, 1950, New York at Pittsburgh, the Giants in the race for the conference title, with a big lead at the half. Then the snow and the Steelers coming back, Burke going out of bounds with seconds left, time for just one play more, two at most . . . The man breaks in and for a second Art thinks he's blown it. Then the guy starts giving it back to him. He knows the whole thing from the inside, like he'd been inside the huddle that day, like he was inside Bill's head, and telling it just the way Bill would have told it, too, in that simple, matter-of-fact way he always talked about what he did on the field, as if the things he did were as simple and obvious as driving a car from here to there. Listening to him Art sees it all again, feels his leg go, feels the snow burning the back of his neck just under the helmet as he lies there, sees Bill floating above him, his face twisted into that funny smile, sees him looking down at him out of that power he had, that secret he knew.

The guy on the other end of the line is Ken LeClair; he worked last season under Burke as an assistant — his first year in the pros. He asks Cooper what he wants to know, but he sounds so jumpy Art's afraid of spooking him. It's just about Bill, Art says, some things about last season, whatever you can tell me. LeClair is silent for a few seconds; it's not something he can talk about over the phone. Cooper says he'll go wherever LeClair says. LeClair doesn't know about that, he isn't sure, he's only out here in the East till the next morning. "You couldn't possibly make it to Dorval Airport in Montreal by seven o'clock, could you?"

By four thirty we were well into Vermont. It was a clear cold night: in the starlight every tree, steeple, barn and shed stood out against the snow-covered hills. But inside the speeding car it was warm enough and we were making beautiful time. Art dozed beside me under a blanket, having instructed me to be sure to wake him for the border.

Above St. Albans the first French sign loomed suddenly in

our lights, a simple PAS DE VIRAGE EN U. Coming as it did without explanation out of the New England night, it might have been the work of some crazy old Vermont sign maker who'd gone off his rocker with the winter and the cold. But soon there were other signs and then we were out of the mountains running low along the shore of Lake Champlain and there were silver glimpses of the lake itself, and I felt the pleasure you feel at coming to any landmark, the sense of being able to locate yourself on the map, to fix yourself for a moment, at least, in time and space. And I began to feel also that special feeling you get approaching a border, even if it was only Canada. Something in the idea that you can move from one place to another, that things can be different for you, and new again.

Near the border I shook Cooper out of a nightmare in which Canadian Mounties were interrogating him in "frogese," a language he didn't speak, and threatening to turn him back as unfit. He was in a cold sweat. The truth was he hadn't ever actually been abroad before — what if he didn't qualify? I told him that he was working himself into a state over nothing, that it wasn't like a real border, it was only Canada. If it was any comfort to him I'd do all the talking.

But when we pulled into the customs plaza, the inspector chose to direct his perfunctory questions at Cooper. Art just smiled sheepishly at him, holding out his hands like a deaf-mute who didn't understand. Well the guy did have an accent but it wasn't so strong you could possibly have mistaken his English for French unless you were Cooper and your nightmare was suddenly coming true. The inspector, his mustache jumping angrily, started cursing at us in rapid French, calling us drunks and anarchists. Finally, shaking his head, he waved us on through.

"Jesus, that was a close one," Art said. "We almost didn't make it."

"Maybe we didn't," I said, coaxing the car back up to full

speed. "Maybe you're only dreaming you made it. Maybe the truth is they've got you locked up back there."

He looked at me sidelong. "Maybe you'd better pull over and let me drive for a while, Jack."

I smiled. "Art, it's only a theoretical question. How do we know anything is really real."

"Oh Rose, for chrissake, come on," he said reaching for the road map.

"Look Art, take a classic example. Suppose you had a guy imprisoned in a cave in such a way that all he ever knew of the outside world was the shadows passing along the wall. For that guy wouldn't reality be those shadows?"

"No Rose, because you're totally ignoring human nature. Sooner or later somebody'd be along to tell the poor stiff the score. And don't try to pretend you don't think you're really sitting here with me. We're both here and we both know it."

"Just because we think so doesn't necessarily make it real."

"Rose, do me a favor, will you? Go out and get yourself hit by a two-hundred-and-twenty-pound fullback in high gear, then come back and tell me he was just a shadow."

"What was it really like, Art?" I said. "The hitting and all."

"Aah, it wasn't that bad. All that violence stuff you read and hear about — people want to think it's like war, so the media gives it to them because it sells. I'm not saying it never hurt, but some days you'd go out there and it would be just like playing a game of touch. For me it was always more the mental aspect. I liked the strategy and I liked the solid feel of a good, sharp block, not because you hurt somebody, but because it was your job and guys were counting on you. For me the best part of a block was the sacrifice. And it was real, Jack. Real enough to make you get down on your knees and pray."

"That you'd win?"

"Well, you never put it that way in so many words. It might not have looked too good, you know. Some of the guys didn't really believe in any of that, but my attitude, being a Catholic, was I'd better play it safe just in case."

At six thirty we crossed the St. Lawrence. Day was breaking cold and gray over the broad river, and the dark, humpbacked hills of Montreal loomed just ahead. We made it to the airport with less than five minutes to spare and ran all the way to the appointed coffee shop.

There were a handful of early travelers at the counter, none of whom glanced up when we came in. We sat down at a table that looked out through the deserted lobby to the parked planes and the expanse of airfield beyond. Seven o'clock came and went. Seven five, seven ten. Then one of the men at the counter swivelled around and came over to our table.

I was surprised by how young Ken LeClair was, a stocky, muscular farm boy, pink-cheeked and square-jawed. He seemed tense and troubled. Clearly he hadn't been expecting two of us.

As we sat down the waitress came by and refilled our coffee cups. The loudspeaker announced a departure, first in French, then in English. LeClair checked his watch and wound it. He told us he didn't have much time. There was a high Wisconsin twang to his voice that seemed out of place in such a solid body. He said he was sorry for dragging us so far to talk to him. He wasn't paranoid and as far as he was concerned this had been his last season in the pros anyhow; but he had a wife and a little girl and as long as he was still thinking of making his living at some level of football he had an obligation to consider their welfare. At the same time he felt an obligation to Burke. Burke had hired him last winter despite the fact that he didn't have much big-time experience. At first LeClair was a little apprehensive about him, but he soon realized that the cold public image wasn't really the man at all. A very private man, yes, the kind of man you couldn't get close to in a million years, but not an insensitive man. Just the opposite, in fact: an extremely sensitive man who used his public image to protect himself. LaClair's wife had just had the baby and the baby had some problems. Somebody else might have tried to back down from the job offer, but Bill Burke went out of his way to help in little ways that meant a great deal at the time.

But LeClair's debt went deeper than personal favors. He had seen his share of coaches who were nothing more than power-hungry egos or would-be celebrities on the make; and he'd had his fill, too, of the ones who tried to make it a religious thing. If that was what religion meant then you could count him out. He said in any field of endeavor, he didn't care which, it was possible to become disillusioned. Then along came one man who made you feel different about it all.

"He had a power," Art said.

"He did, he really did, didn't he?" LeClair said, his voice filling with sudden enthusiasm. "He could look right into you and you know somehow that he knew what you were and that it was all right. He always gave you that. But the thing about it — the thing about him — was that it wasn't a trick. It wasn't anything you could study or imitate. It was just him — the man he was."

LeClair glanced at me and stopped, blushing. His embarrassment made me feel very much the outsider. But I liked LeClair. He had the pink-cheeked earnestness of a young parish priest. I thought that here was a basically gentle, decent soul who had stumbled into the wrong line of work. I had never played football or been close to any football people, except for Cooper, of course, but Cooper was Cooper, and that was different anyhow. Deep down I guess I accepted the stereotype: scratch the surface pieties of any grown man who makes a career out of coaching football, and you'd find a sadistic, ego-maniacal martinet. I assumed therefore that Ken

LeClair must be an exception, not thinking that the qualities that made him seem special to me were qualities I might come to see in others whose lives had been touched by that game.

LeClair sketched the season pretty much as we had already pieced it together: the team potential that Burke had carefully built up over two years had been steadily eroded in the struggle with Greenley. For LeClair it had been a sobering year. He was grateful that he'd had a chance to see what pro ball was all about before he threw away too many years. He wanted to work with people and the game, not to struggle constantly for survival in a crazy world of P.R. images.

LeClair didn't blame Greenley. To him Greenley was just an ambitious managerial type who'd won the backing of the new owners, and would maneuver to strengthen his position even if he had to administer that team to death. The situation in Boston wasn't really so different from most other places in the League he could name, and you could find the same kind of thing in almost any walk of life.

What so disillusioned LeClair was the toll it took on Bill. For Bill Burke was the strongest, most self-willed man Ken LeClair had ever met, and yet this one season had worn him down so far that in the end Greenley could legitimately charge what he had implied all season long: that Burke wasn't up to it, that he was out of touch with the times, that he was unfit to run the team. In the end he could say that Bill had cracked under the pressure.

Art shook his head. He had heard all that talk before and he wasn't buying any of it. He could see Bill getting mad — so mad that he'd make mistakes of temper and judgment — but cracking under pressure, breaking down — never, not Bill.

"I didn't want to believe it either," LeClair said quietly. "But you can't always believe what you want if the facts say different."

"Then fuck the facts," Cooper said. "Maybe if you and the

rest of them that called yourselves his friends had had a little more faith in him, the main fact might have been different."

LeClair sat back looking a little stunned. I watched a plane climb slowly off the runway, drawing a ribbon of black exhaust across the clouds.

"Maybe," LeClair began hesitantly, "you would have been a better friend. Maybe so. But there are things you couldn't know. You didn't have to show up early at Bill's office to wake him out of a drunken stupor before the janitor found him; you didn't try to talk to him about his situation, only to be shouted at for not minding your own business; you didn't have to watch his suspicions close steadily inward, first shutting out all reporters, then the front-office people, then even the members of his own staff, until in the end he'd built a wall around himself. He lived and worked entirely alone with no personal interests whatsoever as far as I could tell, except for his dog, who was always at his side. Towards the end it looked to me as if that icy image he had used to protect himself had hardened into reality."

Art smashed his fist down on the table, making our cups clatter in their saucers. "I don't give a good goddamn how it *looked*," he said. "We didn't come all this way for your opinion of Bill."

Cooper was really steaming. He seemed determined to write LeClair off, but LeClair for his part seemed oddly relieved. For the first time that morning he began to loosen up.

"OK, good enough. What did you come for?"

"That last New York game. You didn't think there was anything strange about it?"

"You mean Bill's charges? That ref business? Bill was down on the refs the whole second half of the season; he seemed to think that they — like everybody else — had it in for him. But I'm the last guy in the world to ask about any of that, anyhow. During the games I was upstairs with a set of headphones, and I wasn't being paid to watch the refs."

"But what if it wasn't the refs at all?" Art said. "What if Bill himself didn't know for sure what it was?"

LeClair frowned. "What what was?"

"What do I have to do," Art said, "tell you everything? You sure are one hell of an informant. What if I told you that last game was fixed? What if I told you we have reason to suspect that one or more of your players helped throw it."

LeClair's face flushed, but his voice stayed steady. "Then I'd ask you what you know about it."

"You wouldn't be able to tell us anything about it yourself?"

LeClair shifted uncomfortably in his seat. "I'm not a fool. I've had my moments of doubt watching games on TV — who hasn't. But as for Boston, as for this year, I was new to the team and known to be loyal to Burke. Nobody would have trusted me with that kind of information."

So Art outlined what we'd been through, from our initial suspicions in New York to our attempts to contact someone inside the team, and for what it was worth, he even showed him the picture of Kauffman's son. Cooper told it all matter-of-factly, as though he weren't angry with LeClair anymore, as though the whole point now was just to impress on him what a lousy informant he had been. But I could hear the underlying disappointment in Cooper's voice. I felt it too. Had LeClair really made us come all this way for so little? And if so, why was he here himself? For despite the apparent impasse we had reached, he was still here listening carefully to Cooper's account. Was there something he was waiting to hear from us? Or was there something he had come to say? Or had he, in his own way, already told us?

I thought maybe I was in a position to know. Because Ken LeClair had told us about Burke and the season, but he had also told us something about himself, about what happens sooner or later to almost anybody. Maybe you dedicate your life to a demanding career, only to discover that the necessary process of working towards success destroys your pleasure in the work itself. Or maybe you put your trust in an idea of yourself or someone else, only to see that idea inevitably shattered on reality. It doesn't really matter how it happens. What matters is that in your self-doubt and your isolation you don't know whether to blame the world or yourself. I didn't know anything about coaching, but I knew what it was to fail, and how you could walk away from someone or something and never know afterwards whether your quitting was a sign of weakness or of strength. And I knew how the worst thing of all was the fear of losing your grip, of giving up, of going under — for in that loss of faith in yourself you came to doubt the reality of your own perceptions.

So I asked him what it really was about this season that had so shaken his faith.

"Aaah, c'mon, Jack," Art said. "What's the use? Let's go."

I didn't move. LeClair stared out the window at the planes taxiing out, red lights flashing under the gray workday morning sky.

We waited.

LeClair cleared his throat. "After that last game and his outbursts to the press Bill disappeared. He didn't tell anyone where he was, but I thought I knew. The spring before, when my daughter was so sick, he had given me the unlisted number for a cabin in Vermont. So I dialed that number, preparing myself for anything, for Bill to refuse to talk with me, or to accuse me of being another of those that had betrayed him.

"I must have phoned the cabin at least a dozen times that day without getting an answer. The last time, late at night, the ringing stopped suddenly with a sharp click, and then silence: after a while I realized that there was someone on the other end. So I said, 'Bill?' After an instant's hesitation the voice came back clear as a bell: 'Kenny, I'm sorry. I thought it was something else.' "

They talked then for a few minutes, mostly about LeClair's

wife and little girl. Then Burke apologized for having to
cut it short, but he had to keep the line open.

"And that was that?" Cooper said scornfully.

"You have to try to understand. For what it was worth I
had called Bill to say that if they tried to force him out, I
would quit, too. But I had also called to thank him for his
help, for the confidence he had shown in me, and to say that
if I had let him down in any way I was sorry.

"At least that was what I intended to say. But I never got
around to it, not the way I had it worked out in my head.
Because it was Bill instead who said those very things to me
— who asked for my understanding and forgiveness, for what
he was and was not, for any wrong he had done or might now
have to do."

"Those were his exact words?" I said.

"Yes."

"Did you have any idea what he was talking about?"

"Only that it was something he had to do alone. He said
he'd just gotten in from working on it, that he was sitting on
it all. He said he hadn't understood at first, but that he knew
now for sure what was going on. It was worse than I could
possibly imagine. But he needed time to finish working it out.
He asked me not to let anybody know where he was. I didn't
begin to know what to think."

"So you assumed he was drunk," Art said derisively. "Or
maybe just stark raving mad."

LeClair looked without defense at Cooper out of his open,
clean-cut Midwestern face. "You have to understand how
it seemed. He was the straightest-thinking, clearest-seeing,
strongest man I'd ever known, and I thought they had broken
him." He hesitated, his eyes fixed on Cooper's. "I didn't accept it until now — couldn't let myself, I guess. But Bill
knew something. Something so bad that for a while the idea
alone almost drove him mad. And two nights later he was
dead."

Nobody said anything for a while.

"That night on the phone," LeClair said, "Bill told me to remember that whatever happened, it was only a game.

"He was a great coach. He didn't make any big mystique out of it, but he knew his stuff, and he knew the secret."

"The secret?" I said.

"Of coaching," LeClair said. "It's simple really. You just have to be able to make people believe that things will go the way you say. You have to believe in the power of your own vision. You just have to have that faith.

"Bill had it. He had it almost until the very end."

NINE

We saw LeClair off to his flight, and then drove on into Montreal. On the way up Art had been all excited about seeing Montreal, but now his heart wasn't in it. I could see how he might be depressed by some of the things LeClair had said, but the depth of his dejection surprised me. After all, we had not only just had our first actual confirmation from an insider that something was up, but LeClair had also given us a list of the players he thought were most likely to co-operate. I was hoping a quick tour of Montreal might lift Cooper out of it, but Art said the whole place looked about as foreign as an overgrown Springfield, Mass. He didn't want to go down for a ride in the Metro, he had no interest in eating a typical "frog" meal.

So in less than an hour we were back on the road again, crossing that strange, flat snowbound plain of Quebec towards the mountains of New England, stretched ahead of us on the horizon like a purple cloud.

Somewhere in Vermont the sun came out, and suddenly we had a dazzling winter day. It occurred to me that under the circumstances it might be a good idea to take a look at Burke's cabin as long as we were up that way. Art didn't see the point; he wanted to get back to Boston and start in on LeClair's list. But he was too downcast to argue it one way or the other.

"Do whatever you do, Rose," he said. "You're going to anyhow."

So we came down off the interstate and turned onto one of those narrow old Vermont highways that wind through the hills. This one followed, bend for bend, a little half-frozen river studded with boulders, each sporting a pristine cap of snow. And the road itself was like a river, with the land and all the things of the land floating past: the trees and the white houses with their neat green trim, the barns built snugly up against them, and blue smoke rising from a chimney and all at once the smell of woodsmoke on the air. And all the while the hills were getting bigger and the snow deeper and we were being carried back into the country, back into the winter.

"Tell me about Bill," I said to him then.

"What about him?" he said.

"I don't know. What it was like back then between you, I guess."

For a minute I thought he wasn't going to say anything. But despite himself his face filled slowly with that private, little smile of his.

"You had to know him. You shouldn't judge him by the way he came across on the TV, that wasn't the way he really was, certainly not back then. Don't get me wrong now, Jack, but the light just had this way of coming off him. It looked as if he was lit up from the inside if you know what I mean. God he was a fine-looking man, don't get me wrong.

"You might have thought that nobody who looked so fine could play, Jack, but he could play all right. He had the feet, quick as anyone's, and he could see the whole field, too. But the thing about Bill was his presence. You had to be there to feel it. It was a mystery to me. He didn't have the super talent or the luck to ever play behind a first-rate team, but he made the most of what he did have and he made us better than we were.

"I should know. I was just a rookie, and I wasn't anything

special. But it was my dream to be there and there I was, not really believing I was there, half thinking every time a cop or some joker with a tie and jacket poked his head into the dressing room they were going to boot me out.

"But they never did. And there I'd be then in that awful silence, my guts churning away and the worry I might be sick creeping up into the back of my throat where I could taste it each time I managed to work up enough spit to swallow. When God created football players he made two kinds: the kind like me that's got to be taped and dressed one hour ahead so he can sit around worrying about whether he's forgotten anything; and the other kind — the kind that won't touch a stitch but a jock and T-shirt till the last possible second. You take one look at a guy and you know forever what kind he is.

"Bill was a late-dresser and it always did me good to watch him. He'd be lacing up his shoes, say, and the shoes under all that gear would look as light as slippers. Then he'd take those first couple of steps in that tentative way players do, the cleats making that quick clicking on the concrete, his uniform tight as a second skin.

"Bill felt the same way I did about the game. It was a pure thing for him, too. We used to talk about it sometimes, maybe late at night, on the train coming home from a game, when the guys were playing cards or trying to sleep. It wasn't like players to talk that way, but I was only a rookie and Bill, well Bill was always himself, and then again we were both from down around Boston so the rest of them figured we were both maybe a little nuts anyhow. But we were very different, Bill and I. Bill had those great eyes while I never could see worth a damn; but — hell — a lineman doesn't have to see, he only has to feel, and I could feel my way as well as any-one and I was a born blocker who loved to block and Bill was the kind of back who never ever took that for granted, and he always knew that if he ever called my number I'd have cleared the way to hell for him."

"And after he called your number? After you got hurt. What happened to him then?"

Art, looking straight ahead at the road, gave a little laugh. "Bill had this dog. I never did exactly have too great a rapport with dogs, but Bill thought the world of this one. He taught him all kinds of pass routes. He used to say as soon as the dog learned to snap the ball I'd be out of a job. Anyhow, when he quit, the year after my knee, he said he was leaving football to spend more time with the dog." Art explained that by then Bill was separated from his wife and he was pretty bitter about it all. She was a blue blood with a kid from an earlier marriage and she was never really at home in Bill's world. Bill could have kept on playing — he still had a couple of good years left in him — but instead he chose to call it quits.

"But why?"

Art was silent for a long time, watching the land coming at us, the hills bigger and ever darker. "I guess I really don't know," he said finally. "I guess I could never understand it." Art said he supposed it was a combination of things. Bill had turned that team around; but when things started backsliding, they blamed him. They always blamed the quarterback — except when they blamed the coach. First they said it was his arm, and then they dragged up a lot of talk from the time when Bill was breaking in with the old Boston club and he was young and cocky and maybe a little foolish in some of the things he did. But his marriage changed him and by the time he went to Pittsburgh he was a different player. They used everything they could against him. "People just never could understand him. They said he was arrogant and a loner, but it wasn't like that at all. Bill just had too strong a sense of himself to pretend he didn't."

Later Cooper lost track of him. Years later he heard that Burke had finally gotten back into football, coaching in a college somewhere. Maybe they never really had that much in common outside of the game. But by the time Bill got back into football Art had already drifted into the bookmaking thing, and for his part he didn't want to put Bill on the spot by contacting him. Or maybe that was just the excuse he gave himself after all those years.

The sun slid down behind the mountains, and the day turned colder. We stopped to ask directions at one of those old country stores with an ancient rusty gas pump out front. Long icicles hung from the rickety wooden porch. Inside it was dark and smelled of dust and wax and a hundred years of history. The girl behind the counter couldn't help us, but an old man sitting near the stove said he knew where the Burke place was. He was one of those old-time Vermonters, with a face bleached white by the winters and eyes crossed from inbreeding. He didn't think there was anything open up that way, but allowed as how he could point us in the right direction if we insisted. "And mind now," he said, "if you should be delayed up thataway on them city tires, don't get discouraged. Help'll be right along just as soon as the mud peaks. Long about the first of May, I should imagine. Unless a bear takes a liking to you first."

I thanked him and bought a little bread and cheese, and we trooped back out to the car. Art was for turning around right there, but I figured the old guy was probably just pulling our leg. It certainly seemed that way as we headed back off into the mountains on an asphalt road plowed clean and dry as a bone. Then the bare pavement ended abruptly and we were driving on packed snow, almost like riding into a Christmas card with the little houses blanketed snugly under clean snow and the frozen streams gleaming like crystal. But then the little houses became cabins and the cabins got fewer and the road got hillier and narrower until it was nothing but two deep tracks cut through the thick, dark woods. By now the sky above the black mountain was a cold, bloodless purple.

Art had had it. He served official notice that if I went one foot further it was all on my account. I pushed on — the snow was so deep now I wasn't sure I could turn around if I wanted to. A minute later I realized I no longer had any idea where the road was. Then we skidded sideways into a snow bank.

It was no use trying to rock or dig the car out, the wheels were spinning uselessly in the air. There was no choice but to go back for help. Art was furious. He was damned if he was going to go walking off into the woods in the dark with me. I said he could do whatever the hell he wanted.

We set off then, tramping through the snow in our city clothes and our paper-thin street shoes. It was pitch black now and absolutely silent except for the crunching of our feet in the snow. It was so cold it hurt to breathe, and the sweat we'd worked up trying to push the car out started to freeze against our skins. Art said it was all very well and good for me to count on walking out of it alive, but he had to worry about his leg. To tell the truth he'd already strained it some, pushing on the car. What if it froze up on him completely? He'd be at the mercy of the elements. I told him it was supposed to be one of the pleasanter ways to go. Cooper said being dead didn't bother him. What got him was the idea of some bear taking advantage of him while he couldn't do anything about it. I agreed it wouldn't look too good in the papers: FORMER STEELER HUMPED TO DEATH BY BEAR. Art didn't think it was funny. If he had to die, he said, at least he'd have the satisfaction of knowing it would be on my conscience forever. If I hadn't insisted on driving up here who knew how many productive years he could still have looked forward to.

"Me?" I said. "What about you? If you hadn't approached me that night in the bar and started with all this fix stuff I would have been somewhere warm and dry right now."

"Nah, Rose," he said. "If you hadn't met me, you'd have probably been somewhere worse off by yourself."

For all our talk we were less than a hundred yards from
a cabin. I followed tire tracks up through a gap in the woods,
and spotted the cabin below. Art came limping painfully up
behind me and together we slipped and slid down an icy path
past a jeep into the pool of yellow light from the cabin window.

Suddenly there came a bloodcurdling howl. Cooper
clutched my arm. A gust of wind rushed through the silent
woods, rattling frozen branches; then again there came that
terrible cry.

"Oh my God," Art whispered. "A bear."

"Don't be ridiculous. Bears sleep in the winter."

"We must have woke this one up."

All at once whatever it was came crashing out of the woods
straight at us. "Oh Jesus, *no,*" Art cried, pushing me headfirst into the snow. I rolled over and struggled to my feet in
time to see him scrambling for his life up into a little tree,
with the wild creature circling madly under him, yelping excitedly. Between yelps it was also flashing a big toothy hound-
dog grin.

"For chrissake, Art," I shouted. "It's only a dog."

"That's easy for you to say, Rose," he yelled back, fending
him off with his foot. "It's not your neck he's after. For
God's sake *do* something."

What could I do? I called to the dog, clapping my hands
and whistling, but every time I got near him he just grinned
and danced away out of reach. Clearly treeing Art was the
most exciting thing that had happened to him in a long time.
His tail was spinning so hard with the sheer, frantic joy of it
he was half airborne. He obviously didn't mean Cooper any
harm. The tree was sagging so low with Art's weight that he
was barely off the ground.

"Art, Jesus, for chrissake, will you just come down? You're
only provoking him."

"Oh beautiful, Rose. That's really pretty, you know that?

First you get me in this jam; then he comes flying out of the woods scaring the living shit out of me and you say I'm provoking him."

Out of the corner of my eye I could see the dog standing listening to our conversation. I made as if to reach for Art, then I lunged. The dog leapt straight backwards, just slipping my tackle, and I was down again in the snow. Before I could get up, an ice-cold woman's voice said, "Hold it right there. Lay a hand on that dog and I'll kill you. I swear it."

She was standing on the cabin porch with the light at her back, a shawl wrapped around her head so that I couldn't see her face, but from the set of her body as she sighted along the rifle she looked like a pretty tough old bird.

"Lady, look," Cooper said, "you got to be kidding. We were just coming up the path there minding our own business when this crazy animal attacked us."

"You in the tree — shut up. And get your hands up high where I can see them."

"But I'll fall."

"Then fall goddamnit. It'd serve you right."

"Look, please let us explain," I said, shivering in the cold. "My name is Jack Rose, and the gentleman in the tree is Art Cooper."

"I don't care who you say you are. I catch you here spying on me one more time, I'm not asking any questions."

"Will you just listen for a minute," I said. "We've never been here before. Our car got stuck just up the road. We were trying to find the Burke place."

"You know damn well this is it."

"Then this is the Burke place. Wonderful. We wonder if we could speak to someone about Mr. Burke. Mr. Cooper here is a former teammate of his."

"There's no one here who could tell you anything about him because there's no one here who even knew him. Now I want you off my property right now," she said, taking a few steps down towards us. "Come here," she called to the dog.

The dog didn't move. *"Argus,"* she shouted at him, "will you do what I say? *Come here."*

The dog cast a longing look back at Cooper and ambled reluctantly to her side. She grabbed his collar and waved the rifle at us. "Now get out of here before I call the police."

"Well go ahead and call them you crazy old bitch," I shouted, too frozen to care — rifle or not — what the hell she did. "And while you're on the phone, tell them to send along someone who can pull out a stuck car."

I started for the path, but Art just sat there motionless in the tree. I thought maybe the cold had frozen him out of his wits. He was staring at the woman and chattering quietly to himself like a mad owl. Then he started shouting. "Of course," he cried, waving his arms at her. "Jesus, yes." There was a loud crack and he dropped from the tree like a sack. For a terrible moment I thought the bitch had shot him, but it was only a branch that had given way.

Art was stretched out on the snow, his eyes shut tight. I bent over him, trying to find out where he was hurt.

"Is he all right?" the woman asked from behind me.

I didn't bother answering.

"Is he really an old football player?"

"Now's one hell of a time to ask," I said without looking up at her.

"Oh go fuck yourself," she said, kneeling down beside him.

Art opened his eyes and lay there in the snow smiling up at her and said, "Hello, Jody."

Now I was sure the cold or the fall or both had knocked him out of his senses. But then I looked at her and saw that the shawl had fallen back off her long dark hair and that she wasn't old at all. And I saw also the way she was staring back at him, shaking her head ever so slightly, fighting back the tears.

A few minutes later we were sipping hot tea before a crackling fire: me wearing some of Burke's old clothes while my own dried; Cooper with an ice bag on his knee, propped up on the couch like a great knight fallen in battle; Argus, Bill's dog, curled up just beneath his prize catch, having his ears stroked by the woman whose name was Jody.

She sat cross-legged on the floor and talked. She had the kind of face that changed from one moment to the next in the flickering light of the fire: at times it looked hard and worn, the face of an older woman with no illusions; at other times, it was the soft dreaming face of a young girl full of secret thoughts. In its own way it was a very beautiful face.

Her full name was Jody Richardson Hastings. Her mother, Catherine Richardson, daughter of a prominent Boston family, had married Bill Burke when Jody was a year old, her father, Robert Hastings, having been killed in an automobile accident just before her birth. For three years they had lived in Pittsburgh. Then one day Bill Burke moved out and got a divorce.

I knew all that about her, but what I still didn't understand was how she had come to be here now in Burke's cabin. She herself said she didn't see how she could tell us much about him. She barely knew the man. She hadn't seen or heard from him since the day he left. She hadn't even heard from him when her mother died a few years before. Then just three months ago, he called. She was living in New York at the time.

"I know this probably sounds really dumb," she said, "but do you know what made me maddest about his calling like that? Not that after all those years he'd finally bothered, not even that he'd walked out on my mother and me in the first place. It was that after all that time I knew it was him — knew it instantly.

"How could I help it? I'd hear him on TV or on the radio in the car. Or I'd hear his name at parties and in bars. Sometimes it was like he was in the very air around me.

"When he called that first time I couldn't bring myself to

speak to him. When he called again I knew I had to. A kid doesn't have one father run over by a car and another walk out on her before she's five without paying a price somewhere along the line, and I had spent a lot of time and effort, not to mention a small fortune, getting myself to the point where I could manage to look at it for what it was. God knows I'd spent a lot of time thinking up things I'd say to him if I ever got the chance. And then there it was — my big test, right?" She stopped and looked up at us, her mouth screwed up into a little smile. "And it wasn't any big deal. I don't know why I ever imagined it would be. I mean it wasn't as if I was really even his daughter."

Jody poked intently at the fire. Art turned his head, watching her from the couch, and when he spoke his voice was very gentle. He said things might have been that way for her, but that wasn't the way they had to be; things could have been different. He said he would never forget the first time he had laid eyes on Jody, at training camp the summer of his rookie year — which was of course his only year, since he never actually became a veteran.

It was a grand sight really, camp, a great place to bring a kid — a veritable three-ring circus, with receivers diving and tumbling; running backs racing by, three in a row, step for step like teams of perfectly matched horses; and guards and tackles hunkering down under their coach's orders like snarling lions. Not to mention the feats of strength and skill: linemen pushing back the blocking sled as if they could plow the earth; the sudden, booming, shot-from-a-cannon, soaring arc of a perfect punt; and of course, last but not least, the beauty of a well-thrown ball.

It was a grand sight, camp, even for a lonely rookie who had no idea what he would do with his life if he didn't make the team.

It was one of those steaming summer afternoons when a lineman sweats off ten pounds easy and they have to towel the ball dry after every play. It must have been over a hundred when they finally came off the field, their sweat-soaked jerseys glued to their skins. There were a few fans hanging on the fences — like black birds of doom, Cooper thought. And there, sittting off to one side in the shade of a tree, were Burke's wife and his little girl.

They were so beautiful they took his breath away. Bill took a couple of the veterans over to meet them, and the little girl, dressed only in tiny blue shorts, clambered happily up into her father's arms. Bill's dog, the original Argus, was there too.

Art hadn't meant to stare. But then Bill noticed him standing there and called him over. The little girl wanted to be held by each of her father's friends, so all those big sweaty ballplayers took turns holding her, passing her from one to the other, some of the surest ball handlers the most awkward now, cradling her with both arms like fullbacks down in close to the goal. Cooper remembered the warm, milky smell of her. He wanted to hold her longer, but he was only a rookie who hadn't even made the team yet. Still, Bill had called him over and introduced him to his wife, saying he was from Boston, too, and had let him stand there with the others and hold his little girl. And Art's heart had filled then to bursting and he felt tears coming to his eyes. Because it was the first sign he'd had — the first sign that he belonged.

And never had he seen a more beautiful mother and child, or a prouder husband and father.

Jody listened to Art with rapt attention, hugging her knees like a little girl hearing a fairy tale in which the lost, abandoned, heroine — who looks in every way remarkably like the little girl to whom the story is being told — wakes up to find herself the true princess.

When Art finished she sat there stroking her dog, her face soft and rosy in the firelight. "It's a nice image," she said finally. "But that's all it is."

"It's the truth," Art said. "And whether you believe this or not, something of Bill rubbed off on you. When you called Argus by his name I looked closely. And that's when I knew it was you."

Jody sat up on her knees abruptly and poked again at the fire. In the sudden leap of the flames I noticed the circles under her eyes and the firm set of her jaw. "If he's had anything to do with who I am now," she said very deliberately, "it's because of what he wasn't all those years to my mother and me — not what he was."

"Why did he leave your mother anyhow?" I asked.

"Who knows what it was, Jack," Art said quickly. "Married people have all kinds of secret trouble hidden away. That's why it's such a holy sacrament."

Jody smiled at Art, then turned to me. "What does any of it matter now? It really doesn't make any difference, does it?"

"But you're living in his house," I said.

"Why not? He left it to me. It's mine."

"You didn't have to come. Not if you feel the way you say you do."

She stroked the dog's neck. "I was at loose ends," she said flatly. "I needed a place to come to. I came partly because I thought the change would do me good, and partly because . . ."

In the silence of the cabin the phone jangled like a rude intruder. It rang once, twice, before she even looked up at it.

"Want us to get it for you?" Art said.

She shook her head. "It's just my friends. They'll stop sooner if no one answers."

Her "friends" were the ones she'd mistaken us for, the ones who'd been harassing her. Sometimes they hung up, sometimes they said things. In the night she'd hear sounds; once she'd returned to find they'd broken in, torn the place apart and emptied boxes of Burke's papers and records. The townspeople acted as if that was what any woman deserved who tried to live off by herself in the woods in the middle of the winter. What they really seemed to think, though, was that she had a touch of cabin fever, that it was all the crazy imaginings of a scared city girl. For a while she'd closed up the cabin and taken Argus back down to New York, but once there she missed the woods and the quiet peace of the place, and thought maybe she had let the whole thing get to her, that she was only using it as an excuse. But she felt like a fool having to go through the charade of carrying a rifle she didn't know how to load or fire. And most of all she hated having to worry constantly about Argus. "You've seen how he is," she said. "He's got a mind of his own."

"You were going to tell us another reason why you came," I said.

She sat there stroking the dog. "It was because Argus was here."

"You're living all alone in the woods because of a dog?" Art said incredulously.

She looked up at him without defense, her eyes glistening as if stung by his words.

"I mean don't get me wrong," Art said. "As dogs go he's basically very nice."

"You don't understand," she said, her voice suddenly on the edge of breaking. "He wanted me to. He said he was all alone. He said Argus was the only friend he had left. He said he worried what would become of him if anything ever happened."

"But for chrissake you didn't have to come *here*," Cooper said. "To the middle of nowhere."

"But I did, I had to. Don't you see? It was all such a mystery to me — who he was, what he wanted, why things had been the way they had. He didn't explain any of it, even then. He just said he knew it was too late to make amends, that he could never hope to make me understand. All he wanted was my forgiveness. So I came here because I was partly responsible."

"Responsible?" Art said. "But for what?"

"For what else? For what happened. For his dying."

"But that's crazy. It was an accident."

"Was it? He told me how to care for 'Gus — about his food, his medicine. He told me about the house, the land, the shack across the stream where he liked to work in the warm weather. He told me where the keys were. He said he knew that the little he was giving me now couldn't begin to make up for what he had taken, but it was all he had. He said it had all been a dreadful mistake and that whatever had happened between my mother and him was his fault. He said that he had never stopped loving us, that whatever I might hear I had to believe that he had only done what he thought best for us. He said he could have explained it all, but that it was too late, that the only thing that mattered to him now in the world was my forgiveness. But I wouldn't give it to him," she said, her face stone-cold. "I wouldn't let myself believe it. Not me. Not then."

"When did he tell you all this?" I said.

She looked at me as if surprised by the question. "Why that night, of course," she said. "That last night before he died."

So that was it. Burke had not only known something about that game, he had known that he might die for it. And she thought in her own way that she was responsible.

And if she wasn't, who was?

TEN

We returned to Boston the next day, our heads full of the new possibilities. LeClair had told us Burke knew something about that game; Jody had taken us one step further: whatever Burke knew, he also knew he might die. Was his death an accident after all? Or had it just been made to look that way?

One thing seemed certain: it was all related somehow to a fix of that game. Cooper was convinced the key now was LeClair's list of names: we had to find one player who was willing to talk. We also had to try harder to get hold of someone who could fill us in on the local betting picture for the past season, particularly the activities of Victor Calabrese, the big sports bookmaker. And I thought we'd better take a closer look at Burke's movements during his last four days, from the game on Sunday to his death Thursday night.

"Sure, sure," Art said, "but we have to do away with the fancy stuff now. The key thing is LeClair's list. That's our best shot."

We went at it full steam all that week, but the going was a lot harder than we expected. To begin with, half the players were scattered across the country for the off-season; two couldn't be traced at all; another was away on a hunting trip. Those we did reach professed great respect for Burke, but they all had reasons for not wanting to talk about it. A running back from Kansas said it was just flat-out against his policy to discuss teammates. A wide receiver in California told us he'd put that whole scene light-years behind him.

Closer to home our luck was no better. A skittish young black cornerback agreed on two separate occasions to meet us at South Shore clubs; both times he stood us up. Another player with an interest in a Back Bay lounge didn't see why the hell he should talk to us; when we dropped by his place to see him personally he told us to go fuck off. Only the third-string quarterback seemed really glad to hear from us. He told us to come right on down that afternoon to the field where he worked out, but it turned out he thought we were friends of Burke's who might help get him traded.

The last man on the list was a veteran linebacker who worked in the off-season as an engineering consultant. We stood around in the basement of his suburban home while he grunted and groaned his way through special exercises to come back from knee surgery. A transplanted southerner with a wry twinkle in his eye, he deftly sidestepped our questions and delivered instead a little discourse on what he termed the hard-boiled practicalities of the situation. What the hell did we expect from these guys anyhow? Half of them were just overgrown kids with a terror of civilian life. Football was their whole world and the one kiss-of-death label in this league was that of troublemaker. Sure, he could say plenty of things about guys he suspected — guys who weren't pulling their weight, guys who were protecting their bodies, guys whose asses he just plain didn't like. But what would be the point? It wasn't a rational system like mathematics or a machine. For a player, playing was the only thing that mattered, and he could damn well guarantee us that come training camp they would all be killing each other for the privilege of impressing Greenley's ass now that he was running the show.

The two zippered scars on either side of his knee puckered

up as he swung his leg gently, testing it. Nope, he didn't think we should expect much from the players. And that included the ones who had sided most openly with Bill. Especially them, especially now.

Progress on other fronts wasn't any more encouraging. Cooper had reached an old friend who thought he might be able to put Art in touch with a high-school pal of theirs now working for Calabrese, but so far nothing had come of it. Nobody we talked to had heard of Kauffman or his son, while Kauffman himself hadn't been able to uncover any connection between his son and Calabrese, though he was still working on it. He was happy to hear from us, though, and eager to send us more money and help in any way he could.

Thanks in part to a phone call Kauffman did make for us, and with considerable help from my lawyer friend, I was able to find out the official details of Burke's death. Unfortunately they only confirmed what we already knew. Sunday night after the game Burke returned to Boston by himself, having made charges in front of the cameras before leaving New York, and repeating them when he arrived in Boston. On Monday at his stadium office he refused to deny or withdraw any of his statements. On Tuesday came the announcement I had heard at Litwin's party, about the commissioner's fine; but by then Burke had disappeared. From LeClair we knew that he was at his cabin in Vermont on Tuesday night, and on Wednesday night he spoke to Jody from there. On Thursday evening, however, he was back in Boston for the meeting at which Greenley told him he was through. Witnesses reported seeing him later that night drinking heavily in at least two places near Saxton. The accident itself was cut and dried as far as the police were concerned. The medical examiner's report showed excessive levels of alcohol in the blood. There was no sign of foul play on the car or the body. There was no suicide note.

Art, who made a point of calling Jody every night, phoned

to give her the latest news. She told him things were fine with her and Argus. Since our visit there hadn't been any more trouble and she was feeling much better.

But for Art it didn't matter whether Bill's death was listed as an accident or not. As far as he was concerned it amounted to the same thing: in one way or another Burke was driven to his death by what happened in that game.

At the end of the week, Art received a call from the guy who worked for Calabrese. He agreed to meet with us. He guaranteed that we would find what he had to say very interesting.

Quinlan's was one of those tough little neighborhood bars with a bare brick facade and those narrow little windows over which the curtains are always drawn shut. But you didn't have to see inside to know the kind of place it was, with battered tables scattered around, crates stacked up against the walls, the smell of stale beer and smoke everywhere, and the TV going at top volume while the tight knot of swaggering, quarreling men out-shouted and out-cursed each other for the sheer sport of it. It was one of those little local places where if you had to be making your maiden visit, you didn't at all mind being chaperoned by the single all-time greatest living neighborhood hero.

The cheers went up the second we came through the door. "Hey Ahtie! Hey Coopah! Ya fuck, ya cock-suckah, ya horny one-legged bastid."

In the midst of the ass-grabbing and general hilarity Quinlan served up bottles of Bud on the house in honor of "the world's foremost un-fuckin'-known free-lance flatfoot and his Ha'vid assistant." And so we sat through round after round, hearing stories from the glory days of Somerville High. How the cheerleaders' legs got better looking every year, how the coach should be fired or the taxpayers given the right to send in plays, how despite the atrocious performance of the current team there was plenty of local talent that Art with all his professional contacts should know about: like the natural-born hitter who'd be a sure-fire blue-chipper the day he just learned to lay off civilians; and somebody's neighbor's kid who was a little hefty right now, but once they got him down around three-twenty and taught him to move could be something else; and somebody's nephew who could make forty-yard field goals like money in the bank if only it wasn't for an allergy that blew him to pieces whenever he got near live grass. Maybe Cooper could put a smart artificial-surface ball club onto him.

The rounds kept coming and it was getting later and later and still no sign of Cooper's friend when the door swung open and a snazzy little guy strutted in, followed by three much bigger guys, all smiling to themselves like a singing group with a smash hit on the charts. The place turned dead silent as the little guy stepped around the room flashing smiles and dispensing greetings like some slick TV game-show host. At least that's what I thought. I thought it was either some second-rate local celebrity or a practical joke. But it wasn't either. It was Victor Calabrese.

He stopped in front of Art. "I swear," he said, "my eyes — they just can't believe this. One of the greatest human products the city of Sommaville ever gave to the outah world. Am I right? Aht Coopah."

Calabrese pulled up a chair, straddling it backwards like a pony. "Yeah, I heard you were back in town and it really is some coincidence bumpin' into you like this because, would you believe it, I myself have been wantin' to have a little talk with you. Yeah, I'm one of those who feel it's the duty of responsible businessmen to take a more active role in the welfare of the community.

"Like just today this kid comes up to me with a proposition — says he wants to go into the ahts. Go on, I says, get the fuck outta here, but this kid he just points to this wall where some prick's spray-painted SUCK SHIT HONKY BASTARD. Well you don't have to be in the ahts to see something like that creates a negative atmosphere. This guy wants to create positivity, and I can see he's enough of a ding-dong to be sincere. What this guy wants to do is paint poems. His paint, his time; all he wants is the wall. Fuck, I can get him all the walls he wants, you know. Anybody seen the pa'kin' lot opposite O'Keefe's funeral pa'lah? RIP THE CHORD, YOUR MOTHER'S IN THE CAN. That's one of his best known works. What does it mean? Who the fuck knows. He don't know himself. What the hell, that's the way it goes in the ahts sometimes."

Not that Calabrese was saying this kid had to be the next Leonardo. "The point is I simply try to help out the local talent. Which was why from the minute I heard Aht Coopah was down from New York I've been hoping to have a word with you — a private word."

Calabrese looked around with a smile and suddenly everybody was falling over each other in their race for the door, Quinlan fumbling to explain he'd been planning on closing early anyhow, to take all the time we needed, to help ourselves. He'd come back down later to lock up.

Then it was just Calabrese and his three grinning goons and suddenly the place seemed awfully big and awfully empty. Calabrese jerked his head and one of his friends stationed himself by the door. Then Calabrese turned to me with that TV smile. "Hey you. Maybe you're a little ha'd of hearin'. I said we wanna talk."

"Anything you got to say to me," Art said sitting there bolt upright in his chair, "you can say in front of him."

"Hey, OK, no problem. I'm just tryin' to consider your privacy, Ahtie, that's all. It's no big secret. I heard what a rotten deal you got in New York just because you went a little overboard on one bet. I wanted you to know that I can always make room in my operation for a class guy."

"I'm through with that kind of work," Art said, stiff as a statue. "That part of my life is behind me now."

"Jeez, really, is that so? I must have got the wrong impression somehow. See I heard you were makin' the rounds, askin' questions, so naturally I just figured . . . but fuck it, if that's the way you feel there are lots of other things I can set up for you."

"I don't want your kind of help."

Calabrese smiled at Cooper, then at his friends. "All right, maybe you don't want any assistance, Ahtie, but everybody can use a word of friendly advice, can't they? You've been away for a while; maybe you don't realize how things work around here now. Like all those questions you've been runnin' around askin'. A lot of people might not like the idea of some guy just comin' in askin' a lot of questions about something that's none of his business.

"You can understand that, can't you, Ahtie? Take my own case for example. I'm a sports bookmaker; I sell an intangible product. In such a highly competitive ma'ket, I work ha'd to build a certain name. Then just say somebody comes along stirrin' up doubts about that name. Well naturally I would have to defend myself, wouldn't I? Even if it was just some fuckin' chump a little overwrought from a certain game."

Art jumped to his feet, reaching for Calabrese. Instantly two of Calabrese's men grabbed him from behind. The third pulled out a gun.

"Ahtie, Ahtie, I had hoped this wouldn't be necessary. I had really hoped that by now you would have gotten the message. But maybe you just need a little audio-visual demonstration of exactly what we're talkin' about here."

Calabrese told the one whose name was Paully to show us what his piece looked like. He told him to stick it up under Art's eyes where he could get a nice close look at it. He told him to cock it and then to make sure Art got the point he had him press the barrel right in against Art's eyeball. Calabrese said that out of consideration for Art's playing past he was asking him one last time as politely as he knew how to stay the fuck out of his business. Then he told them to let Art go.

"Look, Coopah," Calabrese said getting up slowly. "I'd like us to be friends, I really would. They tell me you were a sma't ballplayer in your day — so why don't you wise up. This thing you're doin' now — as your friend, I'm tellin' you, there's just no percentage in it."

Calabrese started for the door. "Oh yeah, jeez," he said, snapping his fingers, "I almost forgot the reason I dropped by here in the first place. Some guy who used to work for me asked me to tell you he couldn't make it tonight. It seems he's not feeling too well right now." Calabrese flashed his celebrity smile. "Hey Rose, you're the Ha'vid kid. Try and talk some sense into this dumb townie here for us, will you, or our next meeting won't be nearly so nice."

After they left Art couldn't stop shaking.

"You all right?" I said. "You sure they didn't hurt you?"

"I'm *fine*," he said through clenched teeth, pressing his hand to his eye.

I got him a drink to steady his nerves. He drank it down. I got him another one, and I got one for myself.

"Did you see that, Jack?" he said, rubbing his eye. "Did you see those guys?"

"I saw it."

"Like they could just walk in here and own me, Jack. Like I was nothing."

We sat there in the deserted bar with our drinks and everything seemed sharper and very different. No one had laid a hand on me, but I felt as if I'd been slugged in the stomach. It was one thing to go along imagining that there were people like that out there; it was something else altogether to have them walk in through the door on you. At that moment, the shock of that fact — of their being real — was more unnerving than any of the threats they'd made.

"We're so close, Jack. They can't know how close we are. They think they can make us quit — but we can't quit now, can we?"

I looked up at him and my face must have shown what I

realized then was my diappointment at the thought of his ever giving in.

Art nodded. "They all think they know me, Jack, but you're the only one who knows me now. You understand why we're going all the way."

"Come on, Art," I said. "This place isn't doing either of us any good."

The next morning we began again from the top, calling the people on LeClair's list one more time. To our surprise the black cornerback agreed once more to meet with us. This time, though, he actually showed up at the appointed luncheonette in Hyde Park. He was a lean, wiry guy with a scowl on his face and a chip on his shoulder. He said Burke had always dealt straight with him despite some hassles he was having with the law. As for helping us about that game, he couldn't get involved personally, but he knew somebody who'd had his eye on somebody else. The guy to talk to was H. D. Carob, the defensive end. We asked if he knew where we could find him. He said, "Uh-huh," and pointed to the window. There was nothing there but the back side of a Coke sign and one of those washed-out wrestling posters. Carob's face glared at us from the poster. The Wild Witch Doctor was wrestling the following night at the Boston Garden.

Neither of us had ever been to a professional wrestling match before, and neither of us had ever seen a crowd quite like the one that came tramping by the thousands up the Garden's concrete ramps. There were frenzied fathers and foul-mouthed mothers pulling at children with haunted eyes; there were wheelchairs, crutches, and sleeveless stumps, quivering spastics and drooling retards, the deformed, the deprived, the depraved — the whole sick underside of the sterling coin of self.

From our cheap seats high up in the second balcony we peered down through a smoky haze to the tiny green canvas ring below. Suddenly the crowd erupted in a standing ovation as Mike McBonner, white and stocky, a former New England champion from Chelsea, Massachusetts, jogged into the ring waving confidently to the crowd. Then came a torrent of boos as — from the Amazon, South America — the Wild Witch Doctor entered the ring, a snarling black giant of a man with thick braids dangling like snakes.

The match itself was a joke. The Wild Witch Doctor immediately started strangling the American with his braids, and for twenty minutes proceeded to stomp, kick, punch, throw, bite, drag and bounce his helpless ass around, off and through the ring. It was so phony it was funny; the only frightening thing about it was the sight of thousands of outraged, screaming spectators clearly believing with all their hearts that this patent farce, taking place right before their eyes, was real. And they continued to believe it right up until the final triumphant moment when the good old plodding American, after being worked over like a piece of raw hamburger for almost half an hour, shook off the Witch Doctor's fatal voodoo trance-dance and, responding to the crowd's deafening cheers, came to life like a pneumatic drill and in one sustained, frenzied, wild burst of crowd-pleasing action bounced back for the final victory.

"Jesus Christ," Cooper said as we made our way down to the dressing rooms. "Did you ever see such a disgusting spectacle in your life? If a real guy had a tenth of that stuff happen to him he wouldn't know it — he'd be dead." Art didn't see how any real athlete, using his own name or not, could lend himself to such a farce. He didn't think we should expect much from a guy like that.

Squeezing our way through the fans surrounding the dressing room door, we told the ex-wrestler standing guard that we wanted to talk to Carob. With a jerk of his thumb he waved us on in.

Carob was sitting off by himself in the corner, guzzling his way through a six-pack of beer. He was a giant of a man, all right. Without his wig on he was very handsome in a massive way, with one of those finely sculpted black skulls. The muscles in his arms and shoulders looked like slabs of glistening marble, the hard veins standing out.

"Well now what have we here?" he said as we approached. "Too old to be huntin' autographs. Too raunchy to be bearin' a business proposition. Which must make you writers, don't it?"

"As it so happens," Cooper said, "we're free-lance detectives."

"Well if I ain't a brass-bound hotel dick."

Cooper muttered something under his breath and shook his head at me. I explained to Carob that Art was a former football player, and an ex-teammate of Bill Burke's.

"Well pardon me," Carob said. " 'Course I should've recognized that fact immediately by that creaking sound I was picking up. We voodoos tend to forget, you hear some rusty gringo creaking along, odds are you got yourself a former Steeler on you hands."

"We aren't here to talk with the Witch Doctor," I said, "but with Carob, the football player."

"Carob, Carob, Carob," Carob chanted. "Oh you mean H. D. Carob, that ballplayer. Well now let me tell you something private about ol' H.D. He's awful sensitive about strangers coming around here asking for him, you understand what I'm saying? Powerful sensitive."

I said a friend had sent us. I said we had some questions that Carob might be able to help us with.

"What kind of questions?"

"About the past season. About the last game."

Carob stuck out his lower lip and slowly toweled the sweat off his face. "Want to know a little secret about H.D.? That H.D.'ll do just about anything if there's a steak in it." Carob glanced at Cooper. "Tin man coming, too?"

I nodded.

"That'll cost you two steaks then."

We went to a place in the North End. Carob took his dining seriously, but then, as he put it, he had to; he was eating for two — his body and his ego. While he solemnly studied the menu, waiters buzzed around the table whispering to each other like teen-age girls. Not until his dinner was finally ordered and the wine had met his approval did he settle back in his chair and announce that court was open. So it was up to me, Art and Carob not being exactly on cordial terms, to explain who we were and why we had come to him.

When I had finished Carob carefully set down his knife and fork and scanned the restaurant in disbelief. "Some guys on the team put you up to this, didn't they? Either that or the joker with the big book's gonna walk up now and tell me I'm on 'Candid Camera,' right?"

"Then you can't help us?"

"Of course he can't," Cooper said. "Let's just forget him, Jack."

"Now just a goddamn holy minute," Carob said. "My lord, Cooper, but you sure are one hell of an impetuous dick. I mean here poor ol' H.D. has graciously gone to the trouble of letting you take him out to dinner, and before he's hardly even seen the meat you're already popping the question and pulling out. Now let's just say, just for the sake of argument, that ol' H.D. might happen to have some ideas of his own in a similar direction. No — let's even go one step further and say he has some very definite ideas about certain people. Now — saying all that — what the hell makes you think you can just come strutting in off the street and expect him to go spouting off the top of his head?"

"You played for Bill," Art said. "You knew the kind of man he was."

"So a good man got a rotten deal and a pure prick like Greenley got ahead. Tell me something else that's new."

"Nah, I'm not going to waste my time trying to tell you

anything. Except this: I've often wondered why with your ability you weren't a truly great player. Tonight I sat up there watching you do your thing and I realized you're not a player at all. You're just another two-bit act."

Carob's eyes narrowed to two crocodile slits. "You know, Cooper, I really do owe you an apology, man. I mean here I've been sitting thinking you were just an ordinary run-of-the-mill tin dick. But under all that rust and grime you're really the original white knight, aren't you? And an intelligent one at that, being as how you're a former snapper and we all know how it takes a superior white intelligence to do something as important as centering the ball. Now poor ol' H.D., lacking in the superior powers of perception, just doesn't see things quite as clearly as you do. Frankly, I don't understand the way he sees things myself. His belly gets all the grub it wants and his ego's already got all the glory it can stomach. So why does he do it? Why does he make a fool of himself wrasslin' around? You know what he says? He says a crowd is a child. He says he likes pleasing children."

"But it's a fraud," Art said.

"Oh man, give me a break, will you? It's like a play. Theater. That's all."

"But you're pretending it's real. You're deceiving those people."

"There isn't anybody deceiving those people but themselves. You couldn't give away what we do. They're so used to being taken they wouldn't show up — they wouldn't believe it was for real. They're begging us for it. Give me a little fantasy, a little thrill; give me another body and life for a while because I'm sick of the one I've got. People want to get off on my physicality — that's cool. The promoter's pleased and I'm pleased and neither of us has to go around pretending it's anything but what it is."

"And you're saying football's the same kind of thing," I said.

"It's not so very different."

"It's real," Art said, raising his voice. "That's all the difference in the world."

"Real what?" Carob said. "It's a business, that's all. It isn't a crusade or Armageddon once a week come Sunday. And it isn't for love of God or country or some fucking city you could be traded from tomorrow, or fans who'll curse you the second you start going bad. It isn't any of that any more than it's for some coach who'll be fired for no good reason by some cheap, meddling ambitious general sonofabitch, or even for some teammate who when it suits him nice and good will up and take a dive. It's a show, that's all. You think it's any different, you're a lot worse off than those poor suckers in the stands."

"All right," Art said, "if you don't give a damn about the game then what about the truth?"

Carob picked up his knife and fork and dug into his steak again. "It isn't any fairy tale out there, Cooper. You stick out your neck too far and somebody'll be right along to chop it off."

"Like Victor Calabrese?" Art said.

Carob stopped in midbite, glaring down at us.

"It was him, wasn't it?" Art said. "It was Calabrese."

"Why don't you go ask our friend Greenley just who it was."

"Greenley? What's he got to do with it?"

"You heard me. I'm not giving you any more than that."

"No," said Art getting to his feet, "I wouldn't expect that you would."

Carob's hand shot out across the table and grabbed hold of Cooper's arm. "Before you take your bleeding old-timer heart out of here, do yourself a favor and wake up, will you. It's a meat market, that's all. They use you up and when they're through with you they get another body. Or don't you even begin to know what it's all about?"

Art jerked himself free of Carob's grasp. "I think I know what it's about as well as anyone," he said. Then without even glancing at me he rushed out of the restaurant. I guess

Carob got a good look at the limp then, because as I got up to follow Art he stopped me with a touch. "You tell your friend it was nothing personal," he said. "You tell him I didn't see about the knee."

But in the car Art didn't want to talk about it, and when we got back to our rooming house there were other things to think about. No sooner had we pulled up than the landlady, Miss McDonald, came running down the steps crying. She was so upset we couldn't understand her, but once we got up to our room we understood quickly enough. The place was a shambles. It looked as though Carob and McBonner had gone at it right there — tables and chairs overturned, drawers emptied out, shelves swept clean.

According to Miss McDonald there had been two men. They had come to the door saying they were doing a background check on us, and before she knew what to think they barged in past her. She hadn't dared call the police or tell anyone till she spoke to us. Art asked her if she remembered anything about them, but she couldn't remember much, except that one was older, the other younger, like us. And yes — she'd almost forgot — just after they'd left there'd been a call for us from a very important-sounding gentleman. Art was supposed to go see him the very next day. She went and got her message pad. Cooper glanced at it and handed it to me. It was Greenley.

The next day was cold and rainy. Art left early for the stadium and Jody called a few minutes later. I told her she'd just missed him. She said she was glad to have a chance to talk to me alone, that Art wouldn't tell her anything about what was really going on. She didn't see why we had to be risking it all by ourselves. I explained as best I could, and tried to tell her a little about Art and me and some of the things that had led us to where we were; but she already knew more than I realized.

"Art told me what happened to your woman. I'm really sorry."

"He shouldn't have told you all that."

"I twisted his arm."

"What else did he reveal under pressure?"

She laughed. She had a nice laugh. "He told me to sing out if you put any fast moves on me."

"Oh brother."

"Jack, be careful," she said. "Please. For Art's sake and your own."

I met Art later that afternoon at Quinlan's and he told me about his visit with Greenley. The guards had ushered him straight in to Greenley's office. Through the picture window behind the desk he could see the empty stadium, about as cheerful in the rain as a swimming pool drained for winter. Greenley lost no time coming to the point. Art had been sneaking around harassing his players. He was the kind of outside troublemaker who didn't have the guts to confront anyone in a position of authority eyeball to eyeball. Greenley demanded to know just what the hell he thought he was up to.

Since Greenley already seemed to know so much about it, Art said, why didn't he just go ahead and tell him?

Greenley said he'd do just that. He knew damn well Cooper had been going around trying to stir up old rumors of a fix. And what had he found out for all his meddling? Nothing. Because there was nothing to find out. Because all those same tired rumors had been checked out through proper channels — by the League's own security division, professionals dedicated to preserving the integrity of the game. What's more, not a single responsible member of the media had dared to make a formal charge. So just who the hell did some nobody like Cooper think he was. If Cooper happened to be in possession of any hard information, any papers or documents for instance, this was his opportunity to hand them over so that they could be processed through proper channels. Otherwise Greenley did not intend to sit back and tolerate any further sabotage of his team.

"Aaah, you don't have to worry about me doing that," Art

told him. "I'm sure you can handle all the necessary sabotaging by yourself."

"If you mean that remark to refer to the failures of your friend Burke this past season," Greenley shouted, "it might interest you to know that I didn't have to lift a finger to undermine his position." Greenley proceeded to give Cooper a little lecture on what he called the facts of life, complete with statistics, the kind of stuff that anyone who wanted to bother could look up for himself, about how the pro game had been declining over the last couple of years; how attendance was down and TV ratings had slipped so far that for the first time the networks were on the verge of cutting back the scale of their commitments, threatening the entire structure of the game. In this crucial year of the renegotiation of the networks' contract, steps had to be taken before the season began — and they were: organizational reforms at the top level — new management encouraged, new ideas developed to make the product more exciting and competitive. Taken all together these measures had helped reverse the negative trend of the last few years. All indications were that when the new contract was signed later in the year it would confirm the fact that the past season had been one of the most successful and significant in the history of the League.

It was against this background that Greenley himself had been recruited. For the sake of continuity the new owners had felt duty-bound to honor Burke's contract, though it was clear from the start he was a problem. His personality, his philosophy, his methods, everything about the man was out of line with the image they intended to project. Wilson Burke seemed to think the game should live or die by its own merits, totally ignoring the long, slow, deliberate process of experimentation and innovation that had kept professional football, of all the major spectator sports, closest to the demands of a modern public's changing tastes. The public had not been allowed to grow weary of the game. Teams no longer had to win to be successful. But someone like Burke couldn't appreciate this fact. Step by step he turned his back on every reasonable opportunity to mold the team along practical lines, refusing to acquire players with greater public appeal, or to make minor on-the-field adjustments in the look of the team, or even to be barely civil to the media. If anyone had betrayed the organization, Greenley said, it was Burke, by not responding to its real needs.

"Those were fine teams," Art told Greenley. "He got the most out of everything he had."

"Like your friend, Cooper, you don't seem to realize what business we're in. Our product isn't victories on a football field — it's entertainment. Sports entertainment."

Art was at a loss for words. What Greenley was saying seemed so logical on the one hand, yet so dead-headed wrong on the other. Maybe football was a form of entertainment — of course, obviously it was — but the thing about it was, even if you did look at it that way, the only reason it had any value as entertainment was because it *was* a sport; because it was something *true*.

That's what Art thought, though he didn't have the presence of mind to put it that way, sitting there in Greenley's office. It was something he had to work out by himself coming back in the car to meet me at Quinlan's. But it was what he would have said, what he should have said, what he still had half a mind to call that bastard up on Quinlan's phone right now to say. But back in Greenley's office he'd just sat there speechless while Greenley informed him that if he persisted in tampering with his team he would see to it that both Cooper and his crony — me — would be prosecuted to the full extent of the law.

"Law?" I said setting down my beer. "What law have we broken?"

"That's exactly what I asked him. He said he didn't have to cite any laws. He said my record — ten years as a gambling hoodlum in New York — spoke for itself. He said he had a pretty damn good idea that my misguided loyalty to Burke was just a front for an infiltration of the team on behalf of gambling elements. I said to him, 'Is that so?' He just grinned. 'Whether it's right or not,' he said, 'doesn't matter. What matters is whether or not I'll have any trouble convincing the D.A.' He said if I persisted in interfering with him, if I tried to compromise his position in any way or talk to one more of his players, he'd personally see to it that there wasn't a state in this country with a team in the League that I could safely set foot in. Then he told me to get the fuck out of his office and not to let him catch me there ever again.

"I stopped at his door. He was already bent over some papers, jotting down notes. Maybe I went too far, but I was too worked up to think straight. From the door I said: 'If you really want to know what I'm up to Greenley, why don't you go ask your friend Calabrese?'

"He raised his head real slow and stared at me. Then he said, 'I thought you were just dumb, Cooper, but now I see you're a goddamn fool.' Then he reached for the phone and had me bodily escorted from the premises."

Art stopped, but it was clear as he sat there with both hands wrapped tightly around his beer that there was more to it. Greenley had told him that if Art wanted to deal in dirt he'd play the same game. He said that Art's friend Bill wasn't exactly pure as driven snow, and that the only thing that would be hurt now by a full investigation was Burke's name.

"I don't suppose he was willing to elaborate on that."

"And waste his breath on the likes of me?" Art shrugged. "What does it matter anyhow? Greenley's just grabbing at straws, trying to scare us off." The important thing, Art said, was that it was all starting to add up. In the first place Greenley knew Calabrese. Art was sure of it. You only had to see the look on Greenley's face. Secondly someone had gotten to a player; Carob had come right out and said as much. That someone just had to be Calabrese. Greenley was obviously trying to cover up something. Maybe he'd been in on it himself, who knew? First the threats from Calabrese, now Greenley. The pieces were starting to fall into place. All we lacked was the name of the player. We were so close to fixing the bastards. We were sitting right on the edge. All we needed now was something to give us that one final push up and over.

It came that night. We got back from Quinlan's to find Miss McDonald waiting with an anonymous message: a man had just called to say "if we were interested in getting into some films," I should call him back right away.

It was Carob. He'd been having it out with ol' H.D. What could he do? Ol' H.D. was just a damn jealous fool who hated like the dickens to see anybody else going around having all the fun. He said he wanted to show us some films. There was just one problem. It had to be that night at the stadium, where the films were locked up.

"So what?" I said. "You can get the keys, right?"

"As a matter of fact," Carob said, "no. Not exactly."

ELEVEN

A thick bank of cloud blotted out the moon. We were driving through countryside now but all we could see were isolated points of light floating in the blackness. In the aqueous light of the dash Carob's skin glowed an eerie blue. He was thumping the wheel of his big Caddy in time to the spacey sounds emanating from the stereo — jazz selected by our host specifically, it appeared, to annoy Art Cooper.

"Look, Cooper," Carob said, "you have simply got to get control of yourself. You go and have yourself a heart attack before we get this over with, poor ol' Rose and me will have made the whole trip for nothing. Now there is just no reason at all for you to be working yourself up into such a frenzy."

"Right," Art said. "And I suppose a break-in is just a regular nightly event for you."

"Oh man, how many times must I tell you. This guy's a friend, a fan. He gets lonely guarding a whole stadium by himself. I drop in from time to time, we talk a little ball, watch some films or whatever H.D. wants him to do. It isn't at all like a real break-in."

"Tell that to Greenley if he catches us."

"The man catches us he won't be listening to you, or to me either."

"Unless he gives you a medal," Art said. "Because if there's

some foul-up you'd have us in there signed, sealed and delivered, wouldn't you?"

Carob turned to Cooper, his voice like inky velvet. "Why
now I guess I would, wouldn't I tin man?" A minute later he
poked Art in the shoulder and told him to leave the worrying
about Greenley to him. The only thing Cooper had to concern himself with was Carob's ground rules for the films.
Carob would tell Art what part of the field to look at, but in
order to keep his own biases out of it, he wouldn't name any
names. Art would get one choice and one choice only. If he
was half the player he was supposed to have been, he should
be able to spot it. When Cooper was ready they would both
write down the names. If they failed to match, we would all
just take our suspicions our own separate ways.

I could tell by the way Art sat there with his shoulders all
hunched in around himself that he didn't like it any more now
than he had at the start. But he knew as well as I did that we
couldn't pass up a chance to see the actual game films,
especially with someone who could point Art in the right direction. The only real question was whether we could trust
Carob, and I didn't need Art's hunched-up silence and his
pointed glances to remind me that I was the one who decided
we had to take that risk.

Carob took a roundabout way to the stadium, approaching
it over back roads from the rear. Half a mile away he turned
off the road and up into the woods, killing his headlights. We
crunched along in the dark on what seemed to be a dirt track.
At the edge of the trees we came to a chain link fence. Carob
switched off the ignition and we crept to a stop. I checked my
watch — it was almost one o'clock. We got out quietly.
Looming ahead of us in the night like a great ship at anchor
was the darkened shell of the stadium.

"Look at her," Carob said softly. "The way she sits there
with that important emptiness hanging over her."

"Just can the poetics, will you, Carob," Cooper said, "because if this isn't a break-in it sure as hell doesn't feel like my idea of dropping in on an old friend."

"Be cool, Cooper. We have to show a little consideration for Stan's position, don't we? We can't just cruise right up in front like he was running an all-night cathouse."

"Suppose he won't go along with it?"

"Stan?" Carob laughed. "I already told you, he's H.D.'s fan."

Carob pulled back a flap in the fence and led the way. We followed him through the hole out onto acres of asphalt. The wind was picking up, sending low-flying clouds scuttling behind the darkened rim and towers of the stadium. Silently we picked our way across a no man's land of ice, broken glass and potholes full of water to the back wall of the stadium. Hugging the wall we continued halfway around the perimeter. Then Carob went on ahead by himself to make sure the coast was clear and to set it all up with Stan, and Art and I were left standing there shivering in the darkness with the wind howling and whistling over the deserted stadium. The place looked like a prison camp with rows of barbed wire strung on top of the fences and NO TRESPASSING — ATTACK DOG warnings posted everywhere. It seemed we waited out there forever before a light finally showed and Carob waved at us to come on in. A minute later we were sipping hot coffee in Stan's office.

Stan was a hefty, hospitable soul, transparently overjoyed by Carob's visit. It was all "H.D. this, H.D. that." Boy, we couldn't know what it meant to him to have H.D. drop in on him like this, we couldn't know what it meant to him to meet H.D.'s friends. And here he'd just been sitting eating his heart out over this item in the paper. Maybe H.D. had seen it — about these two guys who found this suitcase with $93,000 in it.

"Ninety-three thousand dollah's *in cash,* H.D., and the crummy bank gives them a hundred buck reward. You think

I ever get them kind of opportunities? I mean here I am with seven mouths to feed, gahdin' a fifty million dollash property at three seventy-six an hour. And sometimes late at night, just me and sixty thousand people who aren't around, it kinda gets to you. But what can I do? It's not like a stadium's a liquid asset. I mean let's just say I do go ahead and hire a contractor to sta't haulin' off the south end zone. Sooner or later somebody's gonna suspect something, know what I mean? But ninety-three thousand dollah's now — forty-six thousand five hundred per man and you don't hafta declare it either. I tell you it's enough to make an honest workin' man sick."

"Well it takes all kinds," Carob said. "The kind that's dumb and then the kind that just likes to sit around with good buddies enjoying himself watching films."

"You mean all of us?" Stan said, eyeing Cooper and me. "Right now? Jeez, H.D., I don't know. I mean, what if Greenley finds out?"

"Stan, I already told you once — these guys are my friends. What's more," Carob added, letting Stan in on a little secret, "Art here is going to give ol' H.D. some private expert advice. By letting us see those films, you'll be contributing directly to H.D.'s peace of mind and the good of the team. That is unless maybe you don't feel like contributing to H.D.'s peace of mind and the good of the team."

Stan's jaw quivered. "Well *shit*, H.D., if you put it that way — jeez." He strapped on his revolver and gathered up his keys and his walkie-talkie, then he and Carob led the way with flashlights down into a long, damp tunnel that curved deep under the stadium. We came to a couple of steps and a set of locked doors. Stan disconnected the security alarm and we went on through and up a flight of stairs and you could tell right away from the vague smell of mildew and the sudden sharp scent of wintergreen that we were near the locker rooms.

Stan and Carob ducked into an office and Stan held up the

flashlights while Carob searched the shelves of film for the box he wanted. Carob had told Cooper we were going to concentrate on Boston's first few offensive series — the ones that had failed, setting the course for the rest of the game. What Cooper didn't know was which part of the offensive unit he would have to focus his attention on, but here Stan stole some of Carob's thunder.

"I don't see how in the world you can stand lookin' at those New York films again, H.D. If you spend any more time studyin' those same films you're gonna be seein' offensive linemen in your sleep."

"Fuck," Carob said straightening up all at once.

"What's wrong, H.D.? What's the matter?"

"It's not here, that's what's wrong. It's gone."

"But it can't be, H.D. We put it back, remember?"

"Well it's gone now and I've got a damn good idea where we can find it."

"Oh no, H.D., we can't go up there."

"I'm going right now with or without you, Stan, and if you don't give me those keys I'm going to personally rip down every door from here to there." Stan looked as miserable as only a jolly fat man can and made little helpless pawing gestures in the air.

"If you're so worried about us getting caught, the place for you is back at your desk guarding things nice and tight." Carob grabbed the keys and told us to follow him; he was going to need our help. Art and I hesitated. "C'mon," Carob snapped. "We haven't got all night."

We went up two flights to the administrative level, where the floors were carpeted and the walls wood-paneled. Carob led us down a back corridor and let us in through a side door and suddenly we were standing in the very office where Cooper had been that afternoon. Carob tried a locked door off to one side of the room, then slid open one of the windows and we stepped out onto a balcony overlooking the field.

At the far end of the balcony, set in the wall at eye level, was a narrow window. Reaching up to his full height, straining like a weight lifter with all his might, Carob forced it open. "Rose," he said, handing me the flashlight, "I'm gonna give you a boost. You get inside, you open the door." I squeezed in through the window, dropped to the floor of what appeared to be a storage closet and let Carob and Cooper in from Greenley's office. Carob found the can of film in a couple of seconds.

"The sonofabitch," he said.

We rushed out of there back downstairs to the player's level to a room with a projector and screen. I held the flashlight while Carob threaded the film through the projector. He said we were going to have to rush it a little more than he'd planned. He reminded Cooper to pick carefully, that he would get one choice and one choice only.

Carob began with Boston's opening series, running each play over a couple of times for Cooper to get them set in his mind. For each play Carob reeled off down and yardage, the call in the huddle, the type of alignment, and a wealth of information I couldn't begin to follow about the responsibilities, frequencies, tendencies, and idiosyncrasies of each starting lineman from the tight end, Grumm, all the way across to the left tackle, Ohlenberg.

Boston's opening series started from the twenty, with New York already ahead 7–0, thanks to the help of the quick whistle on their kickoff return. The first play from scrimmage went off right tackle for four yards. A quick look-in pass over the middle picked up five more. But on third and one, the middle-linebacker, Woltgen, met the fullback head on for no gain.

"What's Woltgen's key in that situation?" Art asked. "It's the guard, isn't it?"

"Uh-huh," said Carob.

"Davis pulled. Why didn't he follow?"

"Maybe he saw something," Carob said.

"Run it again," Art said.

Carob ran the play over and over in slow motion. Art leaned forward in the dark, searching for some kind of sign in the left side of the line that might give away the direction of the play.

"Go on," he said finally, shaking his head. "I can't see it."

Boston punted the ball away. New York got a break on a pass interference call and before Boston saw the ball again they were behind by ten. The next series was the one that altered the course of the game.

On first down from the seventeen Santinelli ran right end for five yards. On second down Santinelli ran the same play to the left, but this time he was hauled down from behind for a six-yard loss before the play could develop. Cooper and Carob went down the line looking for the reason.

"Davis gets beat to the outside," Art said.

The players flew backwards up off the ground as Carob rewound the film. The play ran again, the projector clicking forward loudly in slow motion. "We use a lot of misdirection on their ends," Carob said. "Davy could have ridden him even wider."

"It doesn't matter. Grumm's man makes the tackle."

"Off a stunt, though."

"I see it. He was Crenshaw's to pick up, wasn't he? Crenshaw clean misses him."

"Look again," Carob said running it over. "Coming up right — now."

"Run it again." Art leaned forward, squinting. On the screen in slow motion we saw the left guard, Crenshaw, missing his block because he was partially tripped up as one of his own men — the tackle, Ohlenberg — toppled back across his legs. Could Ohlenberg have helped losing his feet? Could Crenshaw have got to his man anyhow? Carob kept running the play over and over. But the more I studied it, the more impossible it seemed to me to tell from the film alone what was really going on. As much football as I had watched over the years, there was no way for me to know what it felt like from the inside.

"OK," Art said. "Go on."

The next play, sent in by Burke from the sidelines, was the real heartbreaker: a daringly called, beautifully executed third-and-eleven screen that went eighty-four yards for the score.

"Go, Nattie, go," Carob shouted as Redding gathered in the pass and cut upfield behind his shield of blockers, bobbing and weaving, picking up speed like a downhill skier. "*Do* it baby, *do* it," he cried as Redding broke into the clear, streaking up the sideline. "Oh my, ain't that a thing of beauty. Just *look* at the way the good Lord intended for a screen to be run."

Carob reran the play. With the repetition I saw what he meant, saw the play not as the result of the combined actions of eleven separate men, but rather as the embodiment of something else, something whole, something with a life of its own. The play unfolded with all the flowing harmony and secret inner purpose of a time-lapse film of a blossoming flower: first the disguise of the anticipated long pass, the line setting up to block, the receivers taking off, the quarterback dropping back. Then the deception: the right side of the line letting their men manage to slip through the pocket, the quarterback feigning sudden desperate retreat. And already the receiver drifting out for the ball now spiraling on its way, a wall of blockers forming instantly out of the apparent chaos, the receiver following them upfield now, one hand on the lead blocker's waist, as gently as some guy guiding his date across a crowded room.

A perfect play sprung at a moment when the course of the entire game could have been reversed. A perfect play in every respect but one: it wouldn't stand. On a late flag, the umpire, John Murdock, called holding in the left side of the line.

"Jesus Christ," Art cried. "How the hell could Murdock do that? Even if it was holding, it was too far away from the play to matter. They're not supposed to make that call."

"They're not supposed to," Carob said, "but they can. It's a judgment thing."

"Well what the hell were those damn fools doing anyhow? Why risk a holding call where it wasn't even necessary?"

On the film Grumm, Ohlenberg, and Davis all had their hands in. You couldn't tell from the film whether they were in fact holding because you couldn't feel the pressure. But if it was holding it certainly wasn't any more so than the kind of thing that happened on almost any play. All you knew for sure was that after the penalty Boston was forced to punt from their own end zone, and seconds later, instead of only trailing 10–7, they were down 17–0.

Suddenly the building reverberated like a steel drum with a tremendous metallic boom. I grabbed a flashlight and stepped out into the hall in time to see Stan come running towards me, waving his arms and shouting. He shoved past me into the room. "H.D.," he gasped, his fat chest heaving. "I'm sorry. I really am, but this is it. You gotta beat it right now."

"Stan, what on earth are you talking about?"

"The cops, H.D. Somebody's phoned in a report of vandals. I tried to tell them it hadda be false but they're comin'. They'll be out front in seconds."

Art was on his feet in a flash, but Carob was even quicker, clamping a massive black fist on his shoulder. "Listen Cooper," he said, "I don't know what this is about. I had nothing to do with it."

"For the love of mercy, H.D., can't you guys hash it over later. If they catch you all in here, I'll lose my job."

"Can we make it out the tunnel, Stan?"

"H.D., you know for yourself those doors double-lock from the outside."

"What about across the field then?"

"The gates are all locked, H.D. The only unfenced spot is the corner by the end zone ramp, but that's at least a forty-foot drop."

"It'll have to do," Carob said, pulling Art and me after him. He took off down the corridor and we sprinted right at his heels. Halfway down the hall he dove into one of the training rooms and popped out a second later with a coil of rope. At the end of the corridor he stopped and told us he'd cover our backs; if he didn't make it to the car inside of five minutes we should take off without him. He handed me the rope and the car keys and pushed us out a door.

It was pitch black. We stumbled up a passageway and emerged suddenly into the open stadium. Somewhere nearby sirens were wailing. We started running out across the field. It seemed to take forever, like running in a dream across the floor of an endless canyon. When we reached the far side I gave Art a boost up over the wall into the stands. He took the rope, then pulled me up after him. The sirens were screaming louder now. We rushed up the steps along the edge of the stands, looking for the spot about two thirds of the way up where the drop to the exit ramp was supposed to be shortest. I peered over the side. In the dark it was impossible to tell how long a drop it was.

"Don't let me look," Art said. "How far is it?"

"Not that far," I said, tying the end of the rope to the railing, being careful to waste as little as possible.

All at once a blinding light flashed, and shouts echoed through the stadium. We ducked behind a row of seats while a powerful searchlight at the opposite end of the stadium rapidly crisscrossed the field. We watched spellbound as the beam of light began systematically sweeping the seats.

I crawled back to the wall, keeping as low as possible.

"For chrissake Jesus hurry, Jack. It's coming closer."

I finished tying off the knot and threw the rope over the side. It was short of the bottom — by how much I couldn't tell.

Art took one look over the railing. "Oh my God, Rose, are you crazy, it's got to be at least two hundred feet."

"It looks worse than it is. Go on."

"Jack, I'll never make it. My leg won't hold up."

"You'll make it," I said winding the rope around him. He closed his eyes and swung out over the side.

I went over right after him. The drop at the bottom was less than ten feet.

"You all right?" I said, helping him up.

"I think so," he said; but it turned out he was limping too badly to run.

He leaned on my shoulder for support and we hurried across a back service road to the fence bordering the stadium grounds. Incredibly there were no cops around. Keeping our heads low we followed the fence until we came to a hole big enough to crawl through. Behind me Art hesitated.

"Jack," he panted. "Someone's coming."

I looked up to see a figure chasing after us. First I thought it was Carob — then I saw the glint of metal in his hand.

"Art, run for it," I cried.

It was too late. Art stood up slowly, raising his hands high in the air; I did the same.

The man stopped. We saw the stocky outline of him, we saw the raised gun, but we couldn't make out the shadowed face under the brim of his hat. He played a flashlight across our faces, momentarily blinding us. The next thing we knew he was running away across the asphalt.

"Jesus," Art breathed out.

We crawled through the fence, cut deep into the woods and circled all the way around to the far end of the parking lot and Carob's car.

Cooper's leg and shoulder were hurting, but there didn't seem to be any serious damage. He was against waiting for Carob. Even if Carob wasn't in on it from the start, there was no telling what he might say if the police caught him. But just then Carob himself came crashing out of the woods and slid into the driver's seat and we pulled out. Carob wasn't even out of breath. He said Stan had sent the cops rushing off in the wrong direction. Carob had not only gotten away scot-free, he'd even put the film back in Greenley's office. He had no idea what had gone wrong or who the guy chasing us could have been. But one thing was for sure: the last thing Carob would ever do was rat on buddies.

Art didn't say anything. He just tore off a piece of paper, scribbled on it and handed it, folded, to Carob. Carob glanced down at it, nodded, then reached into his jacket and pulled out his own neatly folded slip of paper. He handed both slips to me. The names were the same: Ohlenberg.

LeRoy Ohlenberg, Carob explained on the drive back up to Boston, was the kind of guy who could make you ashamed to call yourself a football player. Not just because of his miserable, pinched poor-white stinginess — it was the help-lessness of the guy that got Carob. Ohlenberg could hardly spit straight without first consulting the playbook. On the field he was the coaches' creature; off the field he was plain lost. His great expectations for cashing in from football in civilian life were matched only by his complete incompetence. Carob knew for a fact he had made some hopelessly disastrous investment in a hunting lodge back in Arkansas; his own brother had practically skinned the pants off him. In this year's preseason Ohlenberg was depressed about that and about the fact that he wasn't playing much and that he'd had to take a salary cut and that pretty soon he was going to have to hang them up. For a while it looked like he might be cut, then the rumor was they had him up on the trading block, but a couple of injuries in the line just before the regular season made him a starter again.

Ohlenberg was a simple, greedy, embittered guy, a perfect mark for someone as slick as Calabrese. Carob had seen them together more than once. Carob had tried to talk to Ohlenberg about it, but Ohlenberg just told him to stick to his own side of the tracks. After that Carob made a point of keeping an eye on him. He knew that LeRoy was saying more than he should to Calabrese about the dissension on the team, but it wasn't until the New York game that he saw what he'd been afraid of.

It was what Art had seen too, close up and in slow motion. No glaringly bad plays, no flagrant fouls, no grossly bungled assignments, just a consistent pattern of poor, sloppy play. Only in retrospect, under the closest scrutiny, could you see just how significant it was. Because Ohlenberg's worst lapses were reserved for those few key plays of the first quarter, when it was still within Boston's power to alter the outcome. For the rest of the game, Ohlenberg played with reckless abandon, and was even singled out for praise by the TV announcers for his tenacity in a losing cause. But by then, for a disheartened and demoralized team, the damage had been done.

After the game Carob went to confront him, but Ohlenberg had taken off without even changing out of his gear. Carob tried to find him, only to learn later that he had dropped from sight.

For Carob's money, if we were looking for the one player whose performance had most affected the outcome of that game, that man was Ohlenberg.

The question was what to do about it.

"Forget it," advised my lawyer friend when Cooper and I met with him the next night at his house. "No D.A. with his self-interest firmly in place is going to go wading voluntarily into the political quicksand of a sports fix case, certainly not the one in that football-crazy suburban district, unless the evidence is so overwhelming that he's either assured of a victory, or put in a position where he has no choice but to act. And good hard first-rate evidence is the one thing, despite all your efforts, that you lack." Maybe Cooper and I had heard certain rumors, maybe one player looked bad on film and another didn't happen to like him — what of it? It was all circumstantial evidence and hearsay. On the basis of that the police wouldn't arrest anyone, and the prosecutors wouldn't prosecute. At the very least we needed irrefutable testimony backed up by hard evidence — photographs, tapes, checks, receipts, etc. — but for that kind of evidence you almost had to start an inside investigation of a conspiracy before it was even carried out. It was virtually impossible to dig up that stuff after the fact, and make it stick.

Therefore, my friend said, forget it. If he were collecting a fee from us that would be his considered opinion, not only because it was hopeless, but because he'd stand a much better chance of collecting said fee if either of us were around to pay it. From everything we'd said about Calabrese he wouldn't care to bet on our chances. In a race between our efforts to convince an official to investigate, and Calabrese's efforts to stop us, we were by far the dark horse.

"But since you're not paying for it anyhow," he said, "I might as well go ahead and throw in some free advice for what it's worth.

"If you could somehow convince Ohlenberg to come forward — by threatening him, by playing on his guilt or his resentments or his vanity, whatever it might take — if you could just get him to come forward with firsthand evidence, that would be a horse of a different color. Then, depending on the nature of the conspiracy and the evidence, we could set up a meeting with an assistant State or U.S. Attorney; even the D.A. himself might feel compelled to move. It might be the kind of case he would relish: some poor hard-luck football player, preyed on and exploited by rapacious criminal elements, coming forward out of the fundamental goodness of his heart to make a clean confession. Hell, if we could produce a witness like that — complete with a southern accent and maybe a tear or two in his eye — the D.A. might not give a damn about the quality of our evidence."

That was a course that made practical sense and gave us a fighting chance of coming out of it in one piece. Our friend Kauffman was already checking to see if he could find any connection between Ohlenberg and his son, wasn't he? Why not use his resources to locate Ohlenberg while we laid low for a while. There was no point in exposing ourselves more than necessary right now; there was nothing more we could do anyhow until Ohlenberg turned up.

In the car on the way back to Somerville Art nearly went through the roof. "*Cooperate* with Ohlenberg? That friend of yours must be crazy, Jack. Is that what he thinks we've gone through all this for? To cooperate with the sonofabitch who did it?"

"That's what he appeared to be saying."

"Well what about you then? Is that what you think it comes down to?"

I was suddenly angry at him. "What did you expect to happen? Or didn't you ever really think we'd get this far?"

"I don't know. I knew we could do it, Jack, but I guess I just never really thought about how it would work out when we got there."

"Well we're there now, so you'd better start thinking fast." I said we had to decide if we just wanted to see one guy punished, or if we wanted to get to the bottom of it and have the full truth come out. In either case, like it or not, we needed Ohlenberg. Until we got to him we ourselves wouldn't know for sure the truth about that game. Ohlenberg was the only one who could tell us what had actually happened in that game and who was really behind it.

Back at the house Miss McDonald told us that Kauffman had been calling for hours. I called him immediately.

"Where have the two of you been?" he said. He sounded excited. "Is everything all right up there?"

"Yes. We went to a lawyer's. Listen, Mr. Kauffman, there's something we need to ask of you."

"Never mind, forget it. I found him."

"What — Ohlenberg? Already?"

"No. *Him*. The nut. The meshuggener. Collect from Mexico City the call comes, so who else can it be?"

"Your son? You mean he's all right?"

"Thank God, he's fine. You wouldn't believe it if I told you the things that boy is capable of. Now he's working already on some new crazy scheme."

"Mr. Kauffman, what did he say about the game?"

"To tell you the truth I didn't press him for details. They used my name to place the bet, but it was no big deal. He and his friends just picked up on a few rumors: that business about getting to the players was only something my boy embellished for my sake. Which I guess puts the real joke on me, doesn't it?"

"What rumors? Which friends?"

Kauffman went right on chatting cheerfully as if we were talking in two different languages. The main thing was that his son was all right and in touch. Ida and he wanted us to know how grateful they were for everything we'd done. As soon as Martin was safely home and everything had blown over he was going to send us a nice reward to show his appreciation for a job well done.

"Kauffman, listen, this is crazy. You know we got in this to find out the truth about that game. You know Marty can help us."

There was a long silence. When he spoke again all the sporty cheer had drained out of his voice.

"They say you're friends of Burke's. They say you know."

"Know what? What does Burke have to do with it?"

"You tell me. You were using me to try to get at them through my son, weren't you?"

"Kauffman, I have no idea what you're talking about."

"Maybe so. What's the difference? Rose, you're a smart boy, too smart maybe, so listen to me good now because I can tell you this only once: forget that game, do you understand? It can't be done. These people are big — much bigger than you seem to realize. They've forbidden him to see me. They're watching him and they're watching you. If you persist with this you're not only risking your own lives you're directly endangering my son — and I can't allow that. I beg of you, please, look out now for yourselves. Do you understand? Right now."

I stood there listening to the maddening buzz the phone makes when someone hangs up on you. Then I laid the receiver on the hook and went upstairs. Cooper was already in bed.

"Well what did the old man have for us tonight?"

"Art," I said softly, "get dressed. We've got to get out of here."

"What — in the middle of the night? Aren't you maybe over-reacting just a little, Jack? I mean you don't want to start going off the deep end on us like I did in Florida."

"Art, do what I say. Get dressed. Right now."

I started throwing clothes into a suitcase. Art was still getting his things together when I went down to warm up the car. It was a little after midnight and very cold. Art struggled out the door, both arms wrapped around the half-opened, overflowing suitcase. I jumped out of the car and ran up the steps to help him.

"For chrissake, Rose, I'm coming, I'm coming, will you just calm down. One lousy minute more one way or another isn't going to . . ." Suddenly he froze, his mouth half open. I turned and saw the dark car rolling silently towards us. Art slammed into me screaming and as we went down the air exploded. The car roared away with a screech of rubber and then there was silence. I rolled out from under him and picked myself up. There was glass all over the place. Art pulled himself to his knees. Pieces of glass glittered in his hair, and there was a trickle of blood down the side of his face.

"Are you all right?" He nodded. We stood there, getting our wind back. The shots had shattered the windowpanes and the door behind us. Lights were popping on up and down the street. A dozen people would be calling the cops, but the cops couldn't help us now.

I grabbed Art's suitcase. He wanted to explain to Miss McDonald; I told him we'd do our explaining later from the road.

We got in the car and pulled out. In the distance a siren began to wail.

PART FOUR

TWELVE

Before daylight the next morning, having made sure we weren't followed, we arrived at Burke's place in Vermont.

Jody was waiting up for us, the lights of the cabin shining through the woods. She pressed us for details while she cleaned Art's cuts but there wasn't much we could tell her. It was a dark sedan, and the shots came from the passenger side — that was all we knew. Not that Art needed more. It was Calabrese's work for sure. What else could it be? First he threatened us, then the minute we linked Ohlenberg's name to his — this.

"Do you think they really meant to kill you?" Jody asked, dabbing at Art's face with iodine.

"If they didn't," he said, wincing, "I don't know how they could have cut it any closer."

She turned to me with the same question in her eyes.

"I don't have any idea," I said, and I didn't. Maybe the shock still hadn't worn off. I felt as though I'd just woken up from a dream in which I'd been right on the edge of some important realization. An instant earlier everything had made perfect sense; now suddenly it made no sense at all. Why this shooting — why now? If it was Calabrese why had he waited so long? And if Calabrese had acted simply because of our identification of Ohlenberg — how had he found out so fast? And where did Kauffman's call fit into it all?

Art had ready answers for everything. Maybe in the beginning Calabrese hadn't believed we knew enough. Maybe he thought we would scare. After the stadium break-in they must have realized we meant business. Maybe the guy who chased us reported to Calabrese or Greenley, or maybe Greenley himself just put two and two together and warned Calabrese. As for Kauffman's backing out, it stood to reason, didn't it, that the closer we got to the truth the more likely they might try to pressure him through his son. But that didn't matter now, Cooper argued. What mattered was that Kauffman's sudden reversal was all the proof we needed that we were on the right track. Kauffman had said they knew we knew, hadn't he?

"He said a lot of things. He said we were friends of Burke's."

"Well of course we are, Jack. From Greenley's point of view what the hell else are we?"

We had some breakfast, then I called my lawyer friend in Boston. He didn't seem the least bit surprised about the shooting.

"Does anybody else know where you are?"

"No."

"Then keep it that way. There's no point in getting your heads blown off if you can't pin anything on them. I'll see what I can find out about Calabrese, it's possible he's vulnerable on other grounds. Until then stay put. And don't let anyone even guess you're still around."

His advice notwithstanding I wanted to make sure Carob was all right, and to warn him. But there was no answer at his place until that evening.

"Rose? — thank God. You all right? Tin man, too? When I heard what happened man I was scared. Rose, nobody my size should ever have to be that scared. You understand? Ever."

"We've been trying to reach you all day."

"Never mind. Where are you?"

"We're around."

"All right — don't tell me. Just tell me from wherever the hell you are how soon you can be in Boston."

"It's better if we don't move for a while, H.D."

"You'll move. For your own damn good you're gonna move plenty fast when you hear what I have to say: I found Ohlenberg."

"What? Where?"

"Right here in town. I've got him on ice for you but he won't keep forever."

"Is he talking?"

"Is he talking," Carob said, hesitating. "Oh yeah, most eloquently. You'd better come see for yourselves, Rose. I don't want there to be any misunderstanding."

Four hours later, a little after ten o'clock, Art and I pulled into the parking lot of a motel just off the Mass. Pike outside of Boston. Carob answered our knock immediately, and for a second his great body filled the doorway. Then he stepped back. Ohlenberg was sprawled out across the bed, his head slumped up against the wall. There was a dark brown stain running down his chest.

"Oh my God, he's dead," Art said.

"Bet he wishes he was," Carob said. "He's just good and drunk. I pickled him real nice for you so he'd keep."

Ohlenberg wasn't so far gone that after Carob hauled him into an icy shower he wasn't blubbering away in a heavy Arkansas twang telling us we-all should just leave him be. Carob shoved him down into a chair, jerking his thick head upright by a fistful of pale soaking wet hair.

"LeRoy," he said, shaking him hard. "Listen to me. They're here. You understand?"

Ohlenberg nodded. His eyes were narrow red slits. "I knowed it," he said. "I knowed they was comin'."

"Tell them why they're here. They want to hear it from you."

Ohlenberg's eyes began to close.

Carob shook him again. "Tell them."

" 'Cause of what I done."

"What did you do? Say it."

Ohlenberg shut his eyes, grinning. " 'Cause I shot one with the spotlights. I don't care. I hate fox."

Carob reached over to the dresser, where there was a clutter of bottles and glasses, and grabbed a thermos.

"Oh no, H.D., I don't feel so good. Don't make me drink no more of that alkyhaul."

"You're gonna feel a lot worse before I'm through with you if you don't tell them," Carob said, pulling Ohlenberg's head back and pouring black coffee down his throat.

Ohlenberg spit up half of it, laughing. "The warden he said, 'LeRoy, son, you're a big boy now but that don't give you no license to break the law on account of what them fox hunters done that one time to your dog.' I promised him and I ain't never done nothin' I had to be ashamed of since."

"The hell you ain't," Carob said slapping his face hard. "Now take a good look at them. Tell them."

Ohlenberg looked out at us through his glassy, pig-red eyes. His head rolled slightly from side to side. "It's all right, boys. I don't blame you none for comin' to get me. Jest get it over with."

"That's right," Carob said looking up at us. "They've come to get you."

"Because of what you did, isn't it?" Art said. "Because of what you did in that game."

" 'Cause of what I did," Ohlenberg said, nodding again. "Seems more like he sent you 'cause of what I didn't do."

"What do you mean what you didn't do?" Art said. "Who sent us?"

"Vic," Ohlenberg said. "Vic Calabrese, he sent you."

So that was it, just the way Carob wanted us to hear it, from Ohlenberg's own lips. We pulled most of the story out of him before he passed out again; Carob filled in the rest. It was pretty pathetic. As the price for his "loans" the summer before, Calabrese had demanded more and more inside information as the season progressed until finally Ohlenberg got nervous and went to Burke. Burke told him to have nothing more to do with Calabrese; and that might have been the end of it, if Greenley hadn't found out. He told Ohlenberg that Burke should have reported him, and that Greenley could have Ohlenberg thrown out of the League, but he was going to overlook it because he had his own suspicions about Burke and he wanted Ohlenberg to stay in touch with Calabrese as a secret informant. But when Ohlenberg reported that Calabrese was pressing him to "do something" in the New York game, Greenley shrugged him off, telling him that was his problem. Ohlenberg was so scared and confused that when the day of the game rolled around he wasn't in any shape to play ball. After the holding call that cost Boston the touchdown he asked Burke to take him out, but Burke just said the call wasn't Ohlenberg's fault.

After the game Ohlenberg took off for Arkansas and he thought the whole thing had blown over. But yesterday Greenley summoned Ohlenberg to Boston and warned him that two of Calabrese's men were out to get him. Greenley also told him that Burke was gone and he was running the show now, and Ohlenberg better not breathe a word about any of this to anyone. Ohlenberg ended up at the Back Bay bar owned by one of his teammates, which was where Carob found him.

"There was nothing to it after all," Carob said. "I'm afraid we just got taken in by appearances. All of us."

"I can't believe it," Art said, pacing back and forth across the room.

Ohlenberg lay snoring away on the bed, dead to the world. At least, I thought, the dumb sucker had an excuse. What was ours? If we had been taken in, it was by a reality of our own making. For all our trouble, what had we uncovered? A half-assed, bungled attempt by a pair of sharpies to manipulate some poor sap of a player for their own ends; Greenley, the ambitious opportunist, who in his rivalry with Burke had played a little fast and loose with his beloved proper channels; and Calabrese, a big-time gambler looking for a little edge. Both of them, on their own terms, had been leveling with us all along. They'd both tried to tell us to stay out of their business, that we were sticking our necks out for nothing, that there hadn't been any big conspiracy, any big payoff, any fix.

"I can't believe it," Art said again, standing over the bed staring at Ohlenberg. "I just can't."

"Face it," said Carob. "Those are the facts. It's over."

"But there just had to be something to that game. I mean Kauffman's son, Bill's charges, our getting shot at, for chrissake."

That vague, unsettled feeling of a half-forgotten dream took hold of me again. Burke's face flashed in my mind as I had seen it on the day of the game, the network of wrinkles around his eyes as he stared out at the field, the look of utter despair when he turned to face the camera, the knowledge in his eyes. I remembered Kauffman's words: "They know you know. They know you're friends of Burke's."

"The shooting," I said, thinking out loud.

"Sure," Art said. "That's what I mean. Now just take the shooting. Why would Calabrese risk that if he wasn't involved in some way? I mean it just doesn't make sense if there was nothing to it."

"It doesn't," I said. "Unless none of it is what it seems."

"For chrissake, Jack, c'mon, will you? Things are already confusing enough without your going bonkers on us now."

"Look, Art, just listen to me for a second. What if it were someone else altogether — someone else we didn't even suspect. What if they thought we were onto them — that we knew something, something maybe that Burke knew."

"Then the shooting could have been someone else, not Calabrese at all," Art said.

"That whole mixup at the stadium," Carob said. "Somebody called the police. And what about that guy who chased you?"

"Christ, yes," Art said. "And that time they tore our room apart. They've been watching us all along. But who, Jack?"

"I don't know," I said. "But whatever it is they think we know, we don't know it."

"Well whatever it is," Carob said, "you don't have to try to figure it out right here, right now, do you?" Carob advised us to hightail it out of there for wherever that someplace safe we'd just come from was, because for all we knew they might be watching him, too, or even LeRoy. He'd take care of Ohlenberg. We should just get out of there.

We got in the car and hit the road and for a while neither of us said very much of anything, each of us wrestling with the question of what it was they knew, and thought we knew. But no matter what line I took my thoughts kept circling back to the same point — the image of Burke as I'd seen him the day of that game. And remembering that day I remembered, too, the first time I'd seen Art in that bar in New York, sitting there on the stool beside me in that awkward stiff-shouldered way he had of holding himself, as though his body were something he wore, as though it were a suit of armor. Now, just two short months later, there was only the road, the night, and the fact of our presence together through it.

"Well?" I said finally, to break the silence.

"You're asking me, Jack, what I think?" he said, his face all shadows in the dark of the car. "Jesus, you should know better than that by now. Every lousy idea I've had has turned out to be wrong. And now we're nowhere — nowhere at all."

"Nowhere," I said, "except for the fact that you were right from the start that there was something to that game. Nowhere except for the fact that whatever it was, your friend Bill is the key to understanding it."

The light from oncoming cars played slowly across his face, then left him in the darkness again. When he finally spoke his voice sounded very far away. "You're saying now that Bill was in on it, is that it, Jack?"

"You're the one who said it," I said.

He stared straight ahead. In the familiar weight of his silence I remembered all the times he'd been reluctant to talk about Burke's past, or even to speculate about Burke's way of handling the fix.

"It's even coming between us now, isn't it, Jack? Maybe we should just quit while we're still ahead."

"*Quit?* Quit what Art? Quit knowing what we don't even know? Quit being ourselves?" I told him that the only way we could end it now was by finding out what it was we were supposed to know, and if there was something he knew about Burke that might make a difference he'd better tell me now before it was too late. Kauffman had said they knew we were friends of Burke's. Burke had known something about that game and yet he had hesitated to act. Had he been prevented from acting? Or was there another possible explanation.

Art sat there stiffly, watching the road as it came at us out of the night. "There was one thing," he began slowly. "I would have mentioned it before if I thought it mattered any. It's no big deal really. I already told you once how it was when Bill quit playing ball — his marriage busting up, everybody blaming him for the way the team was going."

"I remember. You said there was a lot of talk. What kind of talk?"

"Talk. Just junk, that's all, from when he first broke in with the old Boston club. He was young — he liked the girls and the good times and maybe the crowd he ran around with was a little fast. Hell, we didn't all go through Harvard on a silver spoon, you know. It was a different kind of a time. You met all kinds of people in the service; you knew all kinds of people from the old neighborhood."

"What kind of people?"

"How the hell should I know. Guys. People."

"Gamblers, Art?"

He looked away. "I guess," he said faintly, "a few of them were. But that doesn't mean he did what they said," he said turning to me. "That doesn't mean he ever laid down."

"You never had any reason to believe it?"

"He was my friend, Jack. I believed the best of him."

"And the truth of him?"

I felt his eyes on me in the dark. "I knew him, Jack. You play ball with someone and you know them in ways you don't know anyone else. Just because they said those things once — that doesn't mean anything about any of this now, you know?"

"Maybe," I said. "But we've got no choice now but to try to find out what he was up to, wherever that takes us."

The next day, with Jody's help, I went through Burke's papers. But if I was looking for obvious signs of guilt in the form of unaccounted-for income or expenditures, I didn't find them. To the contrary, the only striking fact that emerged was just how spartanly Burke had lived for a man who worked hard all his life, and how little he had to show for it at the end.

By the end of the day I felt lost completely. Not only did we seem light-years away from finding out what Burke had known about that game and why he had hesitated to come forward with his knowledge, but the man himself seemed more mysterious than ever. I was left with the familiar realization of how impossible it is to ever understand someone else's life. I had a hundred images of Burke, and I couldn't begin to see through them to the man himself.

"He wasn't an easy man to know," Jody said later. We

were sitting in front of the fire with drinks, waiting for Art to get back from his walk with Argus in the woods. The little patch of sky outside the window was turning a dusky pink and the cabin was fragrant with the rich smell of stew simmering on the stove. "I can see him only through my mother's eyes — the way she said he looked when he came for her."

Jody smiled. "That's how she always put it — the first time she laid eyes on him." Jody told me her mother's family had kept a farm in Essex, just north of Boston; it was a beautiful old place that looked out over the salt marsh to the sea. Her mother went there after Richard's death, to await Jody's birth, and she stayed on through the winter, trying to wall out the world and what had happened. But it wasn't easy. Both her family and Richard's were socially prominent, and the world kept intruding.

The accident had been a hit-and-run, and it was covered in all the Boston papers. Which was where Bill Burke had first seen her picture. Billy Burke, at twenty-six a war hero and a professional quarterback, a man's man with a taste for beautiful women and a rakish grin that caught their eye. Bill Burke was the kind of man who knew what he wanted and who took it as if the world were a banquet spread for his pleasure.

That spring an old friend came to visit and brought someone along. It was a beautiful May day and she had taken Jody down to the field behind the house. A warm salty breeze was blowing up from the sea, making deep waves in the tall marsh grass. She said the sun shone on his head and shoulders as he came walking down the hill to meet them. And she saw the way he walked — the purpose in his stride — as if the earth were his. Later he told her that if there had been purpose in his step that day it was because he was rushing to get to her before he forgot everything he'd planned to say. But she knew she was in love with him before he ever said a word.

"I don't think she ever really got over his leaving," Jody said, "though with time I think she came to look on it in the best light possible." Richard's death had been a terrible shock. She and Richard had been vacationing on the Cape. He had gone for an evening walk with his dog, Argus — the first Argus, the same dog that was later Bill's. The car's impact broke both his legs. If whoever had done it had only gotten help, if they'd even just driven on and left him lying there beside the road where someone else could have found him, the doctors said he would have lived. Instead they stopped and dragged him off the road out of sight, where he bled to death. The police eventually tried to charge some local racketeer with the killing, but he came up with a host of alibis, and by then Catherine just wanted to forget.

Bill had the strength she needed, and he made it possible for her to find that strength inside herself. But Bill always felt as if he had to protect her from the world. He was very conscious of having taken Richard's place: Richard had been bright and talented and cultured in ways that Bill seemed to feel he could never measure up to. When things began to go bad in his football career, he turned suddenly against the marriage. Catherine loved him too much to try to hold him against his will, though she kept hoping their separation was only temporary. Years later, just before she died, she told Jody that whenever the phone rang at odd hours the thought would still cross her mind that it was Bill finally calling.

"I guess, although she came to accept it in the end, she never really did understand." Jody laid her head back against the couch, her hair falling in a dark curve against the white of her throat. "When he called me that last night, I thought he was finally going to explain. But he only said that it was too late, that he could never hope to make me understand. So I guess now I'll never know — any more than she ever did."

It was dark by the time Art got back, soaking wet to his knees from chasing Argus all over the woods. After dinner we sat around the table over coffee, thumbing through old photographs that Jody had found scattered among Bill's papers, pictures of Jody and Catherine mainly, but also some shots of Bill from before the marriage, in his uniform during the war, at nightclub tables, everyone grinning and toasting the camera with glasses of champagne.

Cooper pounced on a shot of Bill seated on a train and shouted, "That's my elbow! And that there's the tip of my knee." And then there was a shot of Art himself, clear as day, standing in front of a car that looked not unlike our Chevy in Florida, Art young and gangly under a fuzzy Fifties flattop, gawky and startled, like something newly hatched from an egg.

I looked up from the table and nearly jumped out of my skin: a face was pressed up against the kitchen window peering in at us.

"Someone's out there," I shouted, reaching for my jacket and the rifle. Argus started barking wildly, clawing at the door.

"Jesus, Jack," Art said hanging onto my sleeve. "Maybe you shouldn't go out there."

"It's probably just whoever's been harassing Jody," I said opening the door. Jody grabbed Argus's collar.

"Be careful," she said. "Please."

I stepped out onto the porch. Everything was perfectly still. All I could see was the black line of woods against the night sky. I went down the steps and crunched slowly up the snow-packed path. The wind riffled the tops of the trees, carrying the fresh scent of pine. I walked to the end of the driveway where the road ran like a white river through the trees.

Suddenly at the top of the rise a figure darted out of the woods. I shouted. He stopped for an instant, then took off up the road. I threw down the rifle and started running after him, yelling. Looking back over his shoulder, he stumbled and fell. I came running towards him and saw, too late, the gun.

"Stay away from me," he cried, scrambling to his feet. "Go back."

He was short and thin. He seemed young. I couldn't make out his face in the dark, but I could see how the gun in his hand was shaking.

"Who are you?" I said. "What do you want here?"

He took a step back. "Just stay away from me. I don't want any trouble from you." He glanced past me; Art and Jody were rushing up the road towards us.

"Stay right there," he shouted as they came up beside me. "All of you. Just don't anybody come after me." He started backing away.

"Jack," Jody whispered putting a hand on my arm. "It's him."

"The one who's been spying on you?"

"Yes, but don't you see — it's the guy in that picture, the one you've been looking for."

"Christ. Kauffman," I shouted, taking a step after him. "It's you, isn't it?"

He froze. "Get away from me," he cried. "I mean it."

He was about fifty feet away from us. "Kauffman — Marty — listen to me. We're trying to help you."

"You can't. Not you, not my father, nobody."

"Give us a chance," I said, taking another step after him.

"I didn't know what it was about. They said all I had to do was get the bets down. I didn't know it would turn out like this."

"Like what?" I said, stepping closer. "Tell us?"

He shook his head. "They'll kill me if I talk. They'll kill you too if you don't stop it."

"Stop what? How can we stop?"

"Give it to them. Burke's stuff — the papers. Give them what they want."

I was less than fifteen feet away from him. "What papers?" I said moving even closer.

He started shaking his head wildly. "Oh no. You've got them. I know you do." He held the gun straight out at me. "You get out of here," he cried. "You just get out of here before I tell them where you are." All at once he turned and broke into a run. Half a minute later we heard a car start up. Its taillights flashed red for an instant, then vanished.

We stood there in the road spellbound. "Jesus," Art said at last. "Papers. Stuff of Burke's. What the hell was he talking about?"

"Whatever it is," I said, "they think we have it."

"And the ones who were watching me," Jody said. "It was them all along, wasn't it?"

"That's right — sure. Whatever it is, they had reason to think you might have it; or that it might be here."

"But I've been all over the place already. You've seen all the papers of his I have."

"LeClair," Art burst out. "Don't you remember, Jack? Bill told him that he was sitting on it all, but that he needed time to finish. That night LeClair called, Bill said he'd just gotten in from working on it."

"He could have meant his shack," Jody said. "He told me he used to work there in the warm weather."

"Where is it?" I said.

"It's just across the stream," Art said. "I chased Argus way the hell over there this afternoon before I finally caught up with him."

We went back to the cabin for warmer clothes, flashlights, and the keys to the shack. Then leaving Jody behind to start packing, Art and I trudged back through the woods, with Argus running in excited circles ahead of us. We crossed the stream and climbed the bank and there in a little clearing was a tiny screened-in shack. Around one end of it were muddied patches where Argus had dug down through the snow. The padlock on the door was frozen fast. Art held the light while I worked it open, and we pushed in the door. The shack was empty except for a desk, a chair, a rusted typewriter and a hurricane lamp. There was nothing in any of the drawers, no papers anywhere, but Art, undaunted, started running his hands along the walls, stamping on the wooden floor as he went.

"Jack," he said suddenly, "help me move the desk." As we shoved the desk back the floorboards rattled. "Holy Jesus," Art cried, dropping to his knees, ripping off his gloves. He pulled up the loose floorboards, uncovering a mound of clean sawdust. We clawed down through it and hauled up a canvas sack. With frozen fingers, Art fumbled at the knotted cord.

Inside the canvas sack was a waterproof plastic bag, and inside that bag were bundles of tightly bound folders.

We tore into the papers right there, by flashlight. There was an incredible amount of material, all of it carefully sorted and labeled by Burke:

— Charts recording the performance of each team in the League over the past few years.

— Financial reports, with the data painstakingly broken down for each team to indicate the percent of income derived from television versus live gate and other sources, as well as the comparative success of each team correlated with respect to the size of its particular market.

— Newspaper clippings and private League memoranda documenting the declining position of the League within the sports industry as a whole, as reflected in decreasing percentages of revenues and TV ratings. Official estimates of the economic impact of victories by major-market teams measured in terms of heightened media interest, higher ratings, and increased advertising revenues. Compilations of the administrative steps taken in the past season to strengthen the image and appeal of pro football — among them the new rules and procedures for the organization and assigning of referees.

— Pages of detailed, handwritten summaries of all the games of every big-city team over the past season . . .

— And a plain spiral notebook, which Art opened.

"Jesus Christ."

"What is it, Art?"

He handed it to me. I leafed through it quickly. It appeared to be a comprehensive play-by-play study of half a dozen games Burke had selected in advance. Each of them involved at least one team from a major market. Each was played before a national television audience. In every case, the team that Burke had predicted would win — the team from the largest market — had in fact won. And each game had two further things in common: the same elite crew of refs had worked all the games, and the final outcome was substantially influenced by at least one or more questionable calls. And the name most often circled in red for making those decisive calls, right up to and including the game between Boston and New York, was John Murdock.

"Murdock," I said. "No wonder he was scared shit-faced."

"It was him all along, wasn't it?" Art said. "Bill didn't have anything to do with it, did he, Jack? He just found out. The refs threw it. The fast guys got to them."

"The refs threw it all right, but it wasn't gamblers that got to them."

"But, Jack, they had to. What else could it be?"

"This," I said nodding at the mass of papers spread out on the desk in front of us. Nowhere in those papers was there actual documentary proof, but for anyone who had been through what we had, the conclusion was there to see. "This is what Bill found out, Art. It was the League. The League is fixing its own games."

He stared at me. Slowly he nodded. "Bill's craziness, his charges — then it all makes sense, doesn't it, Prince? He couldn't believe it himself, could he? And he couldn't prove it. But he knew."

Yes, Burke knew. And he knew that he might die for it, too. Why hadn't he taken it to the police, or the D.A.? Had he hesitated out of fear, or had he wanted to confront them directly before he acted? Had they killed him after all? And what would they do now if we dared to come forward with the truth?

THIRTEEN

That night we closed up the cabin and headed south. By morning we were back where we'd started, in New York. It was raining and the city looked gray and bleak in the raw March drizzle. We left Jody at a friend of hers with careful instructions not to tell anyone where she was, then Art and I killed the rest of the day on the street. We needed someone who could get to the right people fast so that we wouldn't have to risk exposing ourselves. I thought that someone was Eliot Litwin.

When he finally let us in that night he didn't look any too happy about it. He didn't hesitate to let us know he'd been in Chicago all day on business, it was late and he was tired. But he sat us down by the picture window in the big room, brought us drinks, slumped down into an armchair and said, "All right, what's so goddamn important that it can't wait till morning?"

I told him what we'd been through and what we'd found out. When I finished he just sat there staring at me over his drink with those green eyes of his. Behind him, through the picture window, the city glittered.

"You do have some idea of what you're talking about, don't you?" he said finally. "You do realize you're not just talking now about a couple of lousy gamblers. I mean, this isn't the kind of thing you throw around casually. Or have you completely lost touch with reality?"

"Eliot, if we didn't know exactly what it meant we wouldn't be here. Two people are already dead because of this. We could be next."

"Those guys? The League? Come on, Jack, they're just businessmen."

"Mr. Litwin," Art said breaking in, "it wouldn't have to be them. Not personally. They're in touch with big gamblers all the time. They've got connections to the kind of people who can take care of that sort of thing."

Eliot looked from one of us to the other. "Do you seriously believe," he began, "that any responsible person, anyone who counts, is going to listen to this story of yours for one minute without some kind of proof?"

"Look, Eliot, listen: We realize that we haven't got any hard evidence. Not yet. But it's out there — we're sure of it. All we're asking for is a chance to convince someone that it's worth looking into — someone with the power to do it right. Someone who can offer us some protection."

Litwin stood up abruptly. "Jack," he said without looking at me, "if you don't mind I'd like a word with you in private."

So I had no choice then but to follow him down that long carpeted corridor past the watercolors and the mirrors to the walnut-paneled study and the solid oak door, which he shut. And it was all there just as I'd left it: the leather chairs, the sweet smell of pipe tobacco, the pictures on the wall. And she was still there, too, looking out at me the way she always had.

Litwin poured himself another Scotch from the private stock in the bottom drawer. "You know," he said, his back to me, "I don't give a damn about your showing up like this. I don't even really mind your bringing someone like that Cooper up here with you. But for chrissake, have you forgotten who I am? Do you think you can just go saying anything to me in front of anybody?"

"Art's my friend. I trust him with my life. And now I'm trusting you, too, Eliot. You know there's something to it, don't you?"

Still not looking at me, he sat down on the edge of his desk and took a good pull at his Scotch. "It's possible," he said wearily. "All too possible. The new contract about to be signed, hundreds of millions of dollars at stake, certain personnel changes — sure. If the networks are involved to any extent, there's no telling where it might end." His eyes snapped up to meet mine. "For your own good I think you'd better just drop this."

"*Drop it?* How the hell can I just drop it?"

"Don't be an idiot, Jack. You can go someplace safe. I'll help you. Things will look different after a while. After a while you can start over as if none of this had ever happened."

"It's no good, Eliot. I can't do that now."

"Sure you can. Why the hell can't you?"

"Because I can't. Because I'm just not that way anymore." I sat down across from him on the couch. "Look, Eliot, remember the last time I was here with you in this room — the night of your New Year's Eve party? Do you remember what you said to me that night? You said you wanted to do something important, something that mattered, something that would really count."

He waited, fingering the rim of his glass.

"This thing they've done, Eliot, one way or another it's going to come out — it has to — and when it does someone is going to get the credit. If you were the one who was instrumental in bringing this thing to light, Eliot, think what it could mean for you."

He gave me a long, appraising look.

"And what would you be risking?" I said. "At worst — you were only doing a favor for an old personal friend."

He nodded slowly, absent-mindedly, as if in the back of his mind he was adding up long columns of figures, then sighed heavily. It had been a long day, he said. Maybe he'd jumped the gun on me; he'd only been concerned about my welfare, about making sure I realized how serious the situation was. But maybe I was right — maybe this was the opportunity he'd been waiting for. He'd have to consult his lawyer first, of course, just to make sure he wouldn't be compromising himself in any way. I understood, didn't I? He did, after all, have a name to protect.

Art and I checked into a place on 57th Street and for the first time in what felt like forever we got a full night's sleep. Litwin called the next morning. It was all set. He was going to approach the D.A. on our behalf, but it would take a day or two at the very least. In the meantime it was important for us to stay put where he could reach us in a hurry if necessary.

"OK, Eliot, just remember: be careful who you talk to. And don't let anyone — I mean anyone — know where we are."

"Don't worry," he said. "I'm handling this now. Just sit tight."

Eliot's reassurances aside, I had no intention of just sitting tight, although that, I discovered to my discomfort, was exactly what Cooper was disposed to do. "Hell, Prince," he said from his bed, "it's out of our hands now, it's over our heads. And I for one intend to rest on my laurels."

"What you're resting on, Art, is your ass. Look, you said it yourself all the way back in the beginning — that we couldn't count on anybody else but ourselves. There's no telling now whether or not the D.A. will come through for us, but either way we'll be in a lot stronger position if we can come up with some kind of clue to who's after us."

"Sure Jack, but what the hell can we do from up here? What have we got to go on?"

"We've got everything we've been through. Maybe there's something we've overlooked." It seemed to me if we just went over it all step by step, plotting the points where our paths crossed theirs, maybe we could fix some aspect of their identity. We had to work our way back from what we knew:

— Kauffman's son spied on us in Vermont two nights ago.

— Someone shot at us in Somerville two days before that.

— Someone — a stocky man wearing a hat — chased us at the stadium the night before the shooting.

Art called Miss McDonald in Somerville and asked her to tell us again anything she could about those two men who had searched our room. But she couldn't remember anything more than before: that the older one was shorter; the younger, taller.

"Christ, Jack," Art said hanging up. "It's worse than trying to find a couple of needles in a haystack. I mean we don't even know what these two pricks look like."

"We know more than we suspect. That's the whole problem. We've just got to come at it from another angle."

"Well you keep them covered from here, Rose. I'll go try coming at them from the bathroom for a while."

I stretched out on the bed and lay there staring up at the ceiling, listening to the sounds of the midday traffic down in the street. My mind was a blank.

"You know I've been thinking," Art said, finally emerging from the bathroom. "Maybe we're taking this whole thing a little too personally."

"Getting shot at isn't personal enough for you?"

"But that's just it, Jack," he said standing over me, "I mean too personally involved at the expense of the overall picture. I mean now you take all your great deductive minds, they were all suckers for the big picture."

"Let's not get started with all that again, all right, Art?"

"But it's like you were saying, Prince. We're supposed to know more than we know we know, right? So maybe what we have to do is go back to the time before we even knew we knew it, if you see what I mean?"

"Not exactly."

"Jack, it's simple — just look at it from the League's point of view. They've got this whole bunch of hand-picked zebras to work the fix, right? But however choice these guys are, they're still only refs at heart. Now if they've got all kinds of security types checking up on gamblers all the time — something as big as this, it stands to reason there must be at least one agent in charge of zebras, don't you think? Maybe that's who Murdock was hiding his crisis of nerves from. Maybe the instant Murdock balked at reporting for that last game he knew this guy would be right on his case. Which brings me to my point: maybe this agent who was internally in charge of keeping things under the lid with respect to Murdock is the same guy who's been externally after us."

I sat bolt upright in bed. "Holy shit, Art, you're right. All Murdock's paranoia — he wasn't just going crazy under the pressure. He was being watched."

"Yeah, I know. I've already deduced out that fact. It's just too bad we can't deduce out somebody who saw who it was."

"But Christ, Art," I said reaching for the phone. "Don't you remember? Both Louise and Shipley's wife saw someone that night of Murdock's death."

I called the Shipleys' but there wasn't any answer. I didn't have a number for Louise and couldn't get hold of one. It was over an hour before I finally got through to Taylor at the lounge in Gladiola where Art and I first met him.

"Assholes!" he cried. "I can't believe my fuckin' ears! Don't tell me you two hot shits are revving up to hit the road again?"

"Taylor, listen, this is important. It's about Murdock."

"You're not still hung up on him, are you? Didn't I already tell you he just wasn't worth it?"

"You told us wrong. I don't have time to explain it all. We think Murdock was in trouble with the League, that he was being watched. Did he ever mention anything like that to you? Or did you ever notice anything strange?"

"Are you kidding me? The only thing strange about John was John. He was always afraid somebody was going to find out how he was carrying on. I told you how it was. From the time he tried to get out of that last game he just went straight downhill."

"That call! You made that call for him, didn't you? Who did you talk to?"

"Hell, I don't know. Some guy."

"Did you write down his name somewhere? His number?"

"Man, I don't even have the name and number of this sixteen-year-old chick I picked up on the beach last night, and was she ever unbelievable."

Art was waving his arms at me, telling me to ask about Taylor's old phone bills.

"Yeah," Taylor said, "I suppose it might be on one of them somewhere."

"Find it for us, Randy," I said, "and I swear I'll schedule Art's next road orgy right through your living room." Taylor gave out a rebel yell that nearly blew my ear off. Before hanging up I asked him how we could get in touch with Louise. He said he didn't know; all he'd heard was that she was supposed to be working at some club over in Miami.

Cooper phoned Confianca. Speaking on behalf of Luis and himself, Confianca said they would be only too happy for the chance to make up for that unfortunate little misunderstanding about Big Art's tab at the El Paradiso. If this Louise Boudreau was in Miami, if it was humanly possible to find her, they would find her for us in a jiffy.

It was late afternoon before I finally got through to the Shipleys. Mrs. Shipley had just gotten back from the hospital; the doctor had sent Jim there for more tests. "I know he'd like to talk to you himself," she said. "You boys' visit was such a comfort to him."

I said we hated to have to bother her at a time like this but actually it was her we wanted to speak to. "That man you saw the night of the accident, what can you tell me about him?"

"Man? What man? I don't recall any man."

"Jim said you saw some passerby."

"Oh you mean that fella. The Good Samaritan."

"Yes, him. The Samaritan. Who was he?"

"Well now I reckon I don't really know. He was a stranger. Said he'd heard the shot and seen all the commotion. Said he'd wait out front for the police. I never gave him a second thought, I was so concerned for Jim. He kept crying that he believed the man he'd shot forgave him, that he knew him for a good man."

"Murdock knew your husband all right, Mrs. Shipley — he knew Jim wasn't the man he was running from. That man may have been the one you saw. Can you remember anything about him, anything at all?"

"Well I don't know. It was all so confused. He was about fifty, I'd say, maybe more — I can't rightly judge people's ages no more. Kind of heavyset. Pleasant lookin' sort of man, though. I'm afraid I just can't recall no more than that."

The sheriff of Gladiola wasn't at his office: I caught up with him at his home. Sure, he remembered us right well: had we found us any murderers yet? He said he hated to have to disappoint us once again but there hadn't been anyone waiting to meet them at the gate in front of Shipley's that night and if he or any of his deputies had seen someone standing around the site of a shooting at four o'clock in the morning they'd sure as hell have gotten his name. He was sorry he couldn't be more helpful. I told him he'd been more help than he knew.

Art made a quick call to check on Jody, then we stayed

off the phone to keep the line open. Night fell and we took turns going down for a breath of air and something to eat. It wasn't until after midnight that the phone finally rang. I beat Art to it. I heard loud music and shouting in the background; then Louise's voice. She wanted me to put Art on right away.

"Oh Jesus, Jack," Cooper whispered, backing away. "You talk to her. Tell her anything. Tell her I'm in the bath. Tell her if I come to the phone now I'll constitute an electrical hazard."

I shoved the phone in his hand. He lifted it slowly to his ear, turning his back to me. "Hello? Yes, I'm all right, Looloo. Yes, I do, too, all the time. Yes, I want to, too, real soon, Looloo."

Art told her that the reason he was calling was to let her know that it wasn't her fault about Murdock getting shot like that, that he'd been in some kind of trouble with the League, that now the guys who'd been after him were after us and that if she really ever thought she might like to see Art again alive in person she could do herself a tremendous service by telling him again about the man she saw at her place that last night with Murdock.

"You did too, Looloo," Art yelled into the phone. "Listen you dizzy broad will you just stop and think straight for once in your life. You said Murdock passed out drunk. Then you said you looked out the window and saw someone parked across the street in front of your girlfriend's . . .

"All right, all right. But even at three o'clock in the morning you must have noticed *something* . . .

"His head did what in the streetlights? Are you absolutely sure now it wasn't you yourself that had the shine on?"

First thing in the morning I called Mrs. Shipley to ask if the man she saw that night had been bald.

"Why I reckon now he was, wasn't he," she said, "just up in front."

Art called Miss McDonald, but she couldn't say for sure whether or not the older man was bald.

We spent the rest of the morning waiting to hear from Taylor. But when the phone rang, a little before noon, it was Litwin. He wanted to see me up at his place right away — alone.

When he let me in this time he was all business. We did our talking right there in the hall. The answer from the D.A.'s was no dice. Without hard evidence that a crime had been committed in their jurisdiction they were under no obligation to act. If we wanted to we could try the U.S. Attorney's office or the FBI, but their response would probably be no different. Otherwise they suggested that we take our suspicions directly to the League.

"Eliot, for chrissake, didn't you tell them how it is? The League is *in* it. For all we know their security people are the ones behind the coverup."

Litwin barely glanced at me. "Realistically now, Jack, what did you expect me to say to them? You can't expect them to go around opening full-scale investigations on the basis of every crazy conspiracy somebody cooks up."

"We didn't cook it up. Somebody shot at us."

"Yes, somebody shot at you; and you and your friend lost a lot of money gambling and you were going around Boston asking questions that could have annoyed any one of half a dozen local hoods. Your friend isn't exactly a model boy scout to begin with; or don't you bother taking the trouble anymore to find out who your friends are?"

"Jesus, you didn't give them our names, too, did you?"

"Jack, come on," he said with a wave of his hand, "these are practical men. Surely you really didn't expect me to go in there telling ghost stories. This is the real world now. If you're serious, sooner or later you've got to trust someone else. Sooner or later you've got to play by the rules."

"And if your game is fixed? What then?"

"So now it's the whole system, is it? Everything. Deliberately fixed against you."

"Not deliberately," I said. "And not against anyone in particular. But fixed all the same."

He smiled. "Then the choice is yours, isn't it? That is, if you yourself still seriously believe what you're saying."

"Meaning that you don't."

He began to rock ever so slightly on his feet. "You came to me as a friend. As a friend I went out on a limb for you — a lot further, under the circumstances, than was necessary. Without some kind of proof, your position is hopeless. If you persist in this on your own I can't be responsible for the consequences. There's no point in our discussing it any further."

He stood there with his head cocked slightly, those green eyes of his on me. Then he reached into his pocket and pulled out a slip of paper. "This is the number of someone who might possibly be of help to you. It came to me from a friend. He doesn't know anything about my visit to the D.A.'s or you and Cooper. All he knows is that you want to discuss certain questions concerning the League. The choice to call or not is yours."

It was midafternoon by the time I got back to the hotel. There still hadn't been any word from Taylor. I told Art what Litwin had said and showed him the slip of paper.

"I guess it wouldn't hurt to call, Jack, would it?"

"I guess not," I said.

I dialed the number. He answered on the first ring.

"I was told to call you," I said.

"Just a minute." He clicked off; then he clicked back on. "I know what you want," he began in a half-whisper. "I can help you."

"How?"

"From inside."

"You're with the League?"

"I can't talk about it right now, do you understand?"

"All right, when?"

He hesitated. "Soon. The sooner the better, but it isn't that easy for me."

"Whenever you say."

"If it were necessary," he said haltingly, "could you possibly be in New York tonight?"

"I could."

He gave me another number where I was to call him exactly at six. When I hung up, Taylor called. We'd never believe what he'd gone through for us. Some crazy lady he'd been with a while back had made off with half his papers. It took him the whole night to sweet-talk her into giving them back. But he had the number he'd called for Murdock.

It was a New York number.

"Seventy-six seven seven," said a girl in a singsong secretarial voice.

"Is he in?" I said, fumbling for words.

"To whom do you wish to speak, please?"

"Who else?" I said, taking a stab in the dark. "Old Baldy himself."

She laughed. "Very funny. I'd like to see you call him that to his face."

"Is he there?"

"Mr. Hanson is no longer attached to this office."

"Can you tell me where I can reach him? It's important."

"I'm sorry. We don't give out private numbers unless you've been cleared through security. Perhaps the commissioner's assistant can help you."

"All right. I'll try the commissioner's office later."

"Oh brother, are you ever off-base. This *is* the commissioner's office."

I set the phone back down on the hook and stared at Art.

"I don't get it," I said. "If the League was behind all the

rough stuff — if they really wanted to stop us — they had plenty of chances."

"They thought we had Bill's papers."

"But now we do have Bill's papers and there's no proof in them — at least not the kind they have to be afraid of."

"Well hell, sure, Jack. *We* know that. But that doesn't mean they do."

At six o'clock I made the call to our contact at the League.

"It can only get worse the longer I wait." He sounded even more anxious than before. "There's a phone booth at the north end of the downtown side of the IRT-Seventh Avenue Chambers Street Station. Be there at eleven o'clock. And make sure it's just the two of you."

"The two of us?"

"You heard me."

"What makes you think there are two of us? I never said there were two of us."

"Well I just assumed . . ."

"You just assumed what?"

"Well you're the ones, aren't you? The ones they're trying to stop." He hesitated for a moment. "Look, I don't have time for games. If you want my help — just be there." Then he hung up.

"Jesus, Jack," Art said, "I don't know. I don't like it."

"All right," I said. "Maybe you should stay behind as a precaution."

"Oh sure, you'd love that wouldn't you, Rose? Play the hero off by yourself so you don't have to get stuck here with me all alone while I worry myself into a heart attack over you."

We got to the station well before eleven and hung around near the phone booth. Just before eleven a train came rattling into the station and squealed to a stop. The doors hissed open and a handful of people got off. Then the doors slammed shut and the train roared off into the tunnel.

The phone in the booth rang.

"Nice to see you," said the voice. "Head west on Chambers."

We started walking west towards the river. It was a dark night, raw and clammy. The streets were deserted. We walked quickly, our footsteps echoing on the pavement, Art limping in the cold. Out on the river a ship's horn moaned, and we got a sudden tarry whiff of the harbor.

Suddenly a man called out to us. He was standing across the street in front of a darkened parking lot. With his long overcoat and attaché case he looked like a conservative young executive.

We crossed the street. He held out his hand and gave us a nervous tight-lipped smile. "I'm sorry to have put you through all this," he said.

"Who are you?" Art said. "How can you help us?"

He glanced back anxiously over his shoulder. "Let's go someplace more private to talk?"

"About what?" Art said. "We've gone far enough for you already."

"I can get you what you need."

"What we need?" I said.

"Tell me what you already have. I can get you whatever other documents you need."

"Documents?" I said.

"I guess so." His smile was like a spasm. "My car's right over here."

We followed him through an aisle of parked cars. Under the harsh streetlights the cars looked like toys, the buildings cardboard cutouts.

His car was parked head-on against a brick wall. We got in and he fumbled the key into the ignition. The starter groaned, but the engine wouldn't turn over.

"Dammit," he said, flinging open the door. "They were supposed to have fixed that."

"What's wrong?" Art asked.

"It's nothing," he said, getting out. He asked me to start it up for him when he gave me the signal. He walked around in front. As he raised the hood his eyes flicked towards the black van parked beside us.

Art saw it then too. I was groping for words when he flung open his door and pulled me out after him. We spun around practically right into the three men blocking our way. Without a split second's hesitation Art drove headfirst into them, taking them by surprise. *"Jack,"* he shouted as they all went down. "Run."

I couldn't move. Then I saw that it didn't matter. A fourth man stood behind the van with a gun on me. The young executive was right in back of him.

The first three shoved us up against the van. Art could barely stand — he'd wrenched his knee and his face was twisted in pain.

"All right," said the one with the gun, "we want the stuff and we want it fast."

"We don't know what you're talking about," Art said firmly. "We don't have any stuff."

The man with the gun stepped closer. He was thick and short and wore a hat. He raised his arm, then slammed the pistol butt down across Art's knee. Art fell screaming in agony. The other three grabbed me from behind.

"For God's sake," said the executive, "take it easy."

"Shut up," said the one with the gun. He wiped his forehead with his sleeve and I got a good look at him then. Under the hat he was bald.

He raised his arm for another blow.

"All right, that's enough," I said. "We'll talk."

"But Jack you can't," Art cried, his eyes squeezed shut, his head rolling from side to side in pain. "We haven't got anything to tell them."

"It's no good, Art. I'm doing the talking now."

"Where are they?" the bald man said to me. "Take us to them."

"I'm afraid I can't do that," I said.

"Suit yourself. It's all the same to me whether your friend ever uses that leg again."

"Jack, Jesus, for chrissake," Art cried. "Just tell them we don't have anything."

"You shut the fuck up now," the bald man said turning on him, "or I'm going to break the other one, too."

"You touch him again," I said without even thinking, "and I'll see to it it's the last thing you ever do."

"Oh you will now, will you?" he said nodding at me.

"You better believe it. The documents and a long letter to the D.A. explaining everything are with people who will know what to do if anything happens to us."

He stared at me, then glanced at the executive. "You're lying. You don't have enough and you know it."

"Oh don't we, Hanson?"

"Holy shit," said the young executive. "Dave, I think we'd better check. If they've got your name . . ."

"Shut *up*," Hanson shouted. "I'm handling it now. He's bluffing, can't you see that? If they had enough, what have they been waiting for? If they had enough why did they risk meeting you?"

They both looked at me. I was in too far to stop. "It's simple," I said. "We'd much rather deal with you than with the D.A."

They both stood there staring at me. Then Hanson broke into a grin. "And to think all along I had you two pegged for a pair of fucking do-gooders. So you want to deal, do you? And if I'm not buying? If I just decide to deal with you my own way for all the trouble you've given me?"

"You'll be a lot better off settling this our way. Because when the shit hits the fan your commissioner's not going to be handing out any medals."

"The commissioner?" he said glaring at me. "The commissioner, Rose, will never know you even existed."

Hanson told the others to get us into the van. They made us lie down, our hands crossed behind our backs. Then they tied and gagged us. Art was weeping silently with the pain. It was the last thing I saw before the blindfold.

FOURTEEN

It seemed as if we lay in the back of that van forever. They drove endlessly, then stopped and drove again. It was hard to breathe, and my arms and legs kept going numb. But however bad it was for me it must have been a lot worse for Art.

We'd been stopped for some time when I heard angry voices. The doors banged open and someone pulled roughly at the ropes around my legs, untying them. They dragged me out and stood me up. Through the blindfold I could see lights, so it was still night. The air smelled wet and salty. I heard them yelling at Cooper to stand up, to move. Someone shoved me from behind, then rushed me down a long, steep set of stairs. I tripped, cracking my head against what felt like a door frame. They pushed me on, then threw me to the floor and loosened the ropes around my hands. I heard Art groaning, begging them to take it easy, to put him down gently. I worked my hands free and pulled off the blindfold. We were in a bare windowless cellar. There were two mattresses on the floor. They had set Art down on one of them. I caught just a glimpse of them as they pulled the heavy door shut, leaving us in total darkness.

Art's leg had swollen up terribly. Working as gently as I could in the dark I tore open his pants leg to his hip, and did what little I could to make him comfortable, but he was more concerned about me.

"Jack, you sure you're all right?" he said, his voice coming in short, shaky bursts. "You sure they didn't hurt you? Jesus, why did you have to knuckle under to them? You didn't have to do it for me. We didn't get into this to make any deals with bastards like these."

"Art, we aren't making any deals."

"But Jack, documents, D.A.s, deals — Jesus — where the hell did you pull all that crazy stuff out of?"

"Where the hell do you think? From the same place I get all my crazy stuff. Don't you see, Art? It's all coming true, just like you said, just like you laid it out at the start in Florida. You said we could flush them out into the open, bluff them into showing their hand. That's just what we've done, Art. They think we have the proof."

"But Jack, they're wrong."

"That doesn't matter now. Whatever the documents are — something Bill had or something they're afraid he had — they believe we have them now. It's essential that they keep believing that. Everything depends on that now."

"Jack it won't work. How can it? You think they're going to take our word for it"

"We know the truth. It'll work, as long as we stick together, as long as we don't let anyone or anything come between us. Do you understand, Art? It's all come down to that."

"Sure, Jack, sure. But what if they don't buy it? What if they call our bluff?"

I said there was no use thinking about that now. We'd know soon enough whether or not they'd bought it. Until then we just had to hold on. I took off my coat and spread it over him and massaged him gently. Gradually he fell off to sleep. I tried to sleep then, too, but I couldn't stop shivering in the cold, my mind going round and round.

The rattling of the lock woke us up. A bare light bulb came on overhead, then the heavy door rumbled open and a cheerful voice sang out "room service."

He was a fat, baby-faced old guy, laden like a mule with towels and buckets of water.

"I don't want to hear no complaints now," he said. "I got nothing to do with these accommodations. I'm just here to see if I can give you a little service."

He checked Art first. Art looked pale and feverish; his eyes glittered. The old guy carefully peeled back his pants leg. The knee had ballooned up even worse during the night.

"What do you think?" I said.

"I seen better looking legs in my life."

He gave Art some pills, then rushed off, bustling back a minute later with a tray of breakfast. While Art chewed half-heartedly at a piece of toast, the old guy set about fastening a makeshift splint to his leg, revealing in the process a sure hand with a roll of tape.

"You a trainer?" Art asked.

"I been around ballplayers before. Whaddaya say we just leave it at that? How you like the toast?"

"Terrific," Art said listlessly. "This is just the little off-the-beaten-track kind of place we're always hoping to discover."

Whatever the place was, it sure as hell wasn't your run-of-the-mill household basement. The windowless cellar felt like the inside of a bunker; the concrete door was at least half a foot thick. I remembered suddenly the salty smell of the air the night before.

"Where are we?" I said. "We're near the sea, aren't we?"

"They'll tell you what you need to know," he said without looking up from his work.

"Who're they?"

"Look, don't make me say no more than I'm supposed to, OK? You'll find out everything soon enough." He finished off Art's leg without another word, then started for the door.

"Listen," he said, hesitating. "I know you guys had a rough night. But try not to worry now, OK?" He pulled the door closed behind him.

"Art," I whispered, kneeling beside him, "I think they've bought it."

He frowned. He didn't know what to think. It was all so confusing. He said I knew I could count on him, but he thought I'd better do most of the talking myself if I didn't mind. He wasn't feeling all that clear in the head just now.

A few minutes later the old trainer returned to say that they were ready. I was to come on along by myself.

I followed him out into an enormous room. The place looked as though it might have once been a nightclub of some kind. There was a long bar and a huge stone fireplace, everything thick with dust and cobwebs. At the far end of the room near the stairs four men were playing cards; they barely glanced up at us. A soft breeze fluttered in through a half open vent near the ceiling. For the first time that year I smelled the early spring scent of the damp earth warmed by the sun.

The trainer led me into another windowless cell, this one richly carpeted and appointed in massive oak furniture. A handsome, well-tanned, distinguished-looking man was waiting at the head of a long table. Sitting there in his three-piece suit he looked as casual as if this were his club and he'd just dropped by for a little chat between corporate meetings. He gestured courteously for me to take a seat. The trainer backed out, shutting the door. I knew it was important now for me to seem in control, but I couldn't help myself. "Cooper's hurt badly. He needs to see a doctor right away."

He barely glanced at me over his glasses. "Mr. Rose," he said in a dead even voice, "I'm certain we share your desire to get this over with as quickly as possible."

"Who are you?"

He gazed placidly at me out of his polished, businesslike

facade. "Let's just say that I'm here to be of service in settling the matter at hand."

"Does the commissioner know we're here?"

He eyed me with cold distaste. "There's no need, Mr. Rose, for the exchange of information that could cause anyone any future problems." He took out a silver pen. "The situation is a relatively simple one. You have the papers. What price do you ask?"

I looked at him. He seemed serenely confident, a man whose every breath betrayed his absolute belief in a world where money and the relations it determined were the ultimate reality.

"Come on now, Mr. Rose," he said with a condescending smile. "I'm sure that you and your friend have had ample opportunity to speculate on what your price might be."

I looked at him for a long moment. "As a matter of fact Art and I are both rather fond of the number fifty-two."

"Fifty-two what?" he said depreciatingly.

"Fifty-two thousand."

He sucked in his cheeks. "Fifty-two thousand. That's a rather large sum."

"Well now that depends on how you look at it. In fact why don't you just go ahead and make it ten times that?"

For the first time a trace of doubt flickered across his face. "That would be over half a million dollars."

"Oh would it? Well how's that sound to you anyhow?"

He lowered his head slightly, studying me over the top of his glasses. "As a ballpark figure, that would not be entirely out of the question."

"For each of us. Which brings it to something over a million, doesn't it? Hell, why don't we just round it off: one million for Art, one million for me."

He leaned forward, folding his hands in front of him on the table. "This is not a joking matter," he said sharply. "I can assure you that if you bargain with us in good faith there's every reason to believe we can reach a mutually satisfactory accommodation."

"There isn't going to be any accommodation," I said. "At least not the kind you mean."

"I'm afraid I don't understand. If it's simply a question of money . . ."

"It isn't a question of money."

He stared at me coldly. "What are you after? What do you want?"

"We want the League's cooperation in exposing the fix."

He sat back in his seat and put down the pen. "You're mad."

"Am I?"

"It's out of the question. It just can't be done."

"It's going to be done," I said. "It's going to be done whether they do it or not."

"Do you really think for a second they're going to let you get away with this?"

"We have friends. If anything happens to us they'll know what to do."

He stared blankly. Then he lowered his head, tapping the table with his pen. "There's no telling how they're going to react." He checked his watch. "How much time do we have to work in?"

"What time is it now?"

"A quarter to one."

"Our friends will be expecting us by six this evening."

"Can you give me more time? Surely you can understand how difficult this is going to be for them."

"I don't give a damn how difficult it is. I want to get Art to a hospital right away. It's simple enough. If you let us go now we'll sit down later with you and the people from the D.A.'s and give you time to figure out the least painful way of making the facts public. That's the only concession I'm making — not that you deserve it, but because I want to get Art to a doctor. You just tell them it's all coming out. They can face up to it now, or they can make it as hard on themselves as they want. I don't see where there's really any choice to be made."

"No," he said, "I suppose not. Except for one thing." He rose slowly, his eyes hard on me. "It remains to be seen whether or not they will choose to believe you."

The old trainer led me back to our cell. Art couldn't believe they'd actually bought it, that they'd really offered us money. I tried to reassure him, telling him that as long as they thought we had proof they couldn't afford not to go along with us.

He lay there frowning up at the ceiling, his eyes shiny, his forehead fiery hot to the touch. "I just don't know, Jack. Everything's turned inside out. I don't know where I am, or what's happening. I don't even know if I'm in my right mind anymore or out of it."

"You're in your right mind, and you've been there all along, since the very beginning. You said we could do it, Art. You said we were going all the way."

"Hell — I was a nut-case then. I didn't know what I was talking about. You don't listen to every nut-case that walks in off the street, do you?"

"Just the ones wearing your number."

He smiled weakly. I grasped his hand, and we stayed like that in the dim cellar, waiting.

They came for us about half an hour later, the man in the suit and the old trainer dragging in a chair behind him. The man in the suit wanted to speak personally to both of us. I didn't want him talking in front of Art, who seemed more disoriented with each passing minute. I said that Art wasn't up to it, that I didn't want him disturbed.

"It's important that you both hear what I have to say," he insisted.

"It's OK, Jack," Art offered. "You shouldn't have to carry it all on account of me. I'll be all right."

"Sure you will," said the man in the suit. "What I have

to say won't take very long." He waited until the trainer had left. Then he pulled the chair closer and sat down. "I've just spoken with the commissioner. The commissioner wishes both of you to know that he is personally indebted to you for bringing this most serious matter to his attention."

"Are you trying to tell us now that this is the first he's heard of the fix?" I said.

"The commissioner would have no difficulty denying any such knowledge under oath."

"Sure he would. That's the way it works in the big time, isn't it? The head man isn't supposed to know what the little guys are doing right under his nose. That way if something goes wrong, no one knows how or why. No one's responsible."

He smiled. "Gentlemen, prior to appreciating the pure nature of your motivation we had no reason to think that any fuller explanation of the situation would interest you.

"The arrangement to which you refer as the fix was engineered by a handful of individuals. They are well-intentioned men who did what they did, however mistakenly, in the belief that they were acting in the best interests of the game. The harassment you have undergone was entirely the work of one of their people, whose acquaintance I believe you have already made."

"You mean Hanson?" Art said.

"That's correct. He was acting completely alone to hide the fact of his personal exploitation of the situation."

"The two-hundred-thousand-dollar bet placed in New York under the name of Kauffman by Kauffman's son?" Art said.

"Mr. Cooper, I am indeed impressed. Hanson apparently first made contact with Martin Kauffman while on assignment in Gladiola. As far as we've been able to determine, Hanson is the only one who used his privileged knowledge for personal gain. The commissioner wants you to understand that he would never have authorized or condoned such harassment. He wants you to rest assured that those responsible will be dealt with most severely, and that you yourselves will be more than adequately compensated for any personal inconveniences you've suffered."

"Jack, did you hear that? It means they're going to do it, aren't they? It means they're going to go along with it."

"Art, it means that they're trying to see if they can buy our support for their coverup."

The man in the suit sat back, crossing his arms. "It may interest you to know, Mr. Rose, that at this very moment we are doing everything in our power to comply with your most difficult demand. The commissioner has merely asked me to use whatever time we have left to explore the possibilities that might exist for an arrangement more consistent with his responsibilities."

"I'd say your commissioner should have worried about his responsibilities a little sooner."

"Look, all right, yes," he said leaning forward. "We made some mistakes. But the commissioner didn't order this — he's mainly a figurehead anyhow. This whole idea just came out of the blue — out of committee. No one seriously intended to implement it — but somehow it got started. What's the use of quibbling over the fine points now? It was a mistake, a short-sighted stopgap measure. In five or ten years the technology could change completely, television might not be nearly so important to the welfare of the game. But for now at least a serious abuse has been exposed and corrected. The commissioner gives you every assurance that nothing like this will ever happen again. For your efforts — however high-principled your motives may have been — you will both be well rewarded. In the light of all this, what interests can possibly be served now by insisting on a full public disclosure? A disclosure that will not only affect the livelihoods of countless innocent people, but far more seriously, cause incalculable, irreparable damage to the image of the game."

"The image of the game," Art cried, propping himself up

on one elbow. "Jesus Christ! You were fixing your own fucking games."

"I believe the word 'orchestration' more accurately reflects the situation, Mr. Cooper. We were not attempting to profit through illegal wagers."

"Orchestration, ballet, call it whatever you want," Art said. "It still comes down to the same thing."

"All right, Art," I said, laying a hand on him. "Take it easy. Don't get yourself all worked up."

The man in the suit sat studying us. "What is it the two of you are really angling for? Are you out to make some kind of a name for yourselves?"

"What we're out for," I said, "is the truth."

"The truth," he said. "And do you imagine that the truth, in a world like ours, is such a simple thing? What matters is that version of the truth which serves the greatest good of the whole."

"You mean that lie, don't you?"

"What difference does it make?"

"Christ — all the difference in the world. If there's no difference between what's true and false then we're just passive spectators, sopping up whatever people like you choose to dish out."

"We already are spectators, Mr. Rose — politically, economically, in every facet of our lives. The rugged individual is just a myth. So the question is, are we interested in our own little personal crusades, or do we work for the public good."

"As defined by whom?"

"Look, let's try to be practical, shall we, Rose. In order for there to be a fraud, there must first be a victim. Whom have we victimized? The networks? They stand to profit substantially from any new contract. In any case, I can assure you their interests would not be served by such a scandal. The advertisers? They're reaching more consumers than ever before. The public then? The public enjoyed the presentation of a more exciting product. What practical harm, I ask you, was done by that?"

"What harm was done? For starters I'd like to ask John Murdock and Bill Burke what harm they thought was done. But they aren't exactly around to tell us, are they? I'd like to ask your hatchet man Hanson just why they aren't."

"We didn't kill them. We were watching them, yes, but as far as their deaths were concerned — in Murdock's case you might say he paid the price for his own compliance. As for your friend, Mr. Burke — fortunately we never had to cross that bridge with him."

"What did you do to him that last night? How did you stop him from acting?"

"We didn't have to do anything at all. Your Mr. Burke, it seems, was not exactly in a position to live up to the courage of his convictions. As I'm sure you must both be well aware."

"Don't you dare talk that way to me about Bill," Art yelled, jerking himself up off the mattress. "You don't have the right."

"All right, Art," I said, easing him down. "I'm handling this."

"But they should know, Jack. They should know how it is."

The man in the suit smiled. He stood up and aimed the smile down at Art. "I'm sorry," he said. "I didn't realize you were so attached to his memory."

"He was my friend," Art cried. "I know what he was."

"Yes, that's right, I'd forgotten. You went back a long way with him, didn't you?"

"All right, Art, that's enough now about Bill."

"But they should know, Jack. They should know why we're here."

"Yes," said the man in the suit. "I'm beginning to see. There's nothing more to be said, is there? I would, however, be less than entirely frank if I did not inform you at this time that while I believe I can promise you that you need fear no more physical harm from our people . . ."

"Why don't you just skip the threats," I said. "Our minds are made up."

"I assure you, Mr. Rose, that this is no idle threat. While you are in no danger from the people directly under the commissioner, there are other parties whose interests must be taken into consideration — parties that might be willing to take certain risks in defense of their interests that the League alone would not."

"Whatever you do, whatever you say, it's coming out."

"Perhaps," he said, lowering his voice. "But you may not be around to see it when it does and it may not go the way you would like. I'm sure I don't have to remind either of you that on the good name of the game rides not only the fortunes of the League, but also the welfare of a multi-billion dollar gambling industry. Their representatives might be willing, shall we say, to present certain facts in a different light. After all, Mr. Cooper worked for bookies; you both bet heavily and lost. Two frustrated losers — a couple of nobodies who were willing to stoop to blackmail to destroy public trust in one of the country's most popular institutions. It might not be impossible for these parties to make the fix appear entirely the work of underworld elements threatening to undermine sensitive contract negotiations, in the light of which your disappearance might well seem a logical result."

"You're bluffing," I said. "You know it won't work. You have until six o'clock to let us go."

He backed up towards the door, shaking his head. "You haven't understood at all what I'm trying to tell you, have you? What you or I or anyone happens to believe doesn't matter now. This thing has gone too far. It's beyond our control." He reached for the door. "You'll have our reply in a short while. For your own sakes I hope you know exactly what you're doing."

"Jack," Art said as soon as he was gone, "you don't think they're really going to try to frame us, do you?"

"They're just desperate, Art. Don't you see? They're trying to use anything they can to break us."

"But there *are* hard guys out there, Jack. I know a lot of people who would do it for them. If they killed us, Jack — it would all be for nothing." There was panic in his voice, a wild look in his eyes.

"All right, Art, just listen to me. What do you think would happen to us now if they found out we had nothing? We have no choice, do you understand? I know you're hurting bad, but you've just got to hold on a little longer."

He shook his head. "Do you think Bill really killed himself like they said, Jack?"

"Who can say? There're too many things about Bill we just don't know. We probably shouldn't have talked about him as much as we did, Art."

"I don't know, Jack. It all feels so scrambled. I don't know what's real anymore and what's not."

"All we can do now is go on what we know between us to be true. All we can do is trust in ourselves."

His eyes were glazed, his face damp with perspiration. I toweled him down with cold water. He lay there staring up with that wide, faraway look in his eyes.

"Do you hear it, Jack? Listen."

"Hear what, Art?"

He smiled. "That first time in the tunnel before the Philly game at their place, they were the champions then, and a huge crowd waiting: me with chills thinking — sweet Jesus — I'd never seen one that big before. And I said to Bill I guessed they'd be throwing out a lot of noise when we took the field. Bill said no. He said the thing about the big ones was the silence. And not understanding what he meant, there not being time to ask because we were already moving out. That was the first time I ever heard it — that hush, when you first stepped out onto the field. You made ten, fifteen, twenty yards before the roar broke over you. I tell you, you didn't know what it was all about until you heard that silence."

It was an hour, maybe two, before they came again. The old trainer barely glanced up at us, he just mumbled that a doctor was coming. Art stirred, waking from a fitful, feverish sleep. "The doctor, Jack? Did you hear?"

The man in the suit entered with a second man. The other man remained by the door, as if reluctant to come in any closer. He was a solemn, grim-looking man with steel-gray hair and a cold stare.

"This is Dr. Dutcheon," the man in the suit said. "He's here to examine Mr. Cooper. Mr. Rose, if you don't mind coming with me."

"I'm staying right here with Art. I'm not leaving."

"Mr. Rose, I know how exhausted you must be. But there's a call waiting for you in the other room that I think you'll want to receive. Your friend will be in good hands with Dr. Dutcheon."

"Dutcheon?" Art said. He raised his head and looked directly at the doctor, his eyes as wide as if he were staring at a ghost out of a dream. I thought for sure he was out of his mind with the fever, but he turned to me with a gentle smile. "It's OK, Jack," he said, touching my hand. "Everything's going to be all right. Go on. Let me talk to the doctor."

I was too tired to think it out straight.

"Come on," said the man in the suit. "Time is short."

I followed him out into the big room. It seemed there were even more men out there than before. In the room with the table there was now a telephone. The man in the suit smiled. "The call will be coming through for you momentarily." He left me, closing the door behind him.

I waited beside the phone. The passing seconds became a minute. A second minute passed; then another. I picked up the phone — it was dead. I tapped desperately on the hook, trying to get a dial tone — nothing. I pulled at the cord —

the unconnected end skidded towards my feet. An instant later the lights went off.

I pounded on the locked door until finally I collapsed. In the dark I dreamed that I was running free through the heart of the city. The streets were thronged with people. I tried to call to them, but no sound came. I grabbed at them, but I was as thin as air. On and on I ran, driven by a burning, searing grief, till the people vanished. One long empty street after another flashed by. Overhead in the lighted windows of great buildings shadowed forms pressed spread-armed to the glass. In the dream I woke bathed in a warm wave of relief, thinking it was only a dream.

There was a blinding glare of light. I staggered slowly to my feet. There must have been half a dozen of them, but I saw only one face — Hanson's.

"Where's Cooper? What have you done to him?"

"I wouldn't worry about your pal now if I were you, Rose. He's made himself a nice little deal."

"You're lying."

"Am I? I'm afraid your pal turned out to be a hell of a lot smarter than you. Smart enough at least to save his own neck. He told us everything."

"I don't believe it. I don't believe any of it."

"Sure you don't," he said, coming a step closer. "But you will."

Out of the corners of my eyes I saw the others crowding in around me, clubs gripped tightly in their hands. I kept my eyes on Hanson.

"In your next life, Rose, try to be a little more careful who you pick for your friends."

I lunged at him. An explosion burst the back of my head. Flames roared in my ears. My eyes were on fire.

Then I was falling through the cool silence of deep, dark water.

FIFTEEN

I lay in a semicoma for close to a week. When I finally opened my eyes everything was an aching blur. They told me there were fractured vertebrae in my neck and cracks in my skull. No one could say for sure whether I would ever see right again. Altogether I was in one hospital or another for about a month.

During that time I never heard from Art. But Jody came to see me every day, and she told me he was all right. He'd called her from Florida. For once in his life, he said, he had enough money to set himself up the way he wanted. He didn't think he should talk to me. Under the circumstances, he didn't see much point in that.

By the time they released me from the hospital it had been decided somehow that I would stay with Jody. She had already rented a place for us, but said it was entirely up to me. She just wanted to do what she could to help me — no strings attached.

The place was in an old brownstone on the West Side. She had painted the kitchen a cheerful red. She had also bought a brass bed and managed to squeeze it into the tiny bedroom. I hobbled carefully from room to room, leaning on my cane, and lay awake nights on the living room sofa.

It was late spring. Within a week I had enough strength to

walk Argus as far as the park. It was good just to sit there feeling the warm sun on my shoulders, breathing in the soft air of the river. I listened to the old women gossiping, while young mothers wheeled their babies past and kids clattered by on roller skates. There was a crazy old man in a baseball cap who transported loads of dried leaves and earth from spot to spot in a child's red wagon. He seemed just as happy with one spot as another. I watched them all. It was good just to not feel anything anymore, no pain, no hurt, no loss; to know that I could just sit and watch.

After a while the headaches began to ease up and I could walk again without the cane.

During that time I didn't think about what had happened. The police seemed to have lost whatever interest they'd had in pursuing the matter, and for my part I didn't want to look at any of it. It wasn't a conscious decision, and I don't think it was fear. You can be hurt in ways you can't begin to know. Outwardly you may seem the same, but inside something as substantial as muscle or sinew has given way. It takes a certain strength of will to shape experience, to hold it together. A man alone cannot make reality. I couldn't look at any of it. It just wasn't there anymore.

I felt nothing. One day I came across a clipping Jody had withheld from me while I was in the hospital. A neat little black box in the middle of the sports pages reported the signing of a new four-year League-Networks contract for a record 800 million dollars.

I read the article with about as much interest as if it had been a year-old weather report.

One night Jody announced that I had wallowed long enough in self-pity. We went to a movie, then a late dinner. When we got back we sat up for a while with a bottle of wine, and I saw how much she wanted us to be happy. And when I came out of the shower and stopped at her door to say good night she was sitting there on the bed naked, her dark hair down around her shoulders, and a woman's question in her eyes. In her nakedness, in her vulnerability, she was heart-breakingly beautiful. I stood in the doorway until finally she dropped her eyes and turned away, her shoulders trembling. There was nothing I could give her then, except to try to say that it wasn't her fault, and that I was sorry. In the end I left her crying in the middle of her brass bed. Argus, thinking we were going out for a midnight walk, followed me down the stairs as far as the front hall.

The next day I called as I had promised, but there was no answer. Neither all that day nor the next, when I stopped by to leave her a note with the address of my rented room.

I spent the days avoiding thinking about what I would do when my money ran out; I spent the nights walking. During those long nights, thinking over everything that had happened, I came to see that what a person is isn't fixed. It's not something you start with, or that you can go out and find. And it's not something anyone can give you, or sell you either. It's what you make yourself, through your active choices or through your passivity. It's the living sum of all the countless bits and pieces of your experience.

For me there were two alternatives: to risk being involved again, or to give up the struggle, cutting myself off until I no longer knew how not to. Either way there was a price to be paid. And that was the fix I was in. But I wasn't the only one. In a world where men were reduced to spectators, where human experience was increasingly artificial and contrived, how could any of us know finally what was real? How could we know what we wanted, or even who we were?

One evening, a couple of days after I moved out, Jody came to see me. She stood in the hallway, tanned and glowing, more beautiful than I had ever seen her. I was glad that at least I could still feel that much. I think she knew it, too, because she smiled. She moved past me into the room, and hesitated. There was no place to sit except on the rickety bed. So she turned to face me.

"I've been trying to reach you all week," I said.

"That doesn't matter. This hasn't got anything to do with us. It's Art. He's sick."

Though I didn't move an inch, I felt myself pull back from her. "You're taking his word for it, are you?"

"Jack, I saw him. He's in Gladiola."

"And he sent you here to tell me."

She shook her head. "He made me promise not to tell you." She put a hand on my arm. "Jack, it's not at all the way he wanted us to think. He doesn't have a cent to his name, and they hurt him, they hurt him badly. His leg's been operated on once already and he's developed massive clotting. They need to operate again right away but he won't let them. Jack, they say this thing could kill him."

"What he did," I said pulling away, "almost got me killed."

"All right. So he did it. He must have been scared, hurt, confused — who knows exactly why he did what he did. He wouldn't talk to me about any of it. He just said he'd done it and now it was done. He said he wasn't making any apologies. He doesn't expect to ever see or hear from you again. He said he doesn't care, that for him it's over. But I can see that it's just tearing him up. I can see that it would mean everything if you went to him now. I don't blame you for feeling the way you do. I'm not asking you to forgive him. But for your own sake, Jack, you've got to find some way to make a peace with it."

"He sold me out," I said.

"Yes, he sold you out. And what about you? You talk about betrayal, but what about your feeling for him? What about your faith in him? You loved that man."

I stood there like a stone, unable to respond.

She brushed past me. From the door she said, "I'm leaving New York tomorrow."

"To go to him?"

"Someone has to."

After she had gone I lay down on the bed. For a long

time I had been convinced that there was nothing left, that it was all over. Now suddenly I was flooded with images. The memories burned inside me, and I forced myself to face them. I remembered our first night on the road, when we'd fled Miami, the Gulf spread out before us all silver and shimmering; I saw him there on the snow-white moonlit beach with his first-rate case of TV on the brain and his Grade-B movie lines saying, "For your own peace of mind, Jack. You don't ever want to quit on somebody without giving them a fair chance." I saw him lying on Taylor's couch, covering his eyes with his hands so that he wouldn't have to look at the delusion of Louise Boudreau, to whom, nevertheless, he felt compelled in all honesty, to admit that he wasn't a football star — at least not that big a one. I remembered him later that same night, on the beach, with the surf washing up around us, telling me what he thought was the worst truth about himself. I remembered the night they shot at us on the porch steps, when his first impulse was to sacrifice himself for me.

No — I had to face it. It was impossible that Art could have betrayed me.

I got up and poured a drink. I lay down again, closing my eyes. For the first time I forced myself to remember how it had been: the rattle of the key in the lock, the old trainer's evasive glance, the man in the suit presenting the other guy — the doctor. I remembered how Art had peered at the doctor out of his fever, how he had repeated his name before turning to me with a reassuring smile to say that it was all right, to go on, to let him talk to the doctor. In that whole nameless place only he had had a name: Dutcheon.

The next morning I went to the library. I thought there were two possibilities: either this Dutcheon was connected with football, or he was someone Art knew through the gambling world. It took me all day to find out that I was wrong on both counts — at least the way I had figured it. I had worked my way back through the newspaper indexes to the late 1940s, just before Art played, when I found the entry: "Dutcheon, Frank — charged in Cape killing."

There in the timeless yellow gloom of the library I read the story of Jody's father's death: how on a quiet back road on the Cape, in May of 1947, he was hit by a speeding car. How in the opinion of the medical examiner he would have lived if he hadn't been dragged off the road out of sight. How the vehicle in question was positively linked to Frank "Dutch" Dutcheon, a South Shore club owner, and reputed racketeer. How the charges against him were dropped at the last minute when the prosecution couldn't disprove his claim that the car had been stolen, or shake his alibi.

The following morning I caught the first flight for Florida. At the Miami airport I rented a car and in the blazing, shimmering heat of a summer afternoon, once again drove that road to the Gulf. I wasn't looking forward to what I might have to do. He'd had some strong reason to lie. For all I knew he might still try to keep the truth from me.

The Gladiola City Hospital was across the park from the sheriff's office. The nurse at the desk said Mr. Cooper had been taken out for the afternoon. She suggested I try either the park or the town pier.

He wasn't in the park. I ran the block and a half to the pier. The pier led straight out across the beach into the dark blue expanse of the Gulf. The sun was low in the sky, but still very warm. At the far end of the pier, beyond the clicking, whining reels of the fishermen, I saw the back of a wheelchair, and on a bench behind it, a woman with long dark hair.

Then Jody saw me and came running. We hugged each other hard.

"I'm so glad," she said, crying a little. Then she kissed me quickly and left me alone with him.

He was sitting slumped over and I thought he must have been asleep, but when I came up alongside him his eyes were open. His leg was stretched out in front of him in a cast. As I looked at him sitting there something caught in my chest. The flesh hung from his bones, and his shoulders sagged as if all the strength had been drained out of him. It took him a minute to realize I was there, and then he just stared up at me. I could see a dozen things struggling in his face — but when he finally spoke his voice was flat.

"You don't look too bad," he said.

"And you don't look any worse than you ever did."

He pressed his lips into a tight smile. "That's what I keep telling these doctors. Maybe you can convince them I came this way."

"I'll see what I can do."

He turned his head away. From where we were you could see all the way up and down the coast, and everywhere you looked was the glazed dome of the sky and the flat plain of the sea.

"You shouldn't have come," he said without looking up. "I told her not to tell you."

"I know."

"I did what I did. I don't need your forgiveness."

"Whatever gave you the idea," I said, "that I came to forgive you?"

He hesitated slightly. "What did you come for then? To gloat over the remains?"

"No. I came to ask you one question. Who's Frank Dutcheon?"

He sat there heavy as a boulder. "I don't know what you're talking about."

"The hell you don't."

He shook his head determinedly. "Can't we just forget it. Can't we just let it lie."

"If you don't tell me — I'll find out. I'll do whatever I have to. You know I will."

"Jesus *Christ*. Can't you just get it through your goddamn

head that it's over, done with, finished. I made a deal. I sold you out! Can't you understand I don't give a damn anymore, about you or anything else. Can't you understand I just want you to leave me alone and get the hell out of my life once and for all."

"Is that so, Art Cooper?"

He stared up at me hard then. I stared back until his face began to go to pieces. He turned away, burying his face in his hands, and I heard the muffled sobs. "I never could lie to you worth a damn, could I, Prince?"

"You didn't do too bad for a while," I said, handing him my handkerchief. "Who was he, Art?"

He blew his nose. "Someone from the old days."

"What did he do to you?"

"Nothing. He just told me something about Bill."

"Bill?"

"It was true, Jack. All along. All those rumors. The year I played, Bill was throwing games."

"Christ. You took Dutcheon's word for something like that?"

"Dutcheon made him do it."

"But Art, for chrissake, how in the world could he have ever forced someone like Bill to do something like that?"

He gave a pitiful little squeak of a laugh. "Easy," he said, wiping at his eyes. "Nothing to it at all. The same way they stopped him from coming out with the truth about the fix." He stopped, his shoulders stiff now, his arms braced against the chair. His voice when he spoke was so small and weak I could barely hear him. "The accident," he said struggling now against whatever it was. "The one that killed Jody's father . . ."

"I know about that," I said, trying to help him. "This guy Dutcheon did it, didn't he? He was the one behind the wheel."

Art looked up at me. "No, Jack. The one behind the wheel was Bill."

So that was it. Standing there on the pier it all came together, just as it had come together for Art the night Dutcheon told him. All the mysteries of Bill Burke's life suddenly snapped into focus: his deliberate pursuit of Jody's mother in his attempt to make amends for his crime, his abrupt abandonment of his family and his premature retirement from the game under the threat of blackmail, his failure to expose the fix, his suicide.

Dutcheon had told Art about Bill, and out of respect for the old days he'd also leveled with him about our situation. The threats were no bluff. The League was going to take its chances fighting us, pinning the fix on gamblers and linking our disappearance to them. In the confusion of his fever and his new understanding of Bill, Art could only think that he was to blame, that he had misled me about the game, about Bill, about everything. So he did the one thing he thought he could do to save me: he told them the truth. He told them that if there was any proof, we didn't have it. He swore that if they let me go he'd never have anything more to do with me or the fix.

In the end it didn't matter to them that we knew the truth, because in the end we didn't count to them for anything. I suppose we owed our lives to that. When Art found out what they'd done to me, he figured it would be best if I just blamed him for everything. He was afraid if I knew the truth I'd keep after them, and he didn't want me risking my life for nothing. I was strong. He knew I'd pull through all right without him.

Art begged me not to tell Jody about Bill. For his sake I agreed, though I knew, just as I think he knew, too, that eventually she would have to learn what Bill Burke had been: a man whose public image, for which he had sacrificed his entire private life, had been a lie. A man who had chosen in the end to die rather than face the truth about himself. What destroyed Bill Burke was not the bad judgment of a cocky young star who ran with the wrong crowd, or the drunken recklessness that sent him speeding down a back road, or the foolish confidence that his cohorts wouldn't blackmail him. What undid him was the decision to let the image of himself prevail over the fact of what he was. So he let a man die who might have lived. In that moment he gained both his terrible knowledge and his power.

Jody and I didn't understand all of it right away, of course. But over time we began to understand, not just about Bill Burke, but about Art Cooper, too.

The time we had left to make it up to him was all too short. We visited him in the hospital, and took turns pushing his chair over to the pier in the late afternoons. The beach would be half empty at that hour, and pitted with footprints. Girls and boys with golden tans and soft southern voices would be flirting in the glow of the sinking sun. One day I rented a couple of fishing rods. "What the hell do you want to put one of these things in my hands for, Rose?" he said. "With my luck I'm liable to hook us a Cuban submarine." But he managed to fish all right, keeping a watchful eye out for the pelicans. The big birds would come lumbering in like old B-17s, pulling up at the last minute and splashing down just below us, their webbed feet paddling through the clear green gel of the water. Cooper couldn't get over the fact that they were just out there flying around like that.

"What do you expect them to be doing?" I said.

"I don't know, Rose, but wouldn't you think anything that big should have to wear a license plate?"

The night I arrived in Gladiola I talked to the orthopedic surgeon. In his opinion Art had to undergo another operation immediately. It wasn't just a question of his ever walking again, or even being free from pain; the longer he remained immobilized the worse the clotting in his leg would get. The doctor warned me that with another operation there was a risk of a clot breaking off and moving up into his lungs. But in his opinion Art had already let far too much time go by.

The surgeon didn't know why Art was so dead set against it. Perhaps he had been counting too much on the initial operation. Perhaps he was just afraid of another one.

But the next morning when the nurse finally let me in to see him Art just laughed. What — him afraid of a lousy operation? What the hell was an operation? All you had to do was show up. It wasn't that big a deal. The long roll down the corridor to the operating room even reminded him a little of the way he used to feel down in the dressing room just before a game. That one final trip to the can, the coach's last words, the cold worry in your bowels, everything going faraway and different. Then whoever pops his head inside the door to call, three minutes. And all falling to one knee, the guys who still believed and, you could bet your sweet ass, most of the ones who didn't, in the name of the Father, the Son, and the Holy all rah-rah, and smacking pads, and you inside of it, being drawn through the tunnel, not wanting to leave that darkness, knowing you would.

What the hell was such a big deal about an operation? If it would make us all any happier he'd have the goddamn thing. The nurse would lean over him with a smile and tell him to start counting to ten. But he'd be thinking instead about what it was like to come running out onto the field on one of those shiny, brilliant autumn days, with the sun so bright it hurt to look, or in the wind, say, or in the rain, with your feet slipping out from under you and it being murder keeping the ball dry. Or on the first unbelievably cold day, with your legs like iron, your touch gone, and each hit stinging so. Or in the mud maybe, towards the end, say, with the taste of earth in your mouth and no way any longer to tell yourself from them.

You'd come out into the crowd stacked up like a canyon wall, the two teams like herds of wild horses, and over it all the fresh, scrubbed feeling as if the whole world had been made brand new that day.

*

Art would have liked it here. Many of the people speak English; he would have liked them and they would have liked him, too. The salt water would have helped his leg to heal, and he could have slowly worked himself back into shape walking on the beach with Argus. He could have talked philosophy with the fishermen, and shopped with Jody in the market; and when he felt like it, he could have helped me some with the book.

The one time we talked about it was the night before his operation. He was propped up in bed feeling well enough, but he was dead set against the idea. He didn't want me risking it. For what? By now they would have covered it all up anyhow. He didn't see any point in sticking my neck out again for that lousy game. And besides he didn't want me dredging up all that stuff about Bill and himself and that goddamn game when he'd lost his goddamn knee for nothing. He wanted me to promise him right then and there that I wouldn't go doing anything foolish like that if he wasn't around to stop me. I told him if he wanted to have any further say in what I did or didn't do he'd just better plan on being around a little longer. I said it would be different anyhow. It wasn't like we'd be doing it all by ourselves this time. We'd just tell our story, that's all. We could even call it fiction. We'd just make sure that the people involved, and anybody who cared enough, would recognize the basic events. What happened after that would be for others to decide.

But I didn't press him about it that night. I knew then what I had to do, and I was sure that once he was his old self again, he would come to see it the same way.

So I didn't press him, except to point out that despite everything else, at least that one game when he'd lost his knee had been on the level. If one thing was for sure, it was that Bill Burke had been trying with all his might to win that one. That game still stood.

"Jeez, that's probably true now, isn't it, Prince?" he said.

And for the sheer satisfaction of remembering, we went over it again: the Giants, the snow, just enough time on the clock for one last play, maybe two at most.

When we came to the end of it Art sat there awhile, then he asked me, just for the hell of it, just saying that I might actually do something as crazy as sit down and write the story, where would I begin? He didn't see where I could make it begin.

"Why, at the beginning, Art," I said. "Where else?"

"You mean like — it was early dawn on a beautiful day in nineteen twenty-six when a big kid subsequently to be christened me was born? You're not talking about crap like that, are you, Rose?"

No, I said I meant about New York and the game and my coming after him on the street like I did. And he lay back against the pillows and we talked about all that for a while, and for that moment, at least, I believe he was truly happy again.

I don't know how I'll get along without him. The night he died some kid came up to me in the hospital corridor. He said he worked for the local paper. He said they'd told him that the man who just died had been something once. He asked me who he was and what his relationship to me had been. I didn't know what to say. So I just told him that Art Cooper played center for the Pittsburgh Steelers in the early 1950s; that he was a big man with a rugged face and a funny, awkward, proud way of carrying himself, and that for a short time, I had been lucky enough to call myself his friend.